Other Gods

The Averillan Chronicles

BARBARA
REICHMUTH
GEISLER

LOST
COAST
PRESS

OTHER GODS: THE AVERILLAN CHRONICLES
Copyright © 2002 by Barbara Reichmuth Geisler

Lost Coast Press
155 Cypress Street
Fort Bragg, California 95437
(707) 964-9520
Fax: 707-964-7531
http:\\www.cypresshouse.com
Book and cover design: Michael Brechner / Cypress House

Library of Congress Cataloging-in Publication Data
Geisler, Barbara R.
    Other gods : the Averillan Chronicles / Barbara Reichmuth Geisler.-- 1st ed.
    p. cm.
    ISBN 1-882897-64-1 (pbk.)
    1. Great Britain--History--Norman Period, 1066-1154--fiction.
I. Title.
PS3607.E37 085 2002
813'.6--dc21   2001029327

Book production by Cypress House
Printed in Canada
2   4   6   8   9   7   5   3   1

TO

BILL

Sᴛ. Matthew

In 1066, William the Bastard, a Norman from France, defeated the English army at the Battle of Hastings. Although by 1086 all rebellion had been ruthlessly crushed, English hatred simmered beneath the surface, and reemerged with the murder of William's second son, William Rufus, in the New Forest. Henry, the Conqueror's third son, was able to partially mollify the conquered peoples by marrying an Englishwoman and restoring the old justice. However, when Henry died leaving a female heir, a foreign empress at that, it surprised no one that war, violence and corruption erupted from the still sick and vulnerable land. The monks of Peterborough wrote of it thus: "They were all accursed and forsworn and abandoned. To till the ground was to plough the sea; the earth bare no corn, for the land was all laid waste by such deeds; and men said openly that Christ and his saints slept."

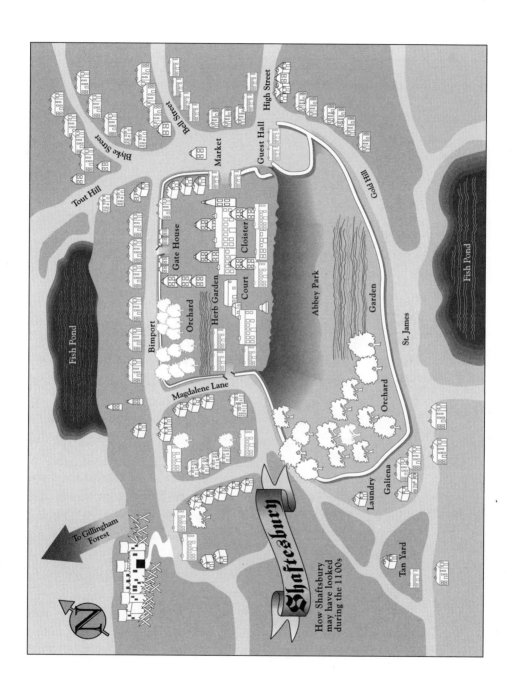

Shaftesbury

How Shaftsbury may have looked during the 1100s

To Gillingham Forest

Fish Pond

Tout Hill

Blyke Street

Bell Street

Market

Guest Hall

High Street

Bimport

Gate House

Orchard

Herb Garden

Court

Cloister

Gold Hill

Abbey Park

Garden

St. James

Magdalene Lane

Orchard

Laundry

Galiena

Tan Yard

Fish Pond

PROLOGUE

FEBRUARY 1139

SHAFTESBURY

THE ABBEY OF THE VIRGIN MARY
AND EDWARD, KING AND MARTYR

She slipped behind one of the massive, carved pillars and watched the column of nuns fade into the gloom of the night's morning. Because she had been late for the midnight services of Matins and Lauds, had deliberately entered after the Gloria of the ninety-fourth psalm, she had been obliged—in accordance with chapter forty-three of the Rule of Saint Benedict—to stand by herself, a single black shadow removed from the series of pairs. Therefore, when the office had ended, it had been easy for her to hide in the shadow of a pillar. She would not soon be missed. Not until they got to the night dorter, and not then until Dame Joan made the rounds and found her bed empty. The old prioress, Dame Aethwulfa, wholly absorbed in forcing her arthritic feet, a tread at a time, up the shallow night stairs, didn't notice that one of her charges was missing. Nor did Dame Joan, the sub-prioress, preoccupied with the busyness of her duties.

Her night slippers made no sound as she crept past the vestment press and into the tunneled darkness of the choir. She was careful not to stumble against the effigies, nine of them there were, memories of the dead, slumbering beneath their monuments.

A rag of moonlight shafted down from the lantern tower and struck the monstrance. The gilding seemed to waver and dance as if in the light of a cresset. Had something moved to create that shimmering? Perhaps the sacrist?

She pressed a hand against the little elf bolt hanging from a cord between her breasts. She hadn't thought it would be so, so scary when she had agreed to it. It had seemed perfectly doable. Easy. But now, here in His place, it didn't seem ... possible. A moan slid through the darkness, circling the upper reaches of the gloom. The hair on her arms raised, and her breathing came labored and shallow. Just the wind, surely. She crept through the choir, stopping every few seconds, melding her body against the wood of the stalls, crouching. The habit is black. No one can see me. With an unknown sense of self-preservation she became aware of her face and ducked it into the black of her veil. Such a long way. It never seemed that far when the priest mounted the two steps to the altar. She stood in front of the gilded sunburst where the reserved sacrament was kept.

She didn't know what she believed about it. She really didn't care. She hadn't wanted to be a nun. Never had wanted to be here. But she was. She reached a hand toward the altar and then stayed it. She couldn't do it. She didn't know if His body really resided in that piece of bread. Didn't see how it was possible, but ... She felt her eyes begin to water. Not tears. Fear. She reached out her hand again. A wall. Her brows contracted. There was a wall. She patted along the solidness of it, scraping her palms on the crudely cut stone; felt the chisel thrusts. She could see no wall. There *was* no wall. She was mad. She was going mad. She tried once more, tentatively this time, and felt the grit, the specks of harder greenstone, cold and real, a massive fortification between where she stood and what she wanted. Holding her knuckles to cover the whispered moan that seeped unbidden from her throat, she stumbled back, then overbalanced and fell. She lay for a moment, winded. The sliver of moonlight seemed to be caressing the gilding again, mocking her. How could she see it if there was a wall? How could the moonlight glint on it? There was no wall. But she had felt... something. Hadn't she? If there was nothing there, then how had she felt it?

Her thoughts traveled again. In her mind's eye she saw Galiena. She had promised. She had promised Galiena, and Galiena had to be honored. Awkwardly, she rose onto her hands and knees, then heavily to her full height. She must have it. Galiena would be waiting. She had heard in the market what they said Galiena was capable of. The dog found by the river. And the child. The rash on John-at-green. The birthmark on Alice's face. She had heard their gossip as Dame Edria stood haggling over the price of pots brought up from Cann.

With a determination born of fear, she mounted the stairs. It was her imagination. She had felt nothing. Tentatively, biting the side of her lip, she stretched out her hand.

This time it was hot, burning, scalding, scathingly hot. Whatever it was burned like fire. Tongues of flame wavered before her eyes, ending the space and undulating like the ice on a pond.

With a whimper she fled, scuttling down the stairs and, heedless, tripping on the raised slab that marked the place where King Canute's heart was buried. For the second time she fell, headlong, hands flat before her. Full length she sprawled on the flags like a penitent after some dreadful sin. She looked back. Now nothing was there but the altar and the monstrance. She would not do it. She had no way to do it, Galiena or no.

So? She would get the bone and the book. That was something, but … A tendril of wind latched around her ankle, and she shivered as she headed for the rood screen. As she passed the sacristy, the little room hidden within the rood screen, she had a thought. The unconsecrated bread was stored here. She could take that. Just a bit. From the small silver box. She unhooked the latchet on the spindled gate and lifted the lid from the box. Breaking off a corner of the bread, she slipped it into the fold of linen she had made ready in her hanging pocket. There was no way Galiena could know that this was not consecrated bread. How could she? And this way, whatever it was that had stopped her, well, it — He — would be satisfied. If…

Darting glances into the gloom, she skidded down the stairs to the nave altar, then made her way toward the small chapel in the north transept that housed the shrine of Saint Edward. Candles, fine beeswax always burning for the saint, were close haloed by vapor. She melded into a shadow and peered at the shrine. The two older nuns were fast sleep where they knelt. It was a duty taken in turn so that the saint was never left alone. Her lips turned at the irony of it. He was with God wasn't he? Really? So he couldn't be lonely, could he? Didn't really need watchers.

This was her week to serve at table — everyone took that in turn — so she had managed to slip the powder Galiena had given her into their cups of watered wine. They had been almost asleep by Compline, and she had seen the abbess glance over at them anxiously more than once, her lips becoming a line of exasperation when Dame Alice lost her balance and had to slump against the seat for strength.

But they were both fast asleep now, slumped against their kneelers with the loose-limbed abandon of sleeping babes.

Her eyes went to the shrine. It was not one of the new gold reliquaries such as she had seen at Winchester, but a leather box with enamel and gold, like leaves intertwining. It didn't seem so terribly evil, what she was doing. The bones were, after all, only bones. She remembered how Galiena had explained it to her in that maddening, superior sort of way, as if she didn't know anything at all. "My dear," Galiena had said, making it sound as if she were saying, 'you slut,' "he is dead. Died long ago. So this will be no harm to him. He is with God. Isn't that what you believe?" And the long, ovate, down-slanted eyes had glinted, reminding her of a snake. "And if he is with God, he can have no need for his bones. And if it is true, as they sometimes say, that on the last day, the day of Judgement, the bones shall be united with the soul, then so they shall be. We shall have returned his bones to him long before that. It is just for a while that I need them. And what harm there? Just borrowing the bones. I do promise you they shall be returned even before they are known to be missing."

The words echoing hollowly across her memory, she tiptoed to the shrine and, with surprising audacity, reached out and touched the box. There was no resistance. She put her hand to the latch and, with no more than a slight clicking, released it and lifted the lid. This was ridiculously easy. She peered into the gilded depths and saw the bones there, neatly arranged, not as if he had died, not as if he was in a coffin, but fumbled all together to fit. "Surely it is not customary to open the reliquary to see if he is in there. No one,"— that had been Galiena's final, convincing argument — "No one will look for the bones. Why would they? And therefore they will not know that they are missing."

She lifted the skirts of her habit, and groped from around her waist the coarse linen bag that had caused her merciless itching since she had put it on before Compline. Feeling squeamish, she reached into the box and pulled out a bone, a little one. Luckily, it seemed no longer connected to the fibers or whatever held it to the other bones. What if it had stuck? Well, it hadn't. She shuddered. Keeping her eyes averted, she thrust it into the bag and firmly drew the strings. She would be glad to be rid of it. With a parting glance at the sleeping, puffing women, she scuttled across the floor.

At the abbess' door, she slid the bolt. Coming out into the picket of moonlight, the cold, clear inrush of air slapped her alert. She could taste it, metallic, on the back of her throat, and clean after the stale incense and burnt wax of the church. The cloister garth was a pale square of chalky white. Keeping to the shadows, she flitted past the carrels, the arched recesses that, in the daylight, were sheltered from the breezes and trapped the sun.

There was a sound; a soft patter as of felted wool on pavement. She flattened herself within the cold stone of a carrel, imagining Dame Joan or the abbess hurrying after her, incredulous to find her sneaking through the cloister. She peered back. No irritated form, skirts held high, bore down upon her.

There it was again, a light hiss, the chinking click of a pebble. She knew of dragons. Could one be here, in the garden? Dropped from the sky on black leathery wings to lie in wait? She had seen the illustrations of Grendel in *Beowulf.* Its scales would glint in the moon-glow; its talons curve like those of her father's hawks, the slathering jaws reeking, noisome. She was a virgin, and the dragon would take her in his claws ... She froze. There it was again. Able to stand it no longer, she looked toward the sound.

A rat. Only a rat, limping toward the garth.

She had lost time. Galiena waited for no one. Rats. The devil's work, rats. Was she doing this for the devil? Well, mayhap she was. One would have thought that the bones and the host would have been enough. But no, Galiena had to have the book, too.

At the edge of the cloister, she gazed across the inner court. In the winter air the ground was at the freezing point. The cobbles were slimy where the night's wind had piled rotting leaves. She had to pick her way to avoid slipping on the hardened frost. As she moved, cold wind blustered up from the park, biting into her flesh and stinging the unprotected bare skin of her hands. Nothing else stirred as she skittered across the open court. She reached the weathered bulk of the infirmary, her feet feeling the crunch of the gravel among the patches of dirty snow. Her eyes, accustomed now to the gloom, could pick out the lighter glow of the paths.

She needed to reach the officina, a little hut where herbs were stored. It looked like a cat crouched, its fur fluffed against the wind. A gnarled rowan tree, still trailing some clusters of bright berries, curved over the doorway. Rowan was used to protect against witches. Well, what if Galiena was.

She pushed the door open. Dry bits of rush swirled in the draft. The air inside felt thick, but blissfully warm. Embers left to prevent mold on the herbs glowed from beneath the curfew.

She found a stool, mounted it, and reached up to finger the sheepskin-covered volumes stored on the high shelf with the poisons. She had been told to bring the slimmest of the volumes, the one of simple, heavy, pale sheepskin. She remembered it; remembered too how it had been carried with all ceremony from the aumbry, the big locked cupboard for books next to the chapter house; remembered how important Dame Averilla had thought it. Biting the inside of her lip, she fingered the leather spines, slid the thinnest book from the shelf, bent down and laid it on the table.

Outside, she struggled through the rumpled clods and fallen branches that littered the orchard, trying to not slip on the stretches of gathered slush or fall into the boggy places. In the outer court, a leaf skeleton, cobweb light, skittered in the mist. She kept to the yeasty shadows of the brew house and the sour-smelling walls of the ewery passage, hoping that no servant, wakeful from the night's ale, needed to answer the call of nature.

At the side of the great gate she could just make out the blurry whiteness of a face. She glanced nervously at the windows of the porter's lodge and of the guest chamber above it. She shoved the book and the bag of linen through the message slot. Dry fingers brushed her hand. The glint of an eye and the brief outline of a face were fleetingly there, then both were gone.

The wind seemed to shift. Tattered voices wafted to her from the nuns' graveyard. Already they had started searching for her! Sparks spiraled from torches and from the iron fire-baskets bracketed to the walls.

Closer than she had thought they could be. She must be in the church when they found her. Otherwise, ... She dashed across the great court, yanked open the north door and ran into the dark quiet of the church. Her feet pattered wetly on the flags as she ran toward the rood screen. Turning toward the nave altar, she blundered into the wooden grille dividing the town portion of the church from that of the lay sisters. God's blood, she had forgotten the grille! She scrabbled along the spindles for the little carved door, finally finding the latchet just as the great south door at the end of the nave opened, letting into the cavernous dark a hushed clicking of fretful voices.

Skidding to a stop, she slumped against the north side of the nave altar, and it was there, in front of the massive rood screen, that they found her.

"Here. Here she is. But Milady, she's dizzy, dizzy and muzzy in the head. Must have wandered through the rood screen somehow after Lauds, and fainted. Probably upset after her penance."

That doesn't seem likely, the abbess thought to herself. No penance known could so easily chasten this particular novice. But why then, she frowned as she released to others the limp body, is her habit wet with dew? And why does she smell damp, damp and earthy, like the night?

Opus Dei

Matins – Midnight – in choir

Lauds – 1 A.M. – in choir

Prime - 1st hour – 6 A.M.* or daybreak – in choir,
directly precedes mixtum, or breakfast

Terce – 3rd hour – 9 A.M.

Chapter Mass** – in choir – followed immediately by

Chapter – in chapter house – about twenty minutes

Sext – 6th hour – noon

Dinner

Midday rest.

Afternoon set aside for labor, study in cloister, or recreation.

None – 9th hour – 3 P.M.

Vespers – sunset – in choir

Supper

Evening Collation (short reading) in the cloister

Compline – 8 P.M. – just before retiring

Not necessarily in choir. To bed.

Absolute silence until Prime.

---

* Times varied with the season and hours of daylight.

** On Sundays and Festivals, instead of Chapter Mass, High Mass is
celebrated at 11 A.M. following chapter but before dinner.

The Abbey of the
Virgin Mary and Edward,
King and Martyr, at Shaftesbury

Abbess: Emma

Choir Nuns*

Dame Aethwulfa – *prioress*
Dame Agnes – *former cellarer*
Dame Alburga – *mistress of ceremonies*
Dame Alice – *assistant to sub-prioress and bursar*
Dame Anne – *in charge of the home farm and the gardens*
Dame Athelia – *in the infirmary, former sub-prioress*
Dame Averilla – *infirmaress*
Dame Avis – *sacrist*
Dame Benedict – *in charge of the gardens*
Dame Berthold – *bell ringer*
Dame Celine – *portress*
Dame Edith – *assistant to the infirmaress*
Dame Edria – *assistant to the cellarer*
Dame Isobel – *in the infirmary; former cellarer*
Dame Joan – *sub-prioress*
Dame Marguerite – *zelatrix – assistant novice mistress*
Dame Maud – *in the infirmary; former infirmaress*
Dame Maura – *mistress of church work*
Dame Perpetua – *present cellarer*
Dame Petronella – *novice mistress*
Dame Thecla – *librarian*

---

* Altogether during this period, more than seventy-six nuns and sisters
  inhabited the abbey. Only the above are mentioned in this work.

Lay Sisters

Sister Cadilla – *assistant infirmaress*
Sister Clayetta – *in charge of the abbess' rooms*

In the Novitiate

Sister Cantile

Sister Helewise

Sister Julianna

Sister Margaret

Sister Mary

Sister Mavern

Sister Theiline

Sister Theodosia

CHAPTER ONE

THE FOLLOWING OCTOBER

1139

ame Averilla was weeding in the herbarium, the welcome autumn sun on her back. August had been wet and miserable. Hail and wind had swallowed the countryside, while famine and war stalked the towns. Here though, even with Allhallows Eve to be had within the fortnight, the Michaelmas daisies and autumn damask roses were aflame in the early morning sun, and she could hear the hum of the bees, bustling about the apples and the clove gillyflowers. Her strong, slender hands rooted with a forked twig in the loamy earth, drawing out the last of the weeds. Even bent as she was she seemed a tall woman, with a long face and the weathered skin of one often outdoors. Her gray eyes held the certain calm of the long professed.

The herbarium cat lay beside her, his body spineless, the tip of his tail twitching just the slightest bit. Though nuns were forbidden pets, the kitchen, the storerooms, the herbarium and officina needed cats to keep down the rodents. Averilla paused to look at him and smiled, revealing a prominent gap between strong front teeth. This mutual reliance is so typical of the community, she thought. Each of us fulfills—A stumbling

1

footfall and a gasping for breath broke through the calm. In some irritation she looked up to find her assistant, Dame Edith, with her feet in the lavender, having already trampled the last of the thyme.

"Dame Averilla," panted Dame Edith, drinking in gulps of air. "It's Dame Agnes. Dame Agnes is – is – " There were no words in the woman's sheltered Norman vocabulary, and she looked, her pale eyes bulging, to her superior in confused entreaty.

Dame Averilla rose, unkilted her habit from the wide leather belt she wore around her tunic, and looked down with resignation at the younger woman. At the best of times, Dame Edith reminded Averilla of a rabbit. When Edith was worried, the resemblance was acute. Her lustrous eyes always seemed to be filled with unshed tears. She rarely spoke more than a timid word or two, and her gestures were a wilted smile, a quick, faded movement of resignation, or a subtly wrinkling nose.

Mentally rebuking her lack of compassion, Averilla blandly asked, "Dame Agnes is hearing voices again?" Her expression remained matter-of-fact as she methodically milked the dirt from her fingers.

"No. No, not this time. The voices are … are speaking. Through her. Her voice isn't even her own — " Dame Edith was interrupted by the great bell, Dunstan, tolling the morning Chapter Mass. Dame Averilla stifled a sigh.

"Dame, you must go to her," Edith pleaded, trying to be heard over the ponderous summons.

"Our duty," Averilla answered, "is in choir for Chapter Mass. And Sister Cadilla is with her, is she not?"

"Yes, but…" Dame Edith's eyes clouded as she peered into the middle distance of her recent memory.

SHE HAD BEEN ABOUT THE EARLY MORNING tidying with Sister Cadilla when Dame Agnes had stumbled down the two steps into the infirmary, a mad look in her eyes. Edith had found it all very confusing. Sometimes Dame Agnes was as sane as the rest of them, eyes clear, her deep dimple appearing and disappearing as the ironies of life amused her. At such times she calmly sang in the church or plied her needle in the Brode Hall, helping the younger nuns with the embroidery for which she was justly renowned. But at other times she was not herself. This time Agnes had torn off her veil and flung it to the floor. Tendrils of gray-black hair clung like leeches to her scrawny neck, and patches of scalp gleamed white as she turned her head to and fro, seemingly searching for something. She had then ripped off her black, wide-sleeved habit. The meager, tight-sleeved undergown of linen seemed dirty.

Dame Edith had edged as close as she dared. She picked up the cast-off habit and, laying it over her outstretched arms, offered it back to Agnes like a deacon presenting a chasuble to his priest. Softly, tentatively, she muttered the gentling words she had been taught to use when dealing with this madness.

When Edith had been within two feet of her, Agnes started to quiver. "Get away from me," she had screeched. "You shall not touch me, you stinking slut." In the dim light of the infirmary, her eyes gaped yellow. "Keep your meddling hands from this body." Her voice hoarse, she pointed at her eyes. "This is fire. Look at it. It burns the soul. Tentacles. Hairy, spider legs." Her eyes narrowed. She snapped her lower teeth in front of her upper lip and wrinkled her nose in a snarl. "My master is … strength … is — " She toppled over then, in a heap, drool sliding down her cheek, her limbs still clenched.

3

"She has fainted?" Edith gaped, both revolted and pitying.

"Aye." Cadilla seemed relieved.

After a few moments, Agnes had reopened her eyes, raised herself heavily to her knees, and stretched out her arms in supplication, staring into the middle distance as if she saw something, or someone. "No feeling," she said in a dreamy voice. "No sadness. Come. Oh. Here. Here he is." She had shut her eyes then, for long enough that Sister Cadilla leaned forward, gingerly, as if with a wild dog, to see if Agnes still breathed. Suddenly, Agnes began to tremble. Her voice was no longer dreamy, but frightened, and again she searched the distance of her seeing. "Misty veils. I can't see you. Where are you?" She climbed to her feet and staggered into the dim arcades where the sick and old lay in rows. "Here I am. I can't see. Where are you?" Sobs racking her whole body, she had sunk to the floor sobbing.

Dame Edith had fled.

"Nay, she shall not soon die, but — " Edith now bleated, squeezing her left forefinger in the fist of her right hand.

"She is in God's hands." Averilla's voice was patient. "We must hurry ourselves to the same place. Sister Cadilla is with her?"

"Yes, but — "

"Our duty is to praise God."

By the time Maurice and Doven had added their lighter, sweeter tones to the bass of the great bell, the two black-garbed women had made their way out of the herb garden, across the inner court and into the slype between the church and the cellarium.

"I think that they told her to take off all her clothes," Dame

Edith whispered loudly, trailing her superior's determined, long-legged gait past the laver where the nuns washed their hands before meals, "and — and she blasphemes. She said things she didn't even know…that I didn't know…wicked things full of horror, as if, as if she was someone, was someone…evil." Sensing rather than seeing disapproving glances, Dame Edith covered her confusion by retrieving a dropped towel and replacing it in the cupboard above the laver. Eyes lowered, they found their places and processed with the others into the church.

2.

NO MATTER HOW HARD AVERILLA tried as she stood with the others in the choir, only a part of her mind heard the abbess' voice, clear and calm and deep:

"Be merciful unto me, O God, be merciful unto me; for my soul trusteth in thee: yea, in the shadow of thy wings will I make my refuge until these calamities be overpast."

Averilla chanted the next line of the fifty-seventh psalm.

"I will cry unto God most high; unto God that performeth all things for me."

But it was rote. She knew she didn't hear the words.

Instinctively, she matched the volume of her voice with those surrounding her. Dear, dear Dame Agnes. What had happened? Why did this madness come upon her? And why not always? Was she possessed? Really possessed? By demons?

The chant moved on with its inexorable discipline. Dame Alburga, the mistress of ceremonies, her wide sleeves flapping, wove her hand, wrist and fingers together, snake-like, as she led them in the deliberate, rhythmless chant.

"My soul is among lions; and I lie even among them that are set on fire, even the sons of men, whose teeth are spears and

5

arrows, and their tongue a sharp sword."

Averilla allowed part of her mind to review what she knew about the other woman. Agnes had entered the novitiate at sixteen, a graceful young woman, but quiet. In any case, Agnes had settled in and shown a tremendous talent with the fine silks and brilliant colors that were embroidered in the abbey's Brode Hall.

Agnes had taken her solemn vows at twenty-three.

Over time they had all come to rely on her quiet competence. Agnes was beloved, too, for the steadiness of her counsel. When one or another of their chaplains was unable to sort out the problems that sometimes beset the more tender souls among them, Agnes could be relied on to listen and — more than listen — hear what the troubled woman was trying to say; to harness the demon that was troubling her life of peace. Above all, Agnes could be relied on to be discreet. She had held most of the positions of trust in the convent, and it was whispered that she would be a good candidate to replace Dame Aethwulfa when the old prioress decided to retire to the infirmary.

Two years ago— before the madness had started— Agnes had been appointed cellarer to fill the vacancy left by the death of an older woman during whose last years the standards had deteriorated. With her usual thoroughness, Agnes had turned the job upside-down, cutting expenses, and forcing Dame Anne to initiate new ways of farming, such as installing those new mills that were moved by the wind. She insisted that the steward and the bailiff show her all accounts and registers, and she questioned incessantly until she understood it all. She even went to the market, a job usually delegated to the assistant cellarer, or even the assistant to the assistant. Over the months, Agnes had become more and more preoccupied and had even seemed perplexed. It was noticed that she was tight-lipped after having been over the books with Dame Joan. "But then, they never did get along," Dame Martha had remarked. In June the madness had started. Agnes had been at the market with one of the novices.

"But then I lost her in the crowd." Sister Cantile, plump and pretty, with skin so fair you could see the blood beneath it, had run, panting, to the main gate. "The Midsummer Market is so crowded. It was just a moment that I looked away and ... and she was gone." Cantile's face had crumpled into tears.

According to Dame Benedict, who had been portress at the time: "We — Dame Martha was helping me, you see — we were in the porter's lodge. The Earl of Gloucester was expected, and with Midsummer and all, there was a deal of coming and going. It was I, I suppose, who saw Dame Agnes first as she came up from the market." Dame Benedict had paused then, and put a hand to where her jowls were just beginning to sag with age. "It was as if someone walked beside her, for she did speak and laugh, very much, I am afraid, as do the maids with their suitors. There was no one with her. Dame Agnes stopped chattering and looked around, distracted, ye wot. She tripped as she came toward us, on a loose rock, but she didn't fall all the way down. Nearer the gate, she looked up and asked us where "he" had gone. We wot not what to say, for we had seen no one. I started to ask her whom she sought when, of a sudden, she started babbling and screaming. We ... we tried to grab her hands, but she fought us. Finally Old Wat from the stable grabbed her from behind and took her to the sub-prioress as was required."

Dame Joan, solid and peg-shaped, had been in her office when they brought Agnes to her. It was the particular duty of the sub-prioress to see that the discipline of the abbey was maintained. It was rumored that Joan had threatened to put Agnes in chains. "You are possessed," Joan had actually said, lips pressed into a thin line. "Pride, Dame Agnes," she had added, "in your own … sanctity — " She had not finished the thought, but had broken off, lifting a square hand to signal for help. Dame Agnes, frantic, had broken away from Wat and fled across the inner court, to burst, sobbing hysterically, into the infirmary.

Dame Averilla had managed to calm and comfort Agnes, but she remembered the frightening perplexity that had seeped into her mind. She hadn't known what to do. Helplessly, she had watched as Agnes continued to fumble and pluck at herself, her eyes lifeless. In the end, she had given Agnes a sleeping draught and tucked her into a shadowed corner where Dame Edith had breathlessly crooned the twenty-third Psalm to her, over and over again.

It wasn't long before Dame Joan had appeared. At the top of the infirmary stairs she had paused, eyes rock hard. "Dame Averilla. You must relinquish her to the bailiff or to the punishment cell. She is a menace."

"She may be ill." Averilla had jutted her chin. "At any rate, now she sleeps."

Dame Joan had descended the two shallow steps. "Dame, something must be done. You, obviously, do not have the courage to do it. I shall take her."

"You shall not." Averilla had wiggled herself fully erect, sure of her strength, taller than the other woman.

"You refuse to obey me?" Joan's face had reddened.

"Obey you?" Averilla had raised one eyebrow, then said, slowly, "My vow is to the abbess."

Joan had opened her mouth to respond, then shut it again. After a moment's silence, the others in the infirmary frankly staring, Dame Joan had turned and left.

The turbulent battle in chapter some days later had disturbed the peace of the whole community. Averilla remembered it now as if it were yesterday.

AS IS SOMETIMES THE CASE in a community close confined, they had been grating on one another all morning. The precentor had hit a wrong note at Prime and someone had hissed. Dame Joan had snapped at the server at mixtum, and the poor girl had dropped her wooden platter. As chapter started, the whole room seemed to be coughing. And Dame Anne, with a face as wind-beaten and tanned as old parchment, had mumbled on interminably about the poor repair of the home farm.

Because it was Friday, the abbess, hoping there were none, had asked for any confessions of fault. When a few minor transgressions had been confessed and easily absolved, Dame Joan had slowly risen. At a weary nod from the abbess she heaved a sigh. "There is one among us, my Lady," she had started, looking around at them meaningfully, "in whom pride is ascendant."

"Shouldn't she tell us herself of her faults?" Abbess Emma's mild voice barely concealed her irritation.

"Nay, Mother, she cannot. She is so entranced—yea, even ensnared—that she herself is unaware. Her pride in her own skills, my lady," Dame Joan's voice had risen, "puts the souls of this whole community into danger." She had waited for the idea to sink in.

"Her stubborn pride," Joan then continued, eyes narrowed, face deceptively calm, "in her own skills threatens to let loose webs of evil among us." She paused then, dramatically. "I speak of Dame Averilla. She it is who stubbornly insists on keeping Dame Agnes here among us, to…to poison our very prayers with her rantings—"

"Surely," the abbess had interrupted, "Dame Averilla is talented with the sick. I have not noticed a fullness of self in her." The quiet voice had tried to cut the heart out

9

of Dame Joan's rage, and, for a moment, the latter had seemed confused.

But only for a moment. Dame Joan looked again at Averilla, and what she saw there seemed to strengthen her resolve. "Aye, Mother, so it seems, but it is these very talents that seem so smooth, so God-given, that threaten the life of her soul. They seduce her, lure her into an overweening faith in herself, in her own powers, in her skills of healing. She has come to believe that she can rid us of any disease. She is blind to the mayhem and turbulence, and indeed heresy that arise from her persistence"

The chapter had erupted then into a babel of clacking voices.

"Mother," Averilla had stumbled through the lower tiers of nuns, and Dame Edith, bless her, reached over with a steadying hand. When Averilla reached the center of the chapter house, she had been surprised to find that she was trembling. "Mother," she said, her voice hoarse as she tried to be heard.

The abbess nodded, and the uproar ceased as the nuns craned forward to hear.

"It is not pride that I have in these skills, which I have worked to learn. It is thankfulness. Thankfulness for being shown a way to help. Thankfulness for being given hands to relieve suffering. Is my faith in these learned skills pride? What I know, I learned from Dame Maud before me. Was her belief pride? Dame Joan says that Dame Agnes is possessed by devils. Is Dame Joan's belief pride? Dame Agnes may be helped, I believe. She is not always . . . ill."

"If it is as you say, Dame," the abbess' words were measured, thoughtful, "how shall we, as a community, distinguish the truth between your opinion and that of Dame Joan?"

Averilla had tried to calm her speech, to wipe out the rising note of panic. She swallowed. "From time to time," she said after a moment, "certain draughts have seemed to make some difference to Dame Agnes. She is not always ill. You have all seen that, have you not?" Averilla had looked around, pleading with the assembled nuns. "After I have given her of this draught? Could we not wait, Reverend Mother, to do anything about Dame Agnes until I have had a chance to seek the advice of Abbess Hildegard at St. Disibod's, under the archbishop of Mainz? Abbess Hildegard is said to be well versed in the healing arts. Her advice might help to distinguish between my opinion and that of the sub-prioress. We then might be able to tell whether Agnes be possessed or ... or, as I believe ... merely ill. Can we but wait to act until we have had Hildegard's learned advice?"

Dame Joan allowed everyone to absorb Averilla's words before speaking again. "I will agree to await counsel," her voice that of one willing to be tolerant. "I would but ask Dame Averilla from what plant she has derived such a beneficent cordial."

"It comes from a spring in Gillingham Forest."

"Not from a plant?"

"N-n-no," Averilla had stuttered. "Er...it is 'living water.' Such the spring is." Her voice had gained volume as justifying words came to her. "Our Lord often described himself as the Living Water. He even used spit."

"But this isn't water blessed by the church, is it? Your 'living water,' the water you give to Dame Agnes comes from a well in the forest, doesn't it, used time out of mind in pagan ceremonies? And probably has a rowan tree arching over it."

Before Averilla could reply, the abbess' calm voice sliced through the room. "You may both be seated, dames."

The following morning Averilla had sent the promised letter. It read, in part:

To the right worshipful and reverend Mother in Christ, Hildegard, by the grace of God, Abbess of St. Disibod from Averilla of the Abbey Church of the Virgin Mary and St. Edward, King and Martyr, at Shaftesbury, a humble handmaiden of the convent in that place; Eternal greeting in the Lord. Most honorable and Reverend Mother in God, I seek your favor and pray you in all haste possible send me by the next sure messenger, your counsel...

There had been no reply. With war raging between King Stephen and the Empress Matilda, was it any wonder that either her letter, or the healer's reply, had gone astray? Her letter had been sent more than two months ago. By now, Dame Joan's patience had undoubtedly worn thin.

Averilla hit a wrong note in the psalm and forced herself to refocus on the office.

CHAPTER TWO

John the mason absently coiled the cord of his plumb line and hooked it onto the thong attached to his tunic. He remembered how Dame Averilla had once watched, fascinated, as he showed her how a plumb line, a hanging rock on a piece of cord, could determine the straightness of the nave wall. "Now I understand." Her puzzled face had brightened with comprehension. Then she had laughed. "This" and she had taken the plumb line in her hand and held it up, "you call your 'regula.' With it you measure the straightness of a wall. With our 'regula' we measure the straightness of our lives." At John's corresponding look of incomprehension, she gave him a mischievous smile. "The regulations that we obey. We call them our 'regula,' our rule. They were written by St. Benedict and are what keeps us from killing each other, cooped up as we are."

His huge hands slack, John now stood·on the temporary wooden landing, halfway up one of the western towers of the church. Work on the twin towers, the last parts of the building to be completed, came to a halt whenever the nuns were at worship. To be sure, it had been different with Abbess Cecily. Though many churches, big churches like this one, might take fifty years to complete, Abbess Cecily had wanted "her church" completed in her lifetime. The men had worked from dawn to dark, making a frightful din, he supposed, for those trying to pray. He welcomed the bits of rest that the new abbess, Abbess Emma, insisted on. From what he had observed, his lads didn't mind stopping, either. They managed to perch when the bell sounded, hands dangling between their knees. The high sound of the women's voices floating up to them made an ethereal drift within the wind. "Gets under your skin, it does," one of the lads had told him without shyness.

John sauntered over to the unfinished wall, put a hand on the solid greensand, and squinted across the downs that undulated south. The morning air was cold and bittersweet, like new wine, and a breeze pricked at the hair on his arm. He liked the invigorating cold of autumn. They, he and his masons, could still work, and the work seemed somehow easier. Soon they would cover the stones with dung and straw to keep the mortar from crumbling in the cold. They would be in time, if something like the hailstorm that had pounded the crops before the harvest didn't blow through. That had been a blow, sure enough. It was rumored though, that the abbess had grain stored at the tithe barn near Tisbury, but he didn't know. He hoped so. Enough chaos in the country without famine. Last famine had been about eight years ago, 1131 it was, with cattle dying in the fields from plague.

As the nuns recessed from the church, it was momentarily quiet. Beside him, a hawk plummeted, and John could hear the wind whiffling in its pinions. Gareth, one of the hodmen, swung noiselessly into view on his rope-hung plank, and started to heave mortar and stone onto the platform. Despite the autumn cool, sweat coursed down his prematurely aged face. No doubt about it, the man was too thin. John knew that, were Gareth to take off the gray drab of his homespun tunic, his ribs would stand out like the beams of a hut. Nor was it just the green-white stone dust that whitened his thatch of hair. He was too old, too soon. Had seen too much. Everyone had. The whole country. People murdered at their plows and tortured for no reason by these Norman wolves. The old courts gone, houses burned, crops trampled and animals stolen. John gave work to as many as he could, but even so, ...

Truth be known, though, they were lucky here in Shaftesbury atop this hill. The sides were steep, sheered by the steady quarrying of rock for the abbey. And that was good. Well nigh impossible to breech. Would take no more than a handful of archers to defend it. The abbey fishponds, at the foot of the hill, would work as a moat. Would slow an invader down, anyway. To confirm the thought, John swerved his glance toward the south pond. Turgold was there, bittle in hand, ramming and beating new slaked lime over the clay. Turgold was one of the few who could construct a proper mist pond. Something about which the Normans knew less than nothing.

But all that made Shaftesbury safe also made her vulnerable to fire. No water. Couldn't blame King Alfred for building there, though. Had his hands full, Alfred had, two hundred years ago. Danish longboats sneaking up the streams at night. Danes at the Battle of Eddington. Almost beat him they had. So when Alfred had won, he built a string of castles to protect Wessex. Shaftesbury had been built far from all the streams. High up. Safe. For his daughter, the first abbess.

As he now watched, the clouds above the downs built and thickened. He frowned. Just like King Stephen and his army, harrying the land; burnt, ruined crops clinging to the wake of his passing. Idly, John's eye followed a figure running and stumbling down the pilgrim track toward the base of the hill. He watched, his interest piqued, not easily able to discern who it was. Dressed in what? A smock? Head uncovered? Strange. And from the abbey. Maybe Dame Agnes? She had seemed

15

quite mad of late. He sighed, saddened. If they needed him for the hue and cry, he would hear soon enough.

Thinking of the hue and cry, John shifted his weight slightly and veered his gaze to the northwestern edge of the town, where stood another tall stone tower. The castle. The bailiff'd be told soon enough if it was Agnes. Bailiff and castle. His grandfer had taken him into the keep of the castle when he had been just a bit of a lad. Had put a gnarled hand on his shoulder, heavy it was, and told him how the Bastard, the one the Normans called the Conqueror, had brutally and ruthlessly, savagely even, subdued the west in 1086. Had then had the wooden tower here in Shaftesbury rebuilt in stone. The bailey of the castle had displaced forty hearths. Forty huts and cots had been demolished, squandered, to make way for the bailey and the new stone keep that watched to the west and the north and, lest they forget, reminded them of the king's power. His grandfer had been forced to help build that tower. His fader had been at hand for the rebuilding of the abbey church when Cecily had determined to enlarge Alfred's stout structure, a different proposition altogether. John had worked on the abbey from the time he was a boy. Like his fader and grandfer before him, he had been a strong worker, and bright, and in time had become the master mason.

Another bell rang. He smiled to himself, and turned. Town'd be lost without those bells. Created a rhythm. Often he'd seen the ploughmen lean against their weathered ploughs to listen to the bells, straining, if the wind was right, for a whiff of the piercing feminine voices borne aloft.

As the wind shifted, the gritty scraping of the hodman, pushing the heavy sludge back and forth in his wooden form, eddied up to John, mingling with the sharper sounds from the market. He looked down. A heavy destrier clopped through the market, scattering squealing children and ragged, chortling fowls. Sheep nagged mournfully from the pen in the cow market.

People yelled, hawking their wares. The smell of hot, spiced pork pasty wafted up from a cook stall. Someone jeered. John swiveled and scanned the crowd, trying to see the sound. "Naaa-na-na-na-na." His eyes narrowed. The market stalls were set cheek by jowl, the braces of wood hung with everything from dried fish to fleeces for sleeping. There, near the fishmonger. There. Though he had known what he would see, the impotent anger rose hot within him. His wife, Alice, a red-brown blotch marring her face, stood fingering the copper and iron pots the tinker had arranged for sale. A crowd of boys danced around her, sticking out their tongues and wagging their fingers in their ears. One scrabbled in the street for a rock, and picked it up to throw at her. John's eyes hardened. He hoisted his belt, pulling at the hammer on his hip. He saw her turn her head to hide the blotch on her cheek beneath a lappet of her veil. The boys banded nearer. The fishmonger looked up. Seeing the danger, he took a warning step toward the boys and shook his slender knife at them. They back-stepped their way through the stalls and ran off, laughing, down Gold Hill.

As John kept a nether eye on Alice to be sure she was safe, he caught a glimpse of Dame Joan marching purposefully down the steps of the guest hall. Curious, he turned to see what she was up to. Glad the master builder has to deal with her, he thought. She never listens. He watched her mingle with the crowd. Her black-and-white habit was conspicuous among the muted earth tones. And she was alone. More and more strange. The nuns never went alone; always had another with them, usually a novice or one of the workmen. No, Dame Joan was, in truth, very much alone. He leaned on the parapet and savored an uncharacteristic and uncharitable curiosity. Up to no good, he imagined, she who was so eager to point out the faults of others. She had stopped and was hesitating, as if searching for someone. Nah, likely not. 'Twas probable she just wanted a bit of a glance around. He would certainly go stir-crazy locked in a house full of women. He continued to watch as Dame Joan ran her fingers along the rims of some wooden bowls set out on a trestle table. John had started to turn his gaze back again to Alice when he noticed that another woman had come to stand beside Joan. He thought they spoke. Couldn't tell, of course, from where he stood, but their movements had a certain … sympathy. Who was it? He squinted. No! He leaned further over. It was, though! Galiena. Dame Joan talking to Galiena? And not just the courtesies of the day. He couldn't believe it. Maybe Joan didn't know who Galiena was. Didn't the nuns hear the rumors from the town? About Galiena? Surely the lay sisters would have told them.

Suddenly, Dame Joan turned and made her way back to the guest hall. The interchange had been so quick he wouldn't have noticed if he hadn't been watching the market just then. He looked back at Galiena. Just to be sure. She had turned her whole body toward him and was looking up and straight at him. Her tailed black eyes looked into his, and she smiled so he would know that she knew he had seen them together. Then she drifted into the crowd. He shook his head. Curious.

As John climbed down steps roughly hewn into the stone of the tower, he shivered. He would not want to offend either of those two women. He would be more than polite when next he met one of them. He might even have to grovel. But the English, and John was English, had gotten used to groveling during the last eighty years since the conquest. He sighed.

CHAPTER THREE

I.

"ho told her to take off her clothes?" Averilla and Edith hurried past the refectory after chapter.

"I, I know not. The, the voices — the ones she speaks to — mayhap."

"How know you this? Heard you them?"

"No, but who else would?"

"Nobody, dame. Nobody, I suppose." As they headed toward the slype, Averilla asked, "And you left her with Sister Cadilla?"

"I didn't want to, I tried to — " Dame Edith broke off, for Sister Cadilla could be seen hurrying toward them. Cadilla was not plump, as was Sister Cantile, but solidly square. A strong brow above bright blue-gray eyes both sharp and observant distinguished her moon-shaped face. When she smiled, which was infrequently, her whole visage softened.

"Dame Averilla" She reached them and stood uncertainly, not wanting to tell, yet knowing she had to, and afraid of the blame. "Dame Agnes has gone off. Shrieking, she was. I was not with her. Only for a moment, ye wist. Seeing to Dame Maud. I went back, and she was not there."

"Calm yourself, sister. Take a long breath."

19

Cadilla breathed in.

"Two breaths, sister."

Cadilla took another breath and continued. "She'd been muttering after Edith left. It sounded like, 'Where are you? I am following. Wait.' It sounded like that. But I paid it no heed, busy as I was."

Averilla sighed. "God will, I trust, be with her."

"But, but—"

"Hush, hush, sister. Be tranquil. Others will hear. Dame Joan would not be pleased." Dame Averilla's face was serene, her step measured, her teeth clenched.

At the cellarium, away from the cloister, Averilla's measured glide lengthened into a stride.

"Agnes has left the infirmary. That we know," Averilla muttered. "We must know where she has gone. If she is in the park or has drifted into one of the stables, no harm will come to her. But all is not as it was. Women are no longer safe. We can search the abbey park, the stables and orchards later. We need first to try to find her in the town. If she is there, someone will have noticed her. Hard to ignore. In her smock, you say?"

The three women had reached the door to the infirmary, which stood open to the fairness of the morning. A gentle cooing and the reek of dung drifted to them from the rounded walls of the dove house.

"Swiftly, before harm overtakes her. The both of you. Ask at the tannery. If none have seen her there, continue on. Do not fear to ask all you see. None shall wonder at you two together so close to the abbey and seeking Dame Agnes. If she went by the Ridgeway or Drove Road, surely someone will have seen her as she passed by."

"Sister," she fixed Sister Cadilla with steady eyes, "You were raised here. The townsfolk well know you. You can ask all those who might not understand Edith."

The two women looked at Averilla blankly and then looked at each other. "I must be seen here," Averilla added, "in the infirmary in case someone finds her before you return. No one will remark if either of you, or both, are missing for a moment, but they, Dame Joan especially, would notice were I missing."

"But, dame," Edith's voice was tentative, "would it not be better if the whole community could help with this search, even perhaps the bailiff? Who knows where Agnes might be?"

"Mayhap. But were the community to be alerted, I fear Dame Agnes would be sent away. Dame Joan would," Averilla eyes took on a steely blue haze, "take this as proof of — of possession. Or worse. And Agnes would be punished."

The two nuns hurried off.

Averilla stood for a moment, then turned in the door to the infirmary. Inside the door, near the lower step, stood a boy, the early vestiges of manhood elongating his form. Averilla didn't notice him at first, blinded as she was by the transition from bright day into shadow. She started when he made a small movement. "Oh, you startled me," she said and then smiled to take away the sting of her surprise. She scrutinized the boy briefly, a memory tugging at her mind. The mop of fiery hair. "Odo, is it not?"

"Aye, dame, but I have much grown since last you saw me."

"Indeed. A sickle leapt out to bite your leg that time, if I remember aright. You never came back. I hope it healed."

"Aye, mistress, I mean, dame. A bloody big scab at first, but never did it fester. This," he held up a finger so she could see his new wound, "I washed with water from the well right off," he said, watching with interest as she unwound the dirty linen.

21

Averilla poured water over the cut, and placed soft, pale-green borage leaves on the ragged flesh. Using her finger, she scooped ointment from a jar and smeared it across the leaves. He looked at her questioningly. She raised her eyebrows. Most who came for healing did not question. They just accepted. To them all healing was a mystery.

"Has piss in it," she said as she replaced the scrap of oiled linen that served as lid. Seeing the horror in his eyes, Averilla smiled and added dryly, "From a goat. And other things."

As she rebound it with clean strips of coarse linen, she smiled and said, "Come again in a few days so I can see how it heals."

"May I do for you something in return?" he asked shyly, flushing in embarrassment.

"The gift is the Lord's," Averilla said, quietly replacing the jar on a shelf. Her mind had already followed Agnes to wherever it was she had fled. Odo did not leave as she expected, but stood shifting his weight back and forth.

"Er, dame?"

"Yes, Odo," she refocused on him.

"I overheard what the, the others said about, about Dame Agnes." Odo looked at his feet.

"Have you seen her?"

"No, no. Is Dame Agnes the one as used to come to market?" Averilla nodded. Dragging one broken toenail through the rushes on the floor, Odo continued. "After my father left, some bigger boys, they called my mother names, and, well, she, Dame Agnes that is, stopped them from beating me."

Odo could, even now, taste the dust of that day bitter on his tongue. He had been on the ground by the time Agnes came upon them. He had started to pray, even though he had told God he would never pray again after his father left. But the blows were coming so fast to his head and to his sides, and the

22

pain was searing through him with such heavy agony, that he had given in to God. The first he knew of his rescue was the clean smell of lavender that had pierced through the heavy taste of earth and dung. Almost immediately the blows had stopped. He had cracked one fast-swelling eye and seen the leather toe of her boot. Emboldened, he had rolled over to watch. She had grabbed the bigger boys by the scruffs of their tunics, blue fire flashing from her eyes, her tongue threatening them with the pie-powder court.

"I would go far to help Dame Agnes," Odo continued after a moment, "no matter what they say of her now."

2.

DAME EDITH AND SISTER CADILLA passed swiftly through the Pilgrims Gate and onto Laundry Lane. A quiet joy was singing in Edith's heart. Glad she was for the unexpected freedom, like a milkmaid after the cows have been milked. She took a deep breath and started down the hill after Cadilla.

Edith had little enough to say to Sister Cadilla at the best of times. There stretched between them gulfs of both language and upbringing. Edith was a Norman and had been raised with the soft Norman French pattering from her tongue. She had even had a Norman nurse, so to her the harsh sound of English meant maids in the kitchen and serfs in huts.

Cadilla, on the other hand, was English. She came from people who had lived here and pushed back the forests, seemingly forever. Her father had the post of Reeve in the town, the go-between, forever fixed between abbey and workers. Cadilla herself had bright blue eyes and very fair skin. Having the natural suspicion of the conquered for the conqueror, the sound of the Norman language seemed, to Cadilla, both affected and far-fetched. "Their words now," she had said once to Sister Mavern, "are indistinct."

The ill-matched pair had been placed together in the infirmary because Cadilla exhibited a strong aptitude for healing, and Edith had a delicate empathy in dealing with the sick. "If we can just keep Edith from crying." Dame Petronella had been unsure. The fact that they did not speak the same language had been ignored. Though Sister Cadilla could understand Dame Edith, Dame Edith understood little English and saw less reason to try. "The English must conform to us, not we to them." Even so, they had learned to communicate with one another through the abbreviated, yet flexible, sign language the nuns used. Imperfect communication though it was, it maintained the quiet.

There also stood between the two women a seemingly insurmountable disparity of class. It had been uncommon until early in the twelfth century for convents to take women from any but the leisured class. Peasant girls were of too much use to their families to be surrendered, even to so important an institution as the Church. In an economy where children were useful and everyone worked from dawn to dusk, a good woman of childbearing age was a treasure. By contrast, there were no nooks or crannies in the social order for the widows or the unmarried daughters of the nobility. There was literally nothing for them to do. It became usual to profess them, willing or unwilling, to one or another of the convents that dotted the southern English countryside. Though the bishops forbade the convents to demand dowries of these women, it was understood that lands, churches, houses and/or stock must be given to provide for the maintenance of the woman or girl being professed.

So the convents gradually filled with ladies, originally the English daughters of the thanes and earls, more recently the daughters of the Norman nobility. These ladies, however, were unused to, or unwilling to perform the hard physical labor that everyday life demanded. Shaftesbury abbey now employed a goodly part of the surrounding countryside in one capacity of service or another, from the exalted position of steward to the lowly, albeit healthy, position of dairy maid. These servants freed the "professed" to "manage" the community, pray, do fine embroidery and, most importantly, sing in church. Female servants who expressed a vocation or obvious piety were increasingly being allowed to make their professions. Since they came without dowries, the work of these women was considered to be their dowry. Both the lay sisters and the novices were called "sister," a different and less prestigious term from the word "dame." The lay sisters did not attend as many services as the choir nuns, and their places were in the nave of the oratory, not in the choir. There was even a separate dorter in which they slept.

Sister Cadilla was all of this and more, for she was unusually well qualified for work in the infirmary. Her mother had versed her, as a small child, in the ways of the herbs and plants that grew in the surrounding woods and fields. The duties she was habitually assigned in the infirmary, such as grinding herbs or watching the brazier, made inadequate use of her considerable learning. Sister Cadilla not only resented the arrangement but felt unappreciated. She refused to believe that Edith's gentleness and empathy was equal in value to her own knowledge of herbs and healing. Though she did not protest the inequity, it was no secret that she held Dame Edith in contempt and that only her vow of obedience kept her from openly rebelling against the injustice.

For Dame Averilla, however, Cadilla nursed no such grudge. Dame Averilla was, perhaps, even better versed in the healing arts than Cadilla's mother had been. Always curious to learn more, Averilla had been known to stop a passing bondsman when she was collecting, to milk his brain for odds and ends of knowledge about plants and animals. She was forever looking up this or that in the herbals. She read Latin, French and the runic, Old English script. "And Dame Averilla seems to know things even when she don't know them. Heals, she does sometimes, where she oughtn't to be able to, with her hands. Just her hands." Cadilla had been in awe.

3.

Now, AS THESE TWO UNEASY COMPANIONS passed through the Pilgrims Gate and hurried down Laundry Lane, they fell silent, not trusting one another enough to speculate about Dame Agnes, and not having enough language in common by which to accomplish it. As they descended the steep path, Dame Edith, hoping not to see Agnes' form there, at least not yet, allowed her eyes to rest on the abbey fishponds where spun light spattered the pinched waves. Hearing Cadilla clear her throat, Edith guiltily moved her glance toward the stream where the women of the village, their lye and clay in pots, pounded their clothes with wooden paddles.

"I see her not."

Near the bottom of the hill their noses were assaulted by the stench of the tannery. Because of its ravenous need for water, the tannery, like the laundry and the fishponds, was placed near the springs that flowed from the hill. Two dogs snapped and grunted as they tore bits of rancid meat from the still fresh hides. Swarms of flies, like black sparks, circled around the curing basins, which were filled with dung from the dove house. One of the men could be seen bending over a vat of fermenting elderberry.

Cadilla went to the edge of the yard. "Warin!" Her high voice carried over the babble sounds. The man looked up.

He was already middle-aged, but a blond growth of beard softened the lines of his face.

He grinned and came to lean against the withey fence where Cadilla stood. Edith could make out the word "Agnes" from the harsh conversation that ensued, but little else.

After a moment, Cadilla rejoined Edith, shaking her head. The path they now took intersected with the Ridgeway, a road by which pilgrims from the west entered Shaftesbury. Above them, an angled palisade of wooden pikes stretched along the rim of the hill.

A rumpled crowd pushed and jostled at the bottom of the hill. Most of the people were filthy. None were fat. A number shouldered furze faggots on long sharpened stakes. These wood gatherers mingled with the pilgrims determinedly making their way to the top of the hill and the town gate.

The two women scrutinized the crowd. Agnes was not here. There was no point in asking. They started up the steep hill to the gate. Halfway up, Edith stopped. Gleaners could be seen, bronze patches on the brass barley stubble. No frail form zigzagged through the fields.

Three men-at-arms stood with the gatekeeper who was busy hitching his stomach over his belt. A heavy cart with a shelf beneath to store hay for the horses carried tiles for village roofs, and would command a high toll, which, from the looks of it, the carter was in no mood to pay.

Just beside the gate, out of reach of the horses' hooves, an old blind beggar sat with his bowl. The skin on his face was stretched taut over the brown hollows of cheek and eye socket. Big-lobed ears jutted from his hairless head and twitched like a cat's as he pieced together the disparate sounds and voices. As another serf, open-mouthed and sly, tried to squeeze past the cart, the beggar rasped, "Hoping to slip by, are ye Matt?"

27

"Shut up you old — " the serf hissed, fumbling in the bundle.

"Mighty heavy load — " The beggar's voice rose, then was cut off as the serf palmed something into the wooden bowl, something that a second later was nowhere to be seen.

Cadilla inserted her question into the roar of confusion. The gatekeeper shook his head. "Agnes ha' na' com this way. Mog 'ere 'ud 'av said some'ut."

As Edith followed Cadilla down the Bimport and through the western part of the town, her mind was truly bewildered. Could Dame Agnes be possessed? To be sure, Dame Averilla seemed certain that it wasn't the devil, and Dame Averilla did know these things. Some of the things Averilla had done… you wouldn't want to say they were miracles. Only the saints had miracles thrust into their hands, and Dame Averilla was definitely not a saint. No. A small smile tweaked the corners of Edith's mouth as she thought of her superior. Dame Averilla was not a saint; she was an enigma. Her family was noble, Edith thought, and old as well, despite the fact that she was half-English. "Her mother," Dame Maura had whispered, "was a Norman lady. Died when she was but a child. Raised by her father, she was. Her old nurse the only female in the castle."

Edith stumbled, and glared at Cadilla's swiftly moving back with exasperation. The stitch in her side hurt. Ladies weren't expected to do this sort of thing. Haring up and down hills after madwomen. Cadilla'd just have to learn to wait.

Though there might be doubt about Agnes in Edith's mind, there was no doubt whatsoever in Cadilla's mind that Dame Agnes was possessed. Hadn't she, Sister Cadilla, seen Agnes with her hair all astart, the ends sticking out nohow and her eyes as wild as the south wind, a funny yellow light to them? And the things she said, using words that no dame should ever know or have heard. And taking off her habit like that? She had just vanished. Dame Joan was right and ought to be listened to. Allow Agnes to stay and it was just a matter of time until real evil would come creeping and entwining itself among the abbey stones. And who would be able to help them then? Sister Cadilla crossed herself hurriedly, and just to make sure, fingered the elf bolt she always carried in the little leather purse attached to her girdle. At the sound of Edith's step behind her, she sighed.

There was no sign of Agnes.

They cut over at Angel Lane and reentered the abbey through the east gate, managing to slip into their places in time for Sext.

CHAPTER FOUR

ame Joan is occupied. With Master Chapman." Dame
Alice glanced at Averilla, her lips prim. Master
Chapman was the abbey's lay steward, and assisted
the prior and bursar in the huge task of administration. He
examined the leases, presided at manor courts, maintained the
legal rights of the abbey and advised on financial matters.

"The accounts, you know," Dame Alice finished, aware of
Averilla's impatience. Dame Alice often kept people waiting.

Averilla sighed. There was nothing to do but stand patiently
with her hands quiet and her eyes downcast. She concentrated
on a dried piece of clover peeking from the rushes at her feet.
Dear Lord, she thought, it is already after midday, and the
longer we have to wait, the farther away Dame Agnes can
go. Who knows what shall happen to her then? I should be
thanking you for your care of her. I do, but you do know
how dangerous the forest is. Lord, there is evil in the forest,
and she is only in her smock. What if she should meet
someone? What will they think? Dear Lord, let the steward
come out now.

The heavy oaken door with its iron rosettes opened and the
steward strode out, a fleshy man with shoulder-length graying
hair and a neat beard. He wore a short blue mantle lined with
gray fox, and polished boots that laced to the knee. "It shall

be seen to," Master Chapman said, half turning to the unseen Dame Joan, and then, with a slight bow to Dame Averilla and Dame Alice, opened the door to the inner court, flooding the room with light. A handsome man, Averilla thought, with those wide shoulders and the scar slashing across his cheekbones, but there was something about him that she couldn't quite like. She thought she had seen dislike in the bailiff's eyes, too, when the two men had been discussing something to do with the abbey.

"Dame Averilla?" Dame Joan stood at the door to the office, effectively blocking Averilla from entering. Her look was calmly inquiring. "I do have much to attend to this afternoon."

"As have I, dame. I would hesitate to bother you were it not desperate. May we speak?" Averilla paused, not wanting to say "alone," which would offend Dame Alice.

"Of course we may speak." Dame Joan tilted her head and calmly stood her ground, deliberately pretending to misunderstand.

Averilla clenched her jaw. "It is a matter of some delicacy, which would, of course, be safe with Dame Alice, but which, if another should come in while we were speaking, might cause unnecessary hurt." To underline the obvious, she added, "May we speak privately in your chamber?"

The chamber they entered was simple yet spacious, and smelled faintly of the herbs that mingled with the rushes on the floor. Averilla could discern both rosemary and lavender as they entered, and wondered, uncharitably, which of the bushes in the herbarium had been raided. An iron-bound coffer stood in the corner, its three hanging locks open and dangling, the keys still in their keyholes. There was only one seat, a sort of bench-stool with carved ends, onto which Dame Joan, placing both long hands on the table, lowered herself, leaving Averilla to stand in front of her in the position of supplicant. As bursar, the job given at Shaftesbury to the sub-prioress, Dame Joan had charge of all of the abbey's money, and had to draw up the accounts for the whole year. Tally sticks were used to calculate the sums, which were then written on both sides of six pieces of parchment stitched together into rolls, each encircled and tied with long strips of parchment. The senior nuns, the obedientaries, inspected these rolls prior to the annual meeting every June.

"Dame?" Dame Joan squared the box of sand used for blotting even with the corner of the table, and narrowed her black eyes.

"I intend not to disrupt your day, but the matter is of some delicacy," Averilla forced her voice to remain even.

"So you have said."

"Dame Agnes — "

"Dame Agnes?" Dame Joan's head came up like a cock with a new hen.

"Dame Agnes is missing." Unconsciously, Averilla held up one of her hands to forestall the exclamations of surprise and irritation. "She is having one of her bad times. When we came back after chapter, she was gone. Sister Cadilla was seeing to something in the infirmary kitchen. She and Dame Edith have searched the ways in and out of the town and the abbey park. They did not find her."

The room was ominously quiet.

"So tell me, sister," the calculated affront, Norman birth to Anglo-Saxon background, "I mean, dame, what you intend to do about this? You are not yourself out searching the fields for her?" The sarcasm was not lost on Averilla.

"Dame Agnes is sick."

"Mayhap. But," Dame Joan's fingers convulsed around one of the tally sticks, "the atmosphere of prayer and quiet that we try to surround ourselves with can so easily be disrupted. When we are jolted from the harmonies of vision by discord and violence — "

"The woman is sick." Averilla raised her voice to be heard over the other.

"Dame Agnes is possessed. I am not blind. I have seen her yellow eyes. I suspected that such as this might well happen. Dame, you become too enchanted by your own talents. You must open your eyes. You are harboring one who is affianced not to Christ, as we should expect, but to something much more ominous."

"She at least refrained from saying Agnes was in league with the devil, but she came close. Very close," Averilla would later tell the bailiff. "Her meaning was unfortunately clear."

Dame Joan stood up and leaned across the table toward Averilla, her black eyes flaming. "She will bring harm to the innocents, to the weak and to the infirm for whom you and I have responsibility. She disrupts their peace. She raves. Dame, I have heard her. One can hear her ravings as far as the park."

"The spells are infrequent," Averilla found herself almost yelling.

"That is my point. Spells. They are spells. She hears voices. Not the voices of the saints, but the voices of 'others'."

"But, dame," a red tide of anger surged into Averilla's mind. She clamped her teeth hard on her inner lip. After a moment she said, "Dame Agnes is, most of the time, very sweet and very pliable. Think, dame, of the years of counsel she has given the abbey, of the respect she has well earned. This... way of being is new to her. She is scared of these voices. She has pleaded with me to protect her from them. She prays fervently to our Lord to save her from them. But they follow and ... and torment her."

"Then we want none of them. None of them, dame. You have made the case against her very ably. I have not the time or the energy to argue with you on this matter. It is very clear to me where my duties lie. My responsibility is to preserve the peace and tranquility of this abbey. You are misled. Look to your pride in this matter, and send for the bailiff without more ado.

Averilla's eyes flashed a green fire. "That, dame, is exactly what I came to ask permission to do."

"See to it, then." Dame Joan reseated herself, drawing toward her across the table the roll of sheepskin on which she had been working with the steward. As it passed it disturbed the neat piles of notched sticks. Joan ignored them. It was an act of dismissal.

Averilla remained standing. "And when she is found?" Dame Joan looked up, her black eyes steely. "I think I have made it quite clear how I feel about this matter. Dame Agnes' presence does not contribute to the health and tranquility of the abbey, or of the souls committed unto our care. There is no — "

"Dame," Averilla interrupted, "even in the village they take care of their sick in mind, with compassion and humor. Most here see Dame Agnes with sorrow and charity, not anger or fear. Their souls' health depends more on how they treat her than on how she treats them." With a perfunctory bow, Averilla jerked open the door, and stumbled into Dame Alice, who had been listening on the other side of it.

"I shall speak with the abbess." Dame Joan's words followed the infirmaress out the door.

"As shall I," Averilla paused to fling back over her shoulder.

CHAPTER FIVE

I.

After Vespers and supper, near sunset, the bailiff followed Sister Theodosia across the inner court in search of Averilla. The ground of the herbarium, when they reached it, was wet from a small rain that had pattered down during Vespers, and the rain-released smell of wet lavender and rosemary, germander and mint scented the air. Robert Bradshaw, creaking of leather, shortened his stride so as not to overtake the diminutive woman whose duty it was to accompany strangers who needed to talk to a member of the community. Past the hedges of lavender, Averilla could be seen, a black, bent form, weeding. She heard him and smelled the horse smell, the coldness of the wind, and the freshness of male sweat about him, but continued to pluck out of the ground the last withered spears before rising to greet him.

"Master bailiff," her eyes smiled at her old friend as she held out both hands. The abbey was a huge enterprise, owning most of the land, houses, farms and churches around Shaftesbury, as well as properties as far away as Devon and Cornwall. The abbess was a baron of the realm, and her bailiff had wide responsibilities. Because it was a time of such uncertainty and little safety, the abbess felt justified in abrogating to Robert

35

powers he would otherwise not need to assume.

"I was just now informed," Robert said. "I was detained in the forest. These are very bad times. Paugh! The king and the empress at each other's throats. And my lord of Gloucester to the north, absent from his lands. It breeds unrest, unrest and lawlessness. Bands of masterless men and outlaws increase fourfold. Things have happened that I am at a loss to explain. A lamb missing from the demesne and a bird maimed. A swan was found with its wings cut. One of Brigold's dogs was slaughtered; just slaughtered and left. The heart cut out. A nasty business. I like it not." He combed his fingers through his short thick hair.

Robert Bradshaw was a fair man, if somewhat abrupt in his dealings with men, and was strangely comfortable in the peace of the abbey grounds. Because of his height — he stood well above average, somewhat under six feet — men perceived well of him even before they came to know him. Ruddy of complexion, he had steel-blue eyes and a barrel chest, which soon, Averilla suspected, would develop into a paunch. His hair and beard were that halfway-between-red-and-gold which, in a woman, is cause for celebration. He had embarrassingly long eyelashes and small hands.

"Those packs of human wolves form a large part of my worry," he continued, "as do these strange occurrences." Averilla glanced up at the sky, which had resumed its interrupted raining. Without words, the two of them sauntered along the mossy paths toward the officina. Sister Theodosia, forgotten, trailed dutifully behind.

After a moment's thought he turned his head toward Averilla. "So, Dame Agnes has disappeared."

"Aye. We searched the abbey and the abbey lands as far as we could, but the farther she goes, the more land there is to search. It is not seemly for us," Averilla motioned vaguely at

36

the habit, "to wander far from the enclosure."

The bailiff scratched his cheek, as if the skin above the well-tended beard was dry and itched. It was a habit he had when he was thinking. Averilla knew it well. They were friends, these two, having been brought into contact over the years upon one matter or another. They saw eye to eye, and their minds knew the same language.

"Dame Agnes," he said at last, choosing his words, "has been in much trouble of late, I think?" He ducked his head under the low lintel of the officina. Even Averilla had to bend a bit to keep the top of her veil from touching the lower edge of the roughhewn plank.

The hut was small and snug, the stone flags of the floor scrubbed and clean. It had a rich, musty smell about it from the bunches of herbs that hung beneath the rafters. There was a slot window on each side of the room, which gave a little light for the work that was done there. The walls were lined with rough clay pots, carefully sealed with wax, parchment and bladders. Cloudy bottles and some large stoneware jars ranged along the shelves. An oaken table butted the wall and held a three-legged pot, several ladles, a mortar and pestle and some flat clay dishes. Robert glanced around for a stool. The fire of apple logs in the center of the room was banked low, but there was still some heat from the embers, which, with the wet afternoon and the coolness of the autumn, was welcome.

"Yes. Agnes has had," Averilla's voice was low and sad, "a strange sort of madness this year past. She will be her old self for weeks, aye, even months at a time, and then she will start to rave and speak gibberish, and ... and she blasphemes. She hears voices and they scare her. I know not whether she is now running away from them, or whether the voices told her to run."

"I think of Dame Agnes with much respect. She has always

been fair and wise, and charitable in her dealings as cellarer. You suspect something foul?"

Averilla stopped and looked at him for a long moment. Sister Theodosia's eyes were wide, her horror palpable. "Yes," Averilla said finally, "and in fearing that, I also fear that which brigands, or — or anyone — might think of her actions and ravings. Mind you, she does no harm, but," and here Averilla brought her lips together in a taut line, "her storms are fearsome. It was while I was at Mass that she disappeared. The voices may have enticed her to do something. I-I cannot say." Averilla, in her frustration, busied herself tying up the last few bunches of creeping thyme. Her back was to the bailiff. "She was only in her smock; no tunic, or wimple or veil. I am much afeared that she may come to harm."

"It is the worse that some time has elapsed. Coming back through Gillingham Forest this afternoon, we came upon a band of masterless men. Surly they were, but nothing more. I let them be. There are too many of them to do aught more." He paused, shook his head and then continued. "Be that as it may, we saw no sign of her. I shall go and see what I can while there is aught of light left to this waning day. We can travel afield on horseback. Mayhap we shall overtake her." He stopped in thought for a moment. "Yet, if she is wily, and intends to evade us, she can. There are caves, you know, in the forest. The tops of the oaks — " He unfolded himself from the three-legged stool and bowed. "If we don't find her tonight, we shall call out the hue and cry on the morrow at first light. With luck we shall find her curled up asleep in the bracken."

"Go with God," she muttered at his retreating back, and made the sign of the cross in the air as he followed Sister Theodosia toward the forecourt.

WHEN THE BAILIFF RETURNED, ABOUT THREE hours later, Averilla was in the warming room. It was comforting there as the evening shadows lengthened. In the frosty days of autumn and winter most of the community could be found warming numbed hands and feet in preparation for the last service of the day, Compline, and the coldness of the night which followed. It was Sister Theodosia again, wide-eyed, who tapped Averilla on the shoulder and bid her follow.

"The bailiff is our friend, child. There is naught to worry you. Perhaps he brings good news of Dame Agnes."

Robert Bradshaw was standing in one of the parlors set aside for visitors. His blew on fingers roughened from riding and chapped from the autumn chill. The low room was spare and clean, with dark timbers holding up the ceiling. Two simple benches stood against opposite walls. The small high window was shuttered against the night.

A crucifix of Norman workmanship hung on the wall. It lacked the intricate traceries and the curling lines of Celtic work. The contorted body and the limp draperies described the excruciating agony the Man had suffered. Robert had been turned toward the crucifix. Averilla could not see his face. "I sometimes wonder," he said harshly, turning to her and nodding his head toward the hanging figure, "why?"

"I—I" Averilla didn't trust herself with more.

"We came upon a babe today. Killed in the forest."

Averilla's eyes squinted in horror. Her hands flew to her mouth. "Killed? You know that? Why? Who? — "

"Aye, I know that. The remains were," his voice was grating, spewed from deep in his chest. "Corla's child. The babe born not long ago, if you remember, with the misshapen arm."

"Wha— I must go to her."

"Nay, dame. Not now. Others are with her. Father Merowald. Some time later. Your respects. Not now." He cleared his throat and narrowed his eyes. When they had both reflected on the enormity of his words, he looked back up at the lonely Man hanging on the Tree. "What profit to Him and to mankind if there still be suffering?" Robert's eyes were angry.

"I, I…" Averilla started, her hands rounding a limp gesture. "I do not know why, either," she said finally as she raised her eyes to Robert's face, from the spider web on which they had been resting. "But, at least, He," she jutted her chin toward the wall, "knows what it is like to suffer. He doesn't just watch us…"

He sighed deeply. "We must be content with that, I suppose," he said at last, fatigue evident in every line of his body. "Dame — " and he seemed for the moment lost. "So," he took a deep breath and shook his head as if a fly buzzed near. "Dame Agnes." He turned his head tentatively, hearing the bell for Compline start its tolling. He brought up from the scrip at his belt a small scrap of linen. "We found naught of her but this, to the north on the road that goes toward Gillingham." It was a piece of linen, torn and dirty, the dried rust of blood fringing one edge.

Averilla took the linen in her hands and felt the smoothness of the flax. "It is from the abbey. It is our work. I know it well." Then, after waiting for him to respond, she asked, "There were no other traces?"

"None. We were on the road, so the footmarks meant nothing. Dame, your bell beckons. We shall have the hue and cry tomorrow. I shall ask at the outlying farms."

"You will let me know…"

"Dame, I shall." He left through the forecourt while Averilla joined the procession for Compline.

3.

SHE WAS DEEP IN A FOREST, A FORBIDDING, unfamiliar forest. Oak branches, wide spreading and round as a man's leg, writhed in the wind, their crippled, lichen-covered arms webbing the sky around her. She was trying to shoulder her way through the tangle of vines and briars, trying to find, trying to find … she didn't know what she was trying to find. Off in the distance, she heard, faint at first, then coming nearer, the insistent tinkling of a small bell. The abbess must be coming, the tinkling nearer now. The abbess would know what she was trying to find. The abbess would help.

As the abbess put a cool hand on her forehead and smiled down into her sleep-fuddled eyes, Averilla started up from her bed. The bed, like all the abbey furnishings, was austere, no more than a framework of boards crisscrossed with leather and supporting a straw pallet. It took Averilla a moment to fumble her way out of the fog of dream and sleep and back into the night dorter, to recognize that it was time for Matins. She was safe on her bed, and the abbess was smiling down upon her with a flicker of worry in her eyes.

After a moment the abbess continued on down the long dormitory, ringing the small bell to awaken the rest of the nuns for Matins. It was about twelve of the clock. In the Abbey of the Virgin Mary and St. Edward, King and Martyr, the nuns had chosen midnight for Matins. The darkest part of the day needed the reassurance of God's presence, the promise of a new beginning. In some houses, the sub-sacrist rang the awakening bell, but Abbess Emma, as had Abbess Cecily before her, awakened her daughters herself.

Averilla, befuddled as she was, made the sign of the cross and commended herself to God. She could remember Dame Petronella, the novice mistress, admonishing them with a no-nonsense shake of the head, "How do you expect the rest of your day to proceed if you don't begin it properly? The first thing you must do is to commit yourself to God. Over and over again. Every morning."

It was so cold. Averilla didn't want to rise. How could she even think of God when she was so cold? Her feet never warmed in bed during the cold months. Like all the rest of them, her hands would start to crack with chilblains as the hoar deepened. Even though she burrowed her head and hands under the coverlet while she slept, she always woke cold.

"Show me Lord, what you would have me do today," Averilla prayed. "Even the cold, Lord, is yours. Let me embrace it and thank you for it." As the rule required, all the nuns slept with most of their clothes on, so rising fuddled in the night took little conscious thought. As she fumbled for her fur-lined night slippers, the memory of Dame Agnes gripped her mind like an aching tooth. Averilla tried to release her worry to God, but couldn't. She felt along her bed to the foot, pulling on wimple and veil from the neat pile on the bedside stool. Then she slumped back to await the deep-throated tones of the small bell, Doven, which would signal the start of the procession down the night stairs.

Led by a junior with a lantern, the snake of nuns wound its way down into the church. Their felted boots made no sound to break the Great Silence as they filed across the transept. Only where the sacrist had lit candles on standards did halos of light pierce the darkness, small glimmerings of grace in the womb-like black. Even the cold gritty smell of stone soothed the senses and those befuddled minds not yet awake. As she paced behind the cellarer and then seated herself in the recess of her stall, Averilla burrowed into the oval of silence.

When the abbess entered, the office of Matins commenced with Dame Alburga intoning "O Lord, open thou my lips;"

42

and the assembled community mumbling out the response, "and my mouth shall show forth thy praise." As they sang psalm three and then psalm ninety-five, their voices lost the night scratchiness, smoothing out and gaining in clarity. Even in the summer season with its shorter nights, chapter ten of Benedict's rule dictated that for Matins a total of twelve psalms be tossed back and forth between the two sides of the choir. The high voices soared into the darkness as if seeking The Presence, becoming the lark's awakening exultation of joy.

Matins and Lauds were sung one right after the other. In the short interval placed between the two services for the necessities of nature, many of the nuns stretched their legs in the cloister. They walked singly or in pairs, wrapped in their thoughts, maintaining the silence, stamping their feet or warming their hands in the long winged sleeves of their habits. As she walked, head bowed, Averilla's thoughts circled Dame Agnes like the miller's horse on the threshing floor. After a moment, she felt the presence of someone beside her and glanced over to find that the abbess had joined her. They accompanied one another, unspeaking. "It's something that you find with surprise as you grow in your vocation," Dame Petronella would always tell the novices. "People hide behind their words. When you are silent with someone, you know their innermost being by how they are and what they do. Small gestures and actions reveal a great deal." The abbess had seen how distressed Averilla was, and was lending her support. Averilla felt the other woman's prayer settle, like a warm blanket, around her troubled spirit.

By the time the sacrist had turned the pages of the Bible and found the passages to be read for Lauds, it was nearly 1 A.M. In some houses, Lauds started later, for it was the service meant for the dawning of the day. At Shaftesbury, however, this abbess, and those before her, had thought it best

43

to awaken the community only once. St. Benedict's rule was gentle, with room for choice and human frailty.

Like Matins, Lauds was a service of sung psalms. The officer of the day sang the first verse, then came the voice of the abbess alone, ringing out the second, and then the full choir batted the rhyming thoughts between them.

Averilla cherished her hours in the choir. As infirmaress, she was often away from the community, bound to those under her care, singing the offices in the small chapel attached to the infirmary. Three times a week, though, Dame Edith took the night duty, and Averilla was free to be with the community. That way, the infirmaress did not become too much isolated from the minds of her sisters. This night, perhaps because of the discord of her dream, Averilla felt herself enclosed by a tenderness that eddied around her like the scent of roses. It had no particular face or voice, only a soft and steady warmth.

CHAPTER SIX

Soon after Prime, the first office of the daylight hours, the abbess settled herself in her lodgings against the eerie hawk's song of the hue and cry and determined to attack the pile of letters that needed response. Mayhap concentration on the accounts would take her mind from Agnes. She was more than surprised when a tap at the door interrupted the quiet. This pause between the morning offices was traditionally a time when each nun attended to private duties. It was unusual for any to impinge on the solitude of another.

At her rather irritated "Deo Gratis," a face peered around the door, followed by the rumpled form of Dame Petronella.

The untidiness of the novice mistress irritated the abbess even more than usual. How could Dame Petronella hope to impress discipline on the novices when she herself couldn't keep her wimple straight? The abbess sighed and privately awarded herself a penance for her lack of charity. The value of this woman, she well knew, was her care of and her concern for the novices, not her fastidiousness. She shook her head.

"Yes?" she said finally, trying to instill the sound of interest into her voice.

Dame Petronella took a few more steps into the room. "It is Sister Julianna, milady."

Again. Mentally, the abbess prepared herself for the worst. Since early the year before, Julianna had become more and more of an irritant to the well-being of the abbey. It had started very much like this. Dame Petronella had come to the abbess with her worries.

At first the abbess had not been concerned. All the novices, in the first year of their novitiate, occasioned this worried look in Dame Petronella's soft brown eyes. Abbess Emma had folded her hands and complacently waited for the recital of all the little nuisances that would be attributed to Sister Julianna.

"She hates it here — "

The abbess' back had stiffened and she had widened her eyes.

" — and … and milady, she has no respect. Even for God."

That had been too much. Emma had furrowed her brow in consternation. Indeed, this was far from the usual tedious litany of minor offenses.

The novice mistress' face had crumpled. "I have erred. I must have. But I know not how. She is lazy, true, but that alone does not account for — "

"Tell me, dame."

"She — she laughs behind the backs of the older nuns. And she has such a wit about her that she has cadged a smile — even from me — at the expense of another."

"Who?"

"Dame Alburga, for one."

Without wholly erasing her frown, the abbess had managed to raise an eyebrow.

"I know, my lady," Dame Petronella had answered the implicit question. We — the long professed — believe Alburga's voice to be that of an angel. But of late, a kind of warble has attached itself to her high notes and she draws out the word *Dominus;* lengthens it so as to make the one word sound indeed as if it is two, nay three, words together. Have you not noticed?"

The abbess had shaken her head.

Petronella had ploughed on, determined to get to the end of it. "And she so mimics that the other novices find it hard to resist laughing. It is a temptation of youth — to scorn — but here it seems overly cruel."

"Aye. Indeed." The abbess had pressed her lips into a thin line.

Petronella had continued. "Though I have seen the like of this rudeness before, usually 'tis naught but a testing, which can easily be erased by the application of a little honest responsibility. But, milady, Sister Julianna just doesn't care."

"And she mocks you, I would guess, though you say it not. Is it so?"

"Aye."

"And hurts you with pointed barbs, though you would not admit to such."

A tear had wended its way down the lined cheek. "But that's not the worst, milady. Nothing — nothing does she take seriously." Petronella lowered her eyes and her voice. "She even mimics the priest at the altar."

The abbess had been horrified. "And the others laugh?"

"No, no. Not at that. It happened only the once. But — "

The abbess had risen, as was her wont, and stood before the fireplace, thinking. "You feel you have done all you can?"

The other woman had nodded.

"I will speak with her."

That very day, the abbess had summoned Julianna to her rooms and purposely kept her waiting. A paltry trick, the abbess had told herself, and I am ashamed of it, but necessary if I am to break through to her.

When finally admitted, Julianna had sauntered into the chamber with the disdain of one used to the rich furnishings attendant on birth and breeding. The girl's eyes had rested on each of the meager appointments. "She didn't actually curl her lip," Emma later confided to Petronella, "but her contempt was ... obvious." Under such scrutiny, Emma had found herself blushing and awkward. She had been ashamed of being ashamed. "I was not made to feel ashamed," Emma had confessed to old Dame Aethwulfa, the prioress, making an ironic little moue. "It was my own doing. I suppose I took too much pride in my 'humility.' In my role as abbess I imposed austerity on the lodgings, yet under the eyes of this raw child, I wanted the protection of gold and silk and jewels. How unreliable is my poverty."

Despite her internal battles, the abbess had forced herself to remain seated, purposely not offering the girl a chair. Julianna had looked her straight in the eye and deliberately trailed her tapered fingers along the carving on the back of the chair the abbess had not offered.

"As well you know," the abbess had begun, "the fourth chapter of the Rule of St. Benedict speaks to the subject of laughter and to the pain caused by evil and wicked words. When I was young, I oft wondered about the caution against laughter. Surely, I then thought, laughter, which brings such a feeling of redress to the soul, can cause no harm." She paused to let the words sink in. "But the Sainted Benedict saw the temptation in laughter; as when a laugh is used against another."

Julianna had looked down. Her lashes, long and strangely curled, had covered her eyes and she appeared unusually demure. "I willingly confess it, milady. I have erred."

"Indeed she said the words," the abbess told Petronella, "but they were glib. There was no ache in them."

"I might be able to control myself better, milady, had I a grain, just a taste, of freedom on my tongue. Is there some task that would let me borrow the trappings of independence for a little time each week?"

The abbess had thought about it and after a moment said, "While Dame Agnes is indisposed, you might be permitted to accompany Dame Edria to the markets each week. Would such an outing make the transition easier for you?"

"I was asking a novice if something was to her satisfaction! Am I mad? How did such a strangeness come about?" The old prioress had only looked sad.

At the time, the abbess thought she saw relief hunkering behind Julianna's eyes, but after the novice had gone, the abbess had wondered if perhaps what she had glimpsed was a hard shard of triumph.

Since June of the previous year, Julianna had been accompanying Dame Edria to all the markets. Emma had hoped that some miracle had occurred and the girl had settled down. Obviously it hadn't.

"Julianna has not settled down as we had hoped?" she now asked.

"Quite the contrary, Lady. If anything, she is becoming more defiant. And disruptive. She enlists the others in her schemes. They have become even more spiteful."

Emma sighed. "She is no closer to a vocation."

Petronella's eyes grew wide. She settled for a concise, "No, my lady," and then blurted out in one sentence, "She has been disappearing. While Edria shops. And she does not return until well into the day."

CHAPTER SEVEN

ater that day, the second day following Agnes' disappearance, tired from the sleeplessness of the night before, eager to hear again from the bailiff, and hating the enforced inactivity, Averilla found herself feeling irritable as she reentered the officina. If they do find Dame Agnes, how will I — how can I — help? The water from the well in Gillingham Forest works a bit, but not enough for Dame Joan's satisfaction. "Nor mine, if I am honest with myself," she muttered aloud. There must be some herb or ... mayhap one of the herbals? King Alfred's *Laece Book* might have something ... Averilla cocked her head and chewed the inner corner of her cheek as she inspected the high shelf where the herbals were stored.

The three sheepskin volumes contained everything that was known about the healing arts: everything from ancient lore and tried remedies to the new thought from the East. From the odds and ends of aged charms to the mystery of wortcunnings, it was all there. Cherished and passed from one infirmaress to her successor. The parchment leaves were well preserved despite repeated turnings. Each infirmaress had added something to the trove, bits of knowledge gathered here and there, observations or thoughts, all written carefully in the margins or sometimes, when much learning had been gathered, a whole signature of new leaves had been added to a volume.

Just recently, when Ailred of Rievaulx had passed through Shaftesbury, Averilla had spent more than a week sitting across from him in the officina, picking from his brain bits and pieces of lore. After the saintly medicus had gone, she had needed four full pieces of parchment from Dame Agnes. Dame Edith had eagerly cleaned the skins with pumice, and polished them with a goat's tooth, knowing that, after Averilla had spent weeks dipping her quill into the bladder of soot and vinegar and writing down the recipes in her crabbed runic hand, she, Edith, would be asked to intertwine the capitals with colors; to create on the pages images of her beloved deer and the faces of small animals peeping through the tendrils of such as rue or mugwort. Averilla smiled as she thought of her assistant, vowing to suggest to the abbess that Edith be given duties in the scriptorium at the next distribution of offices. Averilla would miss Edith's true compassion with the sick, but she could see in her mind the joy the younger woman would feel being assigned to do that for which she seemingly had been created.

Averilla shook her head at the distracting thought and looked again at the high shelf. The creamy sheepskin volumes didn't seem to be there, leaning against one another between the iron stands she used for bookends. She sighed. The cloudy flasks and wax-sealed jars of poisonous mixtures that shared the shelf with the volumes were often replaced hastily. They had probably crowded the seldom-used herbals to the back of the shelf.

Listlessly, she dragged a stool across the room. Her cold fingers fumbled as the stool snagged against a pebble on the floor and fell from her grasp. Muttering imprecations she had learned from the stable lads as a child, Averilla bent to pick up the stool. A smooth shaft of blue-gray glinted against the grit. An elf bolt. Curious. She didn't like the things. Sister

51

Cadilla had one; Averilla had seen her fondling it. She didn't believe in them and wished that Cadilla did not either. She might as well admit it, though; they gave her an eerie feeling just the same, a pricking of her thumbs. Despite the fact that she didn't like having it near her, she put it into the purse that hung from her belt, smiling ruefully at her own wariness. If she was afraid to have it near her body, didn't that mean that she did believe in it? She thrust the thought aside and continued her quest.

She needed to know more. Why did the water help Agnes at all? She had leafed through one of the volumes when Agnes had first come to her, but she hadn't looked in the older book, hadn't sought through the smudged depths of two hundred years ago. King Alfred's *Laece Book*. It was of great value to the abbey. Sent by the Patriarch of Jerusalem to Alfred the Great, who in turn had sent it with other of his translated works to his daughter, then abbess, and her convent at Shaftesbury. There it had remained, safely locked in the aumbry with the other books. Some of the knowledge it contained had been copied, over time, into one of the newer tomes. But not all. Perhaps, just perhaps, there would be some herb, some long-ago knowledge, something the eastern magi knew that would help. She shifted the stool until it touched the table, then mounted it, pulling the long habit away from her sandals. Reaching up, she fingered the bottles on the shelf, tickling her fingers into the cracks between the bottles, touching through to the back of the shelf, delicately moving the jars a bit. The herbals were not there — any of them.

"'S bones, where are they?" Nothing was smooth. "Dear Lord, help me find the books. I know it is but a tiny tuft of worry, but I am tired, and what am I going to do about Dame Agnes?" There they were! Behind the jar of dried witches' bells. She smiled at her own blindness, at the easy answer to her

52

prayer. They were where they were supposed to be.

Averilla hefted the first and second of the heavy tomes down to the table, then put up her hand for the last, the older volume with its crabbed and ancient lore. It was not there. Of course it was — she just couldn't find it. Carefully and with exasperation she took down the poisons: the cool, gritty, pottery jar of dried witches' bells, the small flask containing the juice of deadly nightshade, a squat glazed pot of genestra mixed with hog's grease. Then the bowl of henbane seeds, the jar of larkspur, the tiny golden flask of lily of the valley, which she had used on Dame Agnes. An infusion of monkshood was the last to be removed.

They were all down. All the jars and bottles. She looked at the small collection and back at the empty shelf. A clammy, cold dread writhed up her back. Tears started behind her eyes. Oh, God, help me! King Alfred's *Laece Book,* gone, all because of me. One of the abbey's most precious relics. I insisted that it be stored here. Dame Joan repeatedly protested. Too much access, she had said, and I wouldn't listen. I swayed the Chapter, pulled on their heartstrings.

Averilla had won. The unpretentious book had been carried with full ceremony to the officina, leaving in the nuns a complacent sense of rightness; that their mission was not one of amassing material possessions, but of helping God's poor. She, Averilla, had wanted to test her power against that of Dame Joan. They had been like oil and water against one another since the earliest days in the novitiate. Hadn't she envied Joan her premature appointment to high office? That snake of malicious envy had encircled her heart so that when she, Averilla, had had a chance, she pitted her own popularity against the other's meticulous competence. No doubt about it, she had taken advantage of her office. She had wanted to win. Joan was just trying to protect the abbey. That was what the sub-prioress was supposed to do. It would have been just as easy, Averilla now forced herself to admit, to read the *Laece Book* in the south transept. But she had wanted to prove her power, had wanted to best Joan.

She climbed the stool to look yet again. The book was gone. But how? It should have been just as safe here, for certes. No one came to the workshop but Sister Cadilla and, infrequently, Dame Edith. None wanted to be here. There were no signs of another presence. Putting her dusty hands to her forehead to straighten her rumpled wimple, she burst into tears.

Just then, without knocking, Sister Cadilla banged open the sturdy door and dashed into the hut. Too preoccupied to notice Averilla's distress, she blurted, "Dame Averilla, come quick." She flapped her hand in a beckoning motion. "John the mason. He's fallen. Off the scaffold against the western tower. They are bringing him. The men are. Blue he is. His lips — "

Averilla tumbled off the stool, tipping it over sideways, pulled her skirts high. "Christ be with me," she said, and bolted out of the hut; "Christ within me," brushed past the younger nun; "Christ beside me," and sprinted the short distance between the infirmary and the workroom; "Christ before me." Poor man. Be wrong, Cadilla. Not John the mason.

The earnest face of John's young wife, Alice, with her birthmark, came unbidden to Averilla's mind, followed immediately by visions of her three tow-haired children; the oldest with the gap-toothed smile of just six; the youngest, newborn.

This was too much. Not six months ago another mason, a man called Rab, who had worked on the abbey for the last twenty years, had fallen from the roof. They had all heard his scream as it scored down the side of the church. When they brought him to Averilla on a plank, the back of his skull had

54

felt like an apple in the fall, pulpy and misshapen. There had been nothing she could do. Rab never again opened his eyes, though he lay there for more than a week. A month later, his wife, Corla, had been delivered of a scrawny, misshapen child. Corla had tried to earn their keep. She had made beer, helped with the harvest. Her children left in the care of the eldest, an eight-year-old. Even with all that, she hadn't been able to pay her rent to the abbey.

Master Chapman had asked them to leave. Dame Joan had been matter-of-fact as she brought the matter up to the chapter. "It is indeed unfortunate," she had said, "but we need our rents to be able to support ourselves; to be able to help all the rest who will come … " and she had trailed off.

"If I remember correctly," Dame Agnes' voice had been soft, imperturbable, polite, "our Lord had something to say about widows and orphans."

"Indeed, dame. But it is my duty to make sure that we have enough to survive."

"Is our survival in question?" The abbess had raised one eyebrow.

"Er, no, but … " and Joan had blushed.

The problem still pricked at their collective conscience, festered in their thoughts, sat in choir with them. Corla and the children had been taken in temporarily by one family of masons or another, but no one in the village would have enough to spare over the winter. Sooner or later there would be no where else for them to turn and they would hunker before the doors of the almonry. Their sturdy clothes would turn to rags. The faces of the children would become pinched with hunger and fatigue. Until, finally… And now, Corla's child had been found dead. Oh, dear God.

It was this horrid war. Months on months of it. And the famine and lawlessness that followed. Even the abbey felt it.

They could ill ask starving peasants for grain they did not have to pay the rents they owed the abbey.

Averilla pushed the thoughts away, and forced herself to concentrate on John. "Is aught broken? Does he bleed? Are his arms and legs misshapen? Do they hang strangely?" Her words were flung over her shoulder to the younger, squarer woman.

"I know not. I saw but little." Sister Cadilla stumbled and slackened her pace, cradling her side, gasping her last words after the retreating back. "Dame Edith. She is with him and bade me run..."

His head. It must be his head. Oh, Lord, let it not be his head, Averilla thought. Red meat to keep down the swelling and some willow bark for the pain.

Except for the ugly rasp of his breathing, John's huge frame was limp. Gareth, one of the hodmen, stood beside his master, dirty nails scratching nervously at the leather of his apron, the lines of his knuckles darkened with stone dust. They were carrying him to the infirmary on the plank on which they carted the stone. Stone dust caked the sweaty chest hairs peeking through the leather of John's tunic. The white pallor of death was crouching near, brushing his lips with a blue and bloodless purple. The bruise was starting, indigo and wide, like some sort of spreading fungus. Averilla turned, followed them into the infirmary and pointed to where they should lay him.

"Build up the fire," she commanded Embert, and pointed at the pile of kindling next to the central hearth.

"Hurlbut, get the pallet off that bed." He scurried toward the arcades, where several beds were unoccupied.

"Gilder, now lift him, gentle now, up on the pallet and closer to the fire. That's it. On the pallet, man. He can't lie on the cold stone."

56

"Pillows, Sister Cadilla, under the top of him. Don't bend his neck."

"Dame Edith, fetch linen, and willow bark."

As the burly young men bent gingerly to do her bidding, Averilla turned on Gareth, "Tell me, how happened this?"

"I … I … saw it," Gareth stammered, "from below. He was up on the roof, ye wot, of the west tower, er, as will be. There is no roof there, yet, but some beams across."

Averilla clenched her teeth, knowing that to interrupt the recital would alter it, and might allow him to forget something important. She willed herself to be patient.

"We mun cover the new mortar afore the cold can spoil it. We had strewn the straw already. To protect the mortar, ye wist. And one beam was there, for a winter roof, not permanent. Gilder was drawing up the second beam with a winch and it began to swing to and fro like a bell as being rung. Can happen that. The swaying. Not 'is fault. Embert tried to cross on the other beam to halt the swing. He was too late. Afore any could help, it swayed and hit the master. Tried to catch himself, he did, but in the end …" Gareth trailed off, staring blankly into the embers of the fire, seeing … Averilla sighed, imagining what he saw.

Averilla's whole body tensed as she approached the injured man, her muscles locked, her brain searching for relief. There was none, she knew. She hated wounds of the head. She could do something about the bleeding, and the cuts — bugle, milfoil, samile and loosestrife — her mind quickly reviewed her stores, but as for the rest …

From without, in the forecourt, there could be heard a shrill keening coming closer. That would be Alice, John's wife. Averilla could see Alice in her mind's eye, lappet drawn close to hide her face. Well, the wailing would help Alice, but it would only unsettle the unconscious man, not to mention the peace of the convent. She would have to be gentled home.

"Gilder. Please see to Alice." Averilla's voice was peremptory. "Take her home to her children. Just to be with them. And — and summon some women."

Averilla knelt beside John and watched him for a moment. His breathing had become weak and shallow, his skin pale and clammy. She felt down his legs and arms for fractures, praying that none had occurred. He was still whole. No white shattered bone protruded from bluing flesh. Another coverlet would do no harm. Keeping an eye on the man, she rose and pulled felted wool from the store cupboard and gently folded it over him.

There was a hesitant tread on the stone steps from the forecourt. Averilla looked up, distracted by the quietness of the sound. A small bird-like man entered the room. Father Merowald. He was the parish priest, that is, the priest who sang the masses in the conventual church, for the people of the town and the lay sisters on the nave side of the rood screen. He was a man of a very ancient age with a powerful love of God. Sanctity gleamed through the withered parchment of his skin. He made his halting rheumatic way across the room. Reaching her, he asked, "Dame, may I pray with you?"

Averilla nodded.

He knelt down on the other side of the straw pallet, placing his body carefully so as not to block the heat from the fire, interwove his gnarled and misshapen fingers and bent his head. Latin phrases pattered softly into the darkening room, a litany of supplication and praise and glory for his beloved God; words the man under him could take solace in, words that would, to the mason's faraway brain, provide a glue and drawstring back to this world.

Averilla, too, steepled her hands over the recumbent form, not inches from the parson's. "Oh God," she prayed, "help this man." She tried to focus on the bright light of the Almighty, to see behind her eyes. She knew she should place herself under God and ask for the healing power, that painless fire that could, at the right moments, dwell in her fingers. It wouldn't come. Try as she might, she couldn't get behind her eyelids. There was something tingling her mind, a restlessness of something not done, a problem not solved. Agnes? Of course, Agnes. And the book. She shook her head as if to ward off a fly. Where was the book? Who could have taken it? Her eye rested on one of the iron latches to the store cupboard, and suddenly she knew, as a shudder of anger and—was it fear—poured over her body. The elf bolt. Someone. One of those. She could feel her anger rise within her, a bulging vomit in her throat. How dared they come into her workplace! How dared they defile the purity of even a part of God's house with their blasphemy, with their unbelief? To take that most precious of volumes for their fell purposes."

"My child," Father Merowald patted her hands gently, but when she looked into his eyes, they were firm, firm and commanding. "Whatever it is, let it go. Your anger disrupts the prayer, has no place here." His bright, kind eyes held her gaze, compelling, by force of will, her obedience. "Give it up."

Gratefully, she retreated into obedience. She imagined throwing her anger to the wind at the edge of the park. It was a wrench. "I probably couldn't have managed it," she would tell the abbess, "had it not been John and Father Merowald." She willed her mind to go deep within her; to travel behind her eyes to the bright sparks of sun where her spirit was in the hands of God. Her eyelids started to flutter and she could feel a tingling warmth in her hands, which were still being held between the gnarled, rough, gentle palms of the parson. Together they both rested their hands on the prone man lying before them.

Soft words from the parson's lips ticked against the brokenness, asking only that the will of the Father be done, but suggesting — with time-honored insistence, like drops from a branch in the spring — that this man needed His help. "Thy will be done, of course. But Father, this servant, this man does need your care. There are children, Lord, and a young wife. Not to mention your own needs here in the abbey church."

Averilla's eyes flew open. She didn't think one was supposed to bribe the Almighty.

Father Merowald continued, undeterred by his own gall. He spoke to the Father as a friend, someone who would understand and do something if all the facts were just laid out neatly before him. "Who will we get for the work, eh? There is only John who can well lead these men, with the war battering the country. The others don't have the skill. And you know, Lord, what happens to widows. I needn't tell you. We've been over that one often enough together ..." His words became a mumble, and then a quiet. Averilla knew he hadn't stopped but had gone further in, deeper into the soul of the man. Her thoughts followed.

They stayed there for the rest of the afternoon. Their minds soared between waking and light, in the hands of God, not pleading, but somewhere with the mason; giving him up to a loving God who knew the need better than they did; giving themselves to support and to recognize the need of this fellow human being.

The little light that came through the slot windows waned as the afternoon trickled on. Averilla heard the shutters quietly being closed, and was dimly aware of the bells for both None and Vespers as she and Father Merowald remained undisturbed and still. The sheen of cressets enfolded her bit by bit and shut out all outside her. Her heart opened and overflowed with a sweet thankfulness, even for this difficult moment but mostly for the love of God. She felt herself slide into the star-beam of candlelight where motes danced in the darkness. A scalding anguish seemed to sear her momentarily, and then she felt the prayers from the community like a wall behind her, holding her up, sustaining her and giving strength to the broken man before them. The nuns had fixed their thoughts on John. During the office they would say the words they were meant to say, but they would line them with thoughts for him. Between services three or four nuns would kneel in the chapel next to the shrine of St. Edward. One or two candles would flicker, making of the black kneeling forms, shadows against the stone of the church. They would pray, "Thy will be done; Thy will be done, but Father, please. Not here. On your own grounds." They too would not spare the feelings of the Almighty or those of St. Edward. It was merely a matter of showing him the facts. It always helped. St. Edward had granted them several miracles, as had the Virgin Mary, the Mother of God, their other patron. They didn't question the miracles when they were granted or the wisdom when they weren't. Abbess Cecily had been very firm about that, as had the abbesses before her all the way back to the foundation. It was in God's hands, always in the hands of God.

Suddenly it was over. Simultaneously, Averilla and Father Merowald opened their eyes and looked at the mason. His breathing was even, his color returned.

Father Merowald tried to rise and failed. With a twinkle in his still-bright eyes, he said, "Dame, can you rise?" Averilla found that she could, though the pain in her knees was a heavy, cat-like pain, searing through the numb tingling of her calf. With an answering twinkle, she staggered over to the old man and helped him rise. "Perhaps we both might do with a refreshing cup of your herb tea, Dame Averilla. And you can tell me the news of the convent, for I have been much preoccupied with the affairs of the town."

Averilla placed a pot over the little brazier and, while it was heating, gathered together what she could from the infirmary kitchen to make of their interval a full meal. She knew from looking at him and from having been told, for such things were muttered by the people, that he had little to eat. When his people suffered, as now they did, with this war raging, he, who was their shepherd, refused to be better off than they were. He would never ask for food from the convent, though they had sufficient and it was due him. She took from the infirmary kitchen a round, crusty loaf, warm from the afternoon baking, sliced hunks from it and laid them on a carved and hollowed wooden platter, its grained interior smoothed by years of use. She took out a ripe cheese from the home farm, smooth and golden. There were apples in the basket, and she placed two of the ruddiest, still holding the sun's breath in their skin, next to the cheese. She made the tea with herbs that were always there, choosing chamomile for calmness. There was little more she could do without offending. If she brought in a steaming cup of the broth that Sister Cadilla always kept on the further brazier, all pretense would be gone and he would feel her charity. He would refuse, not from pride, as she knew she herself might do, but because it would be taking something that none of his parishioners could have.

They sat companionably awhile on stools in front of the glowing ashes, the chamomile tea warming their insides. She offered him chunks of the yeasty loaf — not maslin, but oat, for the health of those in the infirmary. The apples, crimson orbs, lay where they had been laid, subtly reflecting the firelight, somehow ripening and expanding in lusciousness through sight. She knew that Father Merowald was savoring, before tasting, the dewy, sweet-apple flavor, the crunch and spurt of juice, the

62

counterpoint of cheese.

As he took the smaller of the two apples and rubbed it against his cassock, Averilla took up a stick to poke the embers. "King Alfred's *Laece Book* is missing," she said softly. She looked up in time to see his head perk up like a dog on the scent of a boar. "Gone from the high shelf. And an elf bolt was on the floor amid the rushes." She was barely able to repress an involuntary shudder. "It was not Sister Cadilla's. I have seen hers."

He carved a hunk of cheese from the round and chewed it reflectively before responding. "I am not surprised. The reeve is missing several lambs from the demesne. But, my child, you haven't yet told me the real agony of your soul. Dame Agnes has gone missing, I understand, and is having one of her bad spells."

"I knew you would have heard. The hue and cry?"

"Even afore that. There is aught that passes me by in the village from word of confidence glibly spoken to common gossip. Many there were that saw Dame Edith and Sister Cadilla. Later, Odo pieced it together for me. He had another mishap?"

"Odo?"

Answering her unasked question, he added, "He wishes to learn to read, and comes to me for it during the waning light. He told me of the good mad dame."

"Think ye that my herbal is somewhat connected to Dame Agnes?"

"Of that I am unsure. But I fear her path may cross something I like not the smell of. Hunger breeds a greedy litter. Her young go squealing into every open hovel."

He rose after his one apple and the bread and cheese. With a flicker of amusement in his eye he reached for another of the apples. "This repast has much refreshed me, dame. I thank you for your hospitality. It pushes out anger. No wonder the bread of the mass is called the 'host.' But I digress. You must tell Robert Bradshaw of your concerns. And of this fall of John's. You are sure it was entirely an accident?"

Her eyes grew wide. "But surely. Who could have aught against John-the-mason?"

"Dame, I know not. But John of all the men on the tower? It is too apt. So. If any word comes slithering under my door, I too shall tell the bailiff. I fear for your mad Dame. It is not safe to be mad in these days. There is little compassion and much fear for such sheep as stray from the beaten path."

CHAPTER EIGHT

At first there was only the red. It shattered the mottled blackness, and then changed and deepened into a faceted scarlet. Like waves tossing against cliffs, it came and went. She knew about cliffs. Had known. Didn't know now. Couldn't find them.

The red was warm against her face; warmer than the constant cold lurking there beside her, lying down next to her, caressing, soothing, like death. Surrounding her. The cold, and the nimbus of red. The red battered away at the beginnings of her as if something in her knew more than she could fathom. She was trembling, too. She could feel the shudders start at the bottom of her feet and slice up her body, but without the regularity of the red.

Then there was nothing. For a long time. As it stole upon her she was glad and welcomed it.

The red of the nimbus crept in again, brighter now, piercing. She flinched from it, shook her head away.

"Simon! Here!" The sound, guttural and grating, forced its way through the red. Irritation surged into her numbness.

"Aye, here in the hut." Those were words. She knew words. Something about them chaffed at her; distressed her. Fear. Was this fear? Acid gnawed at her belly and slithered through her body, growing, strengthening and embracing the cold.

Something blocked the red; distorted it. The heart of the nimbus was gone. She opened her eyes. A face? She knew faces. Not this face. The face leaned toward her, yellow-eyed and gap-toothed. A warm, inner, human stench, the decaying stink of bowels and rotten teeth, overwhelmed her, violated her oneness. She tossed her head from side to side against the hard-packed dirt.

"Waiting fer me, are ye. Just in yer smock. Ready fer me. Then open up, me pretty." Cold, callused hands grabbed at her legs, prodded them open. Cold air streamed in, touched her intimate places. "Nnnnoooooo." She clenched herself, curled and thrashed against the prying hands, afraid for the very realness of self. Self? She was.

"Berthold!" Another voice, gruff, loud, hammered through the silent battle.

Men. These were men.

"No time fer that," said the gruffer voice. Needs fetch 'er to the lady. She'ul be glad to 'ave found 'er, I warrant. Leave 'er. Don't want to get too close to such as that. Plaything of the devil, she is. Or worse."

The face receded. All she could feel was the cold. Why hast thou forsaken … Another face appeared. Hairs stuck out of a bulbous nose; a nose with open pores black with dirt. She tried to crawl to the top of her consciousness; struggled against the encompassing mud which thickened her mind. A stinging pain slashed against her legs.

"Up, ye stupid witch. Stand. We have a meander to find." A sharp snapping sounded within the hut. A lash! She had been whipped! Like a horse! Or a dog! Or a serf! A bright anger flamed against the nothingness and she knew, finally, herself.

There were two men. She had never seen them before, but by the look of them they were not serfs. Their eyes were defiant, and free; tied to nothing. She tried to muster words. Felt her tongue curl against the cracked inside of her mouth. "Leave me alone."

"That brought 'er up."

"Knew it would." One man, the first face, moved behind her as he said it. He squeezed at her breast as he pushed by her. Before she could fumble her way through what that meant, hands grabbed her arms and wrenched them behind her. Coarse cord cut into her flesh.

"No need fer this any more." As he said it the man pulled at the silver chain that hung around her neck, flinging it and the cross that dangled from it behind him. The other man tied a noose around her waist. She butted at him, but was too late and too feeble. She writhed and thrashed, wiggled her body, kicked at a groin. She missed the man and slammed her toe into something hard. Stone? The pain rose, tingling and sharp, through the bones of her leg. She looked down. Her feet were bare. How strange! She was only in her smock. Why? Where was she? She looked around. It was a place she had never seen before. Small. A hut. Made of stone. A lance of sunlight pierced through the unshuttered slot of window. Pierced through the mist outside.

"Ye be comin' with us. Better for ye to come quiet like." She felt the pull of the rope on her waist and struggled after them, rocks piercing the softness of her feet. She didn't belong here. If not here, then where? She was ... she was ... a nun? So, ... how had she gotten here?

Had she taken of the draught? Oh, yes. She remembered, hazily, in a nether part of her mind. After None. Behind the dorter. Under the reredorter, where no one came because of the stink. The leather flask. She had been told to save it for Allhallows Eve. But she hadn't. And she always wanted more. Galiena probably didn't know that. That was all she could remember. After that? They said that she raved for hours after she had drunk of the draught. She never remembered that. Any of it. She had never believed them; had thought they were making it up. But ... often she had awakened to find herself in the infirmary. So many times. And had not remembered. Even that first time. Her last memory would always be of the town. And the street in front of Galiena's house. And she always awakened in the infirmary. And time would have passed.

Agnes stumbled against a root and fell. They lashed at her and she struggled to her feet to flounder behind them further and further into the mist-spattered forest. As she staggered, she heard the voice. It was soft. Not entirely unfamiliar. Not scratchy. Rather pleasant actually. "Where is your cross?" Today there was something mocking about it. Not friendly as it had been before. The hairs on the back of her neck rose. She felt fear. The voice spoke again. "Where is your cross?" She didn't know. She couldn't answer. Why was the voice tormenting her now? She wanted to sleep. "Where is your cross?" The voice was laughing now, triumphant. With the last vestige of strength, as tears of remorse traced down her cheeks, she struggled with her hands, still firmly tied behind her until she could place one index finger across the other. Aloud into the mute forest and at the two trudging men she screeched, "I do have a cross. See, I still have a cross. Against the cross, you are nothing. Do you hear? Nothing!"

CHAPTER NINE

hat night after Compline, her ear cocked, hoping to hear the bailiff's footfall, Averilla watched over John as he slept. He twitched from time to time and moaned softly to himself, but otherwise she was satisfied with his condition. Except for the soft chuckle of the banked fire, the infirmary was still. Rush lights glowed from shallow niches carved into the building, and there was a soft rustling from the corners as mice scuttled about their tiny business. The shadows waxed longer as the oil in the lamps dwindled, longer, but not menacing. When there seemed no more chance that Robert could possibly appear, Averilla's head nodded and she slept.

She was roused from a deep, dreamless slumber by Dame Petronella and Dame Marguerite, who were escorting young Sister Theiline from the dorter with compassionate haste. The latter was retching violently and vomiting. Averilla's brow furrowed in concern at Theline's sudden illness. It had been her experience that when one of the sisters started vomiting, twenty or thirty would follow suit. She dreaded an infirmary full of retching and wretched women. "Do they all have to have all the attention all the time?" Sister Cadilla had been exhausted the last time it had happened.

Sister Theiline, usually more boisterous than not, was as

helpless as a baby bear up a tree after too many green apples. Averilla draped strips of wet linen across the young woman's forehead and offered a sturdy pot to the edge of the bed when the sickness was upon her. Between bouts, Theiline was embarrassingly grateful. Averilla kept her own gorge down by imagining that it was Christ to whom she was ministering. "I never did hear of Him being aught but hale and very healthy," Sister Cadilla had muttered when the technique was first explained to her.

The question of Dame Agnes wiggled to the forefront of Averilla's mind as she wrung out cloths and trotted back and forth emptying chamber pots in the reredorter. It was at first just a creeping wisp of a thought. Then, without intervening logic, she found she had made a decision.

"'Twas I, and I alone," she muttered, swabbing out the bowl, "that could caress Dame Agnes to quietness in her ravings. 'Twas I that she clung to as the ravings were shaking her. My words could coax her, can now coax her from a tree or a cave. Armed men might scare her." There was no question in Averilla's mind. She and she alone needed to go. "I won't ask Dame Joan," she said to herself, squeezing the damp cloth over the pottery basin. "Not again. I shall ask in chapter." Averilla set her lips in a determined line, and forbade herself to remember the eagerness with which she had faced the battle over the *Laece Book*.

The next morning, after the incessant ringing of the "Transgression Bell" at the end of the Chapter Mass, the community processed behind the juniors into the chapter house. Averilla glanced down the cloister walk as she passed, but there was no sign of either Robert or Sister Theodosia coming to fetch her. When Abbess Emma had taken her place, old Dame Aethwulfa, trembling on rickety knees, knelt to kiss the abbess' hand. The old dame's face was like that of an apple too long stored, wrinkled and creased into a withered husk. This daily exercise was the symbolic renewal of the covenant of obedience between the community and the abbess. It was penance to watch the frail old dame slowly inch her way to her knees, holding firmly to the carved lion on the abbatial chair, seemingly gathering strength from it. "But of course she gathers strength from it. Christ was called the Lion of Judah," Dame Petronella had said with some asperity to Sister Julianna, the only one with the courage to question.

The getting up was even worse. Sometimes the old prioress would sway and start to topple. Then the gnarled, brown-spotted hands would scratch and grasp at the abbatial chair or even at the abbess' tunic. Somehow she would manage to clutch at the marble of the chair and clamber, using the carvings as handholds, up its side. Day after day, the community had to watch the whole painful procedure. Dame Alburga had once, with more concern than forethought, asked the abbess why. "Is it wise, Reverend Mother," she had asked, "to put the prioress through this excruciating, um, penance morning after morning?"

The abbess' eyes had held the cold green ire of a sudden, righteous anger. "She needs to do it. We need to have her do it. She makes obeisance not to me, dame, but to God." The abbess had then relented, breathing in a deep sigh, harnessing her own anger, forcing her mind to rehearse her own covenant. "Your job, my dear," the bishop had told her at her installation, "is to shepherd and to teach your sometimes wayward flock. That's why you have a crook, a shepherd's crook," and then he had handed her the heavily jeweled crook.

"My child, my dear child," she had then restarted with Dame Alburga. "We need to be reminded daily of the awesome nature of what we do here. Dame Aethwulfa, I think, demonstrates that as well as any martyr. There are

71

different sacrifices for each of us."

After reading a chapter from the Rule of St. Benedict, the abbess said, as she did every day, "Let us speak about the affairs of our house." This was the signal for the novices to leave and for all the outer doors to be locked. What was mentioned or discussed by the professed nuns was never to be spoken of outside the curved and vaulted walls of the chapter house. The transgressions, the faults, the charters signed, or the presentation of candidates could not be mentioned later. The commemoration of the departed, alone, was to be known by all. Written on the tabula, it would be displayed in the narthex for a day. The abbess gave a short address, shorter today than usual. After that, temporal matters might be broached.

Steeled and resolute, refreshed from deep prayer during the Mass, Averilla stood. "Mother," she said, "I would be given leave to take Dumb Will with me to seek Dame Agnes in Gillingham Forest."

The abbess placed her elbows on the carved arms of the abbatial chair and steepled her hands. "Your concern is understandable, dame. But … there are always calls to pull us out of the cloister. Can the infirmary do without you? How does the mason?"

"Well, Mother. He slept the night through. He left with his good wife for their house this morn. His head throbbed, his fingers trembled and he was as wobbly as a newborn colt, but he was anxious to be with his kith and kin."

"And away from a house full of women." Dame Maura could be counted on to release the tension.

"I imagine we shall see him back high on the scaffold within a fortnight."

"Um. There is none in your care who need your skills above those of Dame Edith and Sister Cadilla?"

"No, Mother. Those in our care will profit more by Dame Edith's gentleness than by my distracted ministrations. My mind is much entangled by Dame Agnes."

The abbess looked around at the faces of her flock. Some were dreaming; others were attentive. As she turned, the better to assess the mind of the old prioress, she felt, rather than saw, Dame Joan's resistance. "Dame?"

"Mother, may I speak?"

"Has it to do with the present matter?"

"It has."

"I hated to see her start up that way," Dame Petronella lectured Dame Marguerite as they hurried back to the novices in west walk. "Who does Dame Joan think she is? Pride — pride and position — that is what it is. Eating her up, I daresay. Always had a thing about Averilla. From the first day in the novitiate. And dear old Dame Aethwulfa. Can little keep charge of her assistant. What with her age upon her and her old eyes."

Dame Joan made her way to the center of the floor and faced the abbess. "Dame Averilla spoke to me on this matter. We, as a community, need to consider how seemly it is for one of our number, even with the accompaniment of a guardian, to go off into the woods. Is this the job of an enclosed? Should not we have the patience to allow the hand of God to reveal itself? What can one of us do that cannot be done by the bailiff and his men? I suggest that Dame Averilla oversteps herself."

Dame Aethwulfa had started to scratch away at the carved arm of her chair. She hated conflict. When any disagreement broke out among the community, the nuns knew she would start scrabbling away at the chair. The abbess shifted slightly on her throne. A flush of annoyance splashed across her high cheekbones.

"Dame Averilla?"

Averilla's voice, when she answered, trembled. "I can explain the reasoning that led me to this present request. Sometimes Dame Agnes, as the spells were coming on her, would come to me seeking solace. From time to time I have been able to gentle her, or at least hold her while she raved, letting her words flow off me. I thought only that mayhap, just mayhap, my familiarity might speak to her, might draw her out of her covert. The bailiff's men could well scare her. That is all." Averilla didn't retake her seat but stood, choosing her words.

"As for the other, more serious, allegation, I trust the wisdom of God, but Mother," the entreaty in her eyes and voice commanded the attention of even the most bored, "He gives each of us skills, or mayhap just a way of thinking. It might be that mine is the skill that is needed right now." Averilla bowed her head and made her way back to her seat.

Abbess Emma looked around at the faces ranged in rows on the hard stone benches. She'd had to learn to read those faces. It was the hardest part of being an abbess. An abbess was not duty-bound to ask for a vote, but things worked immeasurably better if there was agreement within the community. Sometimes, she knew, the nuns didn't want to voice what they felt. At those times, it fell to her to discern from their eyes and hands what they wanted and to take their stance for them. At other times, when the dissent was palpable, she would ask for a vote.

"Mother." Dame Joan still stood, her strong form compelling the will of the chapter. "All Dame Averilla says may be true, but ... " She let a pause sink in, to allow those who had been listening to remember her words, "we should give the bailiff and his men, those whose job it is, the simple courtesy of our confidence in them."

Dame Joan had compelled the will of the chapter. The abbess could see it. "Dame Averilla," she said, "you are refused permission to travel in Gillingham Forest to seek Dame Agnes. We will await word from the bailiff." Averilla bowed her head.

When chapter was over, Averilla walked to the infirmary alone. At the top of the infirmary steps she hesitated, resting her hand on the cold hard stones.

She watched as Sister Cadilla bustled among the sick, tucking a coverlet here, picking up a chamber pot there, stooping to spoon some broth into the waiting mouth of old Dame Maud, eager as a bird for her sustenance. Averilla's eyes were warm as she looked at the younger nun. How little she understood her. How little anyone understood anyone. She or Dame Joan.

"Sister Cadilla," she began as she came down the steps, assuming a briskness she did not feel, "has all been well during chapter?"

"Aye, that it has, dame."

Averilla nodded, and then, as if another thought had caught her, fumbled in her scrip to bring out the elf bolt she had found on the floor of the workroom. "Sister? Can you perchance tell me anything that I ought to know about this?"

Sister Cadilla glanced at it briefly. Then she turned away briefly to pour liquid from a flask onto finely carded wool. With her back to Averilla she said, "No, dame, that I can't. You've seen mine, I know. I have caught your eyes upon it many a time. It isn't something that you put much truck in, I imagine. My old dam gave me mine. For her I cherish it, sort of a keepsake."

"Not a touchstone? Not a talisman? Or an amulet?"

"I wouldn't know about them." Truculence crept into her voice.

"What I mean is, do you expect any... any help from it?"

"How should I, with all the saints and such to guard over me? And the angels?"

"I wouldn't know about that, dame. With Father Merowald to take care of their souls, what would any need from a stone?"

To Averilla's ears the words sounded hollow — rote passages, publicly acclaimed. Nothing was going to be gained from Sister Cadilla on this matter.

CHAPTER TEN

I.

After Vespers, Averilla, muttering vaguely about autumn cleanup, scuttled off to the sanctuary of the herbarium. Her bruised spirit ached for the crisp solitude and the numbing solidity of the soft, cool earth between her fingers. A rain had ticked against the walls of the abbey church at midday. It had been sped along by a high, crooning wind, which had blown skirts and tossed veils as the nuns hurried through the damp, leaf-strewn garth and across the cloister. The work in the cloister carrels had been halted for the misery of the day and the lack of all but a thin, nacreous light. Sometime after None, the rain had dribbled off into a dank mist that climbed out of the clammy vegetation. Smoke from village fires had curled up within the mist. Together they created a murky soup.

Averilla, as she scurried to her nest, expected nothing more than the solace of dripping leaves and a drizzled quiet. There had been no word from Robert all day, and that meant he had found no trace of Agnes. At the corner of the infirmary wall she stopped, soothed by the mellow color of the hedges outlined against the flatness of the day. Bryony and bittersweet berries peeped from between the russet and gold of intertwined blackberry leaves. Plump little finches and tomtits flitted, brown and comfortable, among the branches. Their staccato movements dimmed slowly as they gorged themselves.

She drank in a deep breath of the quiet and plunged between the drooping bushes. With one deft movement, she kilted her habit and started to pull up the spent and soggy plants. Earlier in the fall she had carefully wrapped the various seeds in linen and placed them in rush baskets to be plunged again into the earth with the coming spring.

Weeding released the tension that had been cramping her neck and shoulders since midmorning. Methodically, using a wooden fork, she mounded debris in the corner farthest from the hut and the infirmary wall. She would build a bonfire two days from today on Allhallows Eve. Then the garden would be neat and orderly again, cleared of the bedraggled vegetation. Since ancient times a bonfire had been lighted on Allhallows. It was a pagan ritual, dedicated to the old gods, but still she followed it, as would the rest of the countryside.

Many of the flowers, not as hardy as the hedges, had wilted with the rain. The once soft, spear-bright petals were now opaque. Leaves that had glowed ruddy in the spring, their edges tinged with crimson, now held only a dim translucence, like watery, half-cooked onions. Her mind drifted, catching at a straw of memory that seemed to frequently recur to her. She was only four in the memory, living in her father's manor with her nurse. It had been an autumn day, she remembered...

I dawdle behind the high table, the only table, just now, in the great hall. The other tables, the trestles, are taken down after we break our fast. The way to the solar, where I have been sent, is behind the high table. It is my father's place, the high table. He always sits there. Often alone. I drag my fingers along the soft wool of the hanging. I always do that.

78

The softness reminds me...

I climb the spiral stairs to the solar, taking one step at a time. My legs are short. The stairwell is narrow and dark, even with the thin morning sun straggling through the slot windows. Fire baskets jut from the walls above my head. They are empty of flame, so it is cold. But at least the long-clawed creatures that writhe there on the walls when the baskets are lit, ("Shadows, only shadows", my nurse repeats), are hidden in the daylight.

The stairs are wedge-shaped, and narrow, so narrow toward the center. I cling to the outside wall. "An intruder, any intruder, would be forced to fight up the stairs. His sword arm would be on the wrong side," my father has explained.

"Who would they be, Fader?" I ask, have asked, not understanding. "Who would come into the hall that you do not want? This land is yours. You have said this, haven't you? Fader?"

He answers as he always does, "Aye, Maid. Yes and no." And then he says, "Hush," and cuddles my head next to his chest. I put my fingers in my mouth, but he cannot see them, cannot correct me, and I nestle into the warm, scratchy smell of his beard and feel the soothing thumping of his heart next to my body.

Later, I run down the stairs and slip out of the hall and into the bailey. No one pays any attention to me. My nurse stands talking to a tall man. She tilts her head up at him. Her wimple falls back. She shades her eyes from the westering sun and does not see me. I scamper behind the back legs of a horse, the man's horse, I guess. The beast is huge and lifts one hind leg, tilting the hoof, relaxed, resting on his other legs. His tail switches at a fly, then arches, and the great cord unfurls from beneath his belly. He is going to pee. I scramble into the stable. I don't want pee splattering my new, long gonnelle. With tight sleeves. My very first. The stable is hot, hot with the length of the day and the warm, clean smell of horse and dung. I climb to the loft and squirm into the hay, like a fish slipping through the coverlet of the water. A fly buzzes. The smith clangs at the forge. My nurse laughs. A goose objects. The mice scrabble somewhere near. I sleep.

A shaking wakens me. My nurse, her face haggard, spits words at me, so fast that I do not understand them. A tear slips from beneath her spider-web lashes and melds into the freckles on her face. How could anyone so old have freckles? I smile up from the hay and hold ou t my arms, and she hugs me fiercely.

"What would she say, your moder? Your dear moder. What would she say?" My nurse looks to me as if for an answer. My moder. Other children have moders. I do not. The word is never spoken by my father.

"They look like mush."

Averilla, startled from her reverie, whirled around to find Sister Helewise, one of the newer novices, pushing aside the wet shrubbery. Like Averilla, Helewise was raised in the north. Averilla found herself pleased to see the frank and winsome younger woman. "Like a breath of wind," Dame Petronella had exulted a few months after Helewise had taken her simple vows. At the time, one of the other novices had been launching into a convoluted rationale for the Rule of St. Benedict. Helewise, with a bored drawl, had interrupted, "We need the Rule because we're human. That's why." Petronella had had to scold the interruption, but she had gloried in the no-nonsense insight.

Now, without thinking, Sister Helewise tucked the hem of her skirts into her belt, and tugged at the ragged plants with vigor, seeing and understanding without having to be told, what Averilla was about.

"I miss this," she blurted into the dampened silence. "There was a small plot in the bailey at home." Helewise paused and Averilla did not fill the vacuum with words. The novitiate could be very hard to adjust to, even for women bred to be seen and not heard. "My — my mother loved it and taught me to value the growing things. I need this." She attacked the plot of ground with renewed vigor, her knowledgeable fingers plucking the spent annuals and clearing around the more hardy bushes.

Averilla watched. The girl was deft. Her hands were capable and strong, wide for a woman. "You, too, have a joy in the growing things."

"Aye, dame." A flush brightened Helewise's pale features, and her hands flew to her wimple, muddying its pure whiteness. Averilla smiled, for she too, often could be seen in less than a holy state of repair. Dame Petronella had despaired of teaching Averilla to walk, not run, and to watch her hands and feet and her flighty words.

"Could I help you sometimes? I'd be glad of it. It is the 'nots' of cloister life that prick at me so. The not being able to ride, and the not being able to … to run across a meadow." She paused and looked over the rolling downs, brownish gray, undulating into the distance, obscured here and there by the newly shredded mist. "The obedience, I guess, is hard for me."

"I know. The obedience scratches at the soul. Sometimes I feel that I wear a hair shirt in my mind. Such chaffing prods me to the freedom of this garden. I asked in chapter today if I could go into the woods to seek Dame Agnes. It was refused." Averilla felt a sense of relief as she spoke aloud of her rejection. It seemed as if she agreed or at least had bent herself to it. "Sometimes I think we know ourselves not very well at all." She paused, surprised. Here she was, speaking with candor to one of her sisters. The nuns rarely talked except during recreation. They had been taught to avoid the patter of unnecessary words. "Keep your mouth from evil and wicked words. Do not be excessively talkative. Do not

81

speak vain words or such as move to laughter," Dame Petronella never tired of quoting to the novices sections of the Rule of St. Benedict. She would often add ominously, "Too many confidences breed particular friendships. You must learn to speak your innermost thoughts to God, and to God alone."

"But you were not in the chapter meeting earlier and will not know of that discussion. I should not have mentioned it."

Sister Helewise chose to change the subject. "I always think the ground looks forward to winter; to not having to spend itself in giving, like a mother with too many babes. We had a bitch once who had a litter of ten. Ten puppies. She looked so tired and dismayed as they started to grow, and were yet still gnawing and suckling and pushing their little paws in and out on her belly. I think the earth must feel so at the end of the days of summer, completed, yet at the same time — "

Dunstan thunked at them from the bell tower, ringing them in to supper. The deep bass was deadened by the woolen batting of smoke and fog. Right after the sound of the bell came the mournful sound of the shepherd's horn, which summoned the sheep home, allowing each to trot off to its own byre or pen.

"Oh, dame, I forgot," Helewise said, muddying her cheeks with her hands, "the meaning of my errand. The abbess bade me bid you to sup with her in her lodgings. I was to return with your response."

"Then perhaps," Averilla rose and slapped the mud from her hands, "we had both better go. Sister, you have refreshed me."

"I think I miss the talking even more than the weeding." Helewise's eyes, under the wimple, were unusually shy.

"Mayhap. We all do."

2.

AT THE ENTRANCE TO THE ABBESS' LODGINGS, UPSTAIRS above the parlours, Sister Clayetta was dusting a small table with a goose wing; her movements slow and deliberate. Hearing the whisper of Averilla's habit, she turned. "Her ladyship has been expecting you," she said, and opened the door.

The austere furnishings of Abbess Emma's lodgings contrasted starkly with the wealth of the abbey. "It is said that were the abbess of Shaftesbury to marry the abbot of Glastonbury, they would own more land than the king himself." Alburga needed "her" abbey to have a "certain primacy." The simplicity of the lodgings were a reflection of Abbess Emma rather than an expectation imposed upon her. The abbess of Shaftesbury controlled extensive property: lands, manors, churches — even whole towns. She was expected to entertain religious and secular dignitaries. She was a baron of the realm, and it was considered proper that her rooms reflect her rank and degree. Very few days passed wherein some earl or baron was not being entertained, listened to and often counseled within those walls. Abbess Cecily, born to such a life, born a FitzHamon, reveled in the glory of her power and built the abbess' rooms to reflect this. Abbess Emma, also born to such a life, recoiled from the pomp and nothingness of the trappings of power.

Sister Clayetta took pride in Emma's humility. "She was real, she was. Didn't want to do it. It isn't always that way, you know." Emma had been truly reluctant to assume the crook and ring after her election as abbess. "They often pretend, ye wot, those elected to abbess. Pretend like they don't want the job, when all the while they can't wait to get the feel of that heavy ring around their fingers and the glories of a kitchen all to themselves. No, they push it away with one hand while pulling it toward them with the other, like the merchant with his gold for the church. They mew and blink their eyes to the floor, like newborn kittens. I've seen a lot of them, I have."

Sister Clayetta, a bent apple-doll of a woman, had taken care of four abbesses before Emma. "But with Dame Emma as was, I could hear her locked away in that bed chamber. It wasn't only the sobs, for she didn't know then that I had to be near her always. She thought she was alone. She pleaded with Him," and here Sister Clayetta had raised her rheumy old eyes to the ceiling, and had clucked her tongue, "about the cup and all." In the end, Emma had taken the office with good grace and the calmness that came from a hard-won peace. "Her face was white, I tell ye, white as the down on a swan's belly. For weeks. And sometimes she trembled. Didn't eat but a bite here and there. But she bent to it. She did bend to it. In the end. She had to."

This deep inner peace had both caused Emma's election and saved her from it. In the early days of her abbacy, she had grasped at her peace in desperation, refusing to forfeit that which had brought her to the abbey in the first place. Peace still eddied around her, like the wash caressing a rock rising from the sea. It was this inner peace that, above all else, her flock cherished. As the years had passed, the calm tranquility seated in the being of the abbess had radiated out, creeping into every creature and cranny of the abbey. Any of her sisters welcomed the chance to spend a moment in her presence. It was said that her serenity could calm the most belligerent of barons. She was often called in to try to bring about a meeting of minds, to cajole, even in these days of discord and war, opposing views into concord. So, it was with joy and some apprehension that Averilla had straightened her habit and climbed the enclosed circular stairway that wound next to the cellarium and parlours to the abbess' lodgings, which were above them.

At the "Deo Gratis," Averilla entered and bent to kiss the abbatial ring. Emma was a tall woman, tall and willowy. Her fingers were long and slender, so slender that the ring she wore for the glory of her office slipped and turned, made, as it was, for a woman with a much wider hand. Green eyes, the green of early spring, pierced through the most devious of rationalizations, until, after a moment, the dimple on one side of her mouth would wink at the miserable sinner in companionable understanding. The novices said you could tell the way the wind was blowing by how much of the dimple showed as the abbess went about her duties during the day. Long, unusually black eyelashes fringed her eyes. She used them from time to time to hide her thoughts from the men with whom she had to barter and persuade. Other abbesses often lost money and property through lack of canny dealings. Emma was rarely slighted in a bargain. Under her administration, the Abbey of the Virgin Mary and St. Edward, King and Martyr, at Shaftesbury had seemingly flourished.

"You called for me, Mother?"

"I was hoping," the abbess rose from behind the table at which she had been working, "that you would sup with me, for my mind is perplexed and I would be glad of your counsel."

She motioned Averilla to another table, well polished and set beneath a glazed window. A fire in the new hearth set into the wall bristled and spat with the still-green apple wood from a tree in the kitchen garth. There were silver candlesticks on the table. Averilla had seen them before. Their bases were square and richly wrought, with curving vines and mythical beasts etched into the silver.

Where Abbess Cecily had had hangings on all the walls, some embroidered with geometric or circular motifs, brought, it was said, from the Holy Land after the fall of Jerusalem, Abbess Emma had only the well-rubbed paneling and the rushes on the floor. Averilla wondered idly to herself what had become of those tapestries at the death of Cecily. Had they gone back to the FitzHamon family, or were they carefully stored somewhere in the abbey? The room boasted no other furnishing than a crucifix over the fire and three armed stools, deeply carved.

A door in the far corner led to a chamber where the abbess sometimes slept. When she could, Abbess Emma chose to stay in the dorter with the community, but sometimes the exigencies of entertainment forced her to sleep here. "Her chamber, she'd keep it as bare as a monk's head if it war up to her. 'Cept that chamber is the one as is given sometimes over to ladies and such when they abide with us. The lady abbess, she chooses to sleep on a pallet on the floor, she does. Keeps it rolled up under the Queen's bed." Queen Matilda, mother of the Empress, had once stopped at Shaftesbury for more than a fortnight. An ornate and richly carved bed had had to be acquired to house her majesty. It was used, more frequently than not, by the wives of nobility as they traveled through a country bare of any other hostelries. "Has me remove all the hangings, she does, until one of them comes to stay," Sister Clayetta had confided. "She keeps not even a hanging or a stool. Naught but a straw pallet and the crucifix for comfort, with that bed looming over her. Fair worries me, it does."

Two white trout in a mustard sauce lay nestled in a copper dish on the brazier. There was an almond pea soup and a Lombardy custard. It was an incredible indulgence, and Averilla wondered briefly whether the abbess ate this way by herself always. But no — she knew that the abbess was usually with them in the refectory. When she needed to entertain, though, there was the abbatial kitchen, from which she and her guests were served, as there was also a separate kitchen that served the needs of the infirmary. There were pigeons tonight also, succulent, richly browned, and the smell of mingled red wine, vinegar, cinnamon and currents tickled the nose. To accompany them was a frumenty, coarse wheat porridge, sweet with honey. Averilla was surprised at her own eagerness for the spiced and rich food.

"I asked you here to sup with me," the abbess said, dismissing with a small motion the lay sister whose week it was to serve at the abbatial table, "because of all the things that are happening, disruptive things, and because I need your advice." She frowned, then reiterated. "So many things. John the mason?"

Averilla sighed deeply. "I think he will be well. It is a miracle."

"Oh, thank God. I am so glad, so very glad. He is a good man. What would we begin to do without him? And what would his wife and children do?" She paused then and looked at the plain wooden crucifix from which she seemed to gather strength, and said, "I am concerned about Sister Julianna."

Averilla narrowed her eyes.

Instead of continuing, the abbess asked a blessing on the food and then picked up a spoon and knife to serve from the brazier at her left hand. She obviously expected them to talk through the meal, as those at court did.

"Sister Julianna has had a hard time accustoming herself to the needs of the cloister. If you remember, she came to us somewhat reluctantly, or so we feared at the time. Both her parents had been killed, and King Henry had, as is right and proper, taken on her guardianship. But when Henry died, Stephen grasped, along with the treasury at Winchester, the right to be her guardian. Then, rather too quickly to my mind, she was offered to us." Emma concentrated on lifting off the skin of the trout with her eating knife. Daintily, she slid the white flesh to the side and pulled the bones away. "Of course we accepted her. How could we not? For duty and pity's sake, if for naught else. But we hoped that Julianna, as often happens, might develop a vocation."

"It has not happened. Dame Petronella, as you perhaps remember, brought her concerns to the obedientiaries some time ago. I then talked to Sister Julianna and, hoping that she was merely restless, hampered by the enclosure, I, with the approval of the chapter, decided to send her with Dame Edria to the market. It seemed a good solution all 'round. With Agnes ill, Dame Perpetua was finding her new job of cellarer overwhelming. She couldn't handle the visits to the market along with everything else. As assistant, Dame Edria was the natural choice. She is competent in the market, has gone with Agnes for some years, and has a clever head on her shoulders. But naturally she could not go alone. She needed a companion, and yet no one else could be spared. This need of Julianna's seemed fortuitous. Perhaps, we thought, the exercise, the sense of freedom, might make the enforced enclosure less burdensome. It seemed at first to work well. Or so I thought. Her step seemed lighter. And the unpleasantness that we had noticed, I assured myself, had disappeared."

Delicately, the abbess cut the squab in half with her eating knife. She chewed reflectively, sucked the grease off her fingers, and wiped her fingertips on the edge of the tablecloth, as was customary.

"It was not to be," she resumed her recital. "Dame Edria came, after some months, to report that Sister Julianna was not behaving with the strictness of conduct that we require of those sent into the town. Edria had been tolerant at first, knowing as she did of my concerns, thinking that Julianna just needed to become accustomed to the yoke; that she would soon adapt herself. When the situation worsened, Edria became concerned."

"What was Julianna doing?"

"That is just it. We do not know. First she did nothing except immerse herself in the sights and sounds of the market. Apparently, she was useless with the bargaining and purchasing. Edria said Julianna made it quite clear that she considered it beneath her. She helped carry the purchases with great reluctance, pawning off most of them on Dumb Will." The abbess fluttered her hand as she took a sip of watered wine from her goblet. "But that is not the crux of the problem. After some months, she started to go off on her own. She would leave Edria, on some pretext or other, and Edria would see no more of her until they met at the east gate to return to the abbey for Vespers."

"They spent the whole time in town separated from one another?" Averilla's brows contracted into a straight line. She could hear Dame Petronella in her mind: "And if you are outside the enclosure, you must have another with you. Your own reputation and that of the abbey depend on it." Petronella had turned her back to them for a moment, muttering to herself, but they had all heard, "Without so much as mentioning the small matter of your own safety."

"Outside the abbey walls? Indeed?"

"Indeed. The first time, Edria excused it. But then ... It happens not every Market Day. However, if she does disappear, Julianna is always waiting for Edria at the gate when Edria has given up waiting for her and returns. Frequently, the errands she has been assigned have not been completed."

"Why has Edria not brought this up to chapter? Before it had flowered we might have done something."

"I know, I know. But that cannot now be helped."

"And you suspect?… " Averilla dipped her spoon into the thick soup.

"I know not. I am at a loss."

The soup was no more than lukewarm, but the taste was creamy and delicious. "Edria really has no idea where she goes or what she does?"

The abbess chewed reflectively for a moment and then, long fingers pointed toward the center of her lips, wiped delicately with the cloth. "None."

The room was passively quiet for a long moment. With a hiss and a chink, a piece of burnt wood fell from the pile of logs in the fire. Averilla put her spoon in her bowl and held her sticky fingers up out of the way of the long sleeves of her habit. "I wonder." She paused. "I was just with Sister Helewise. She seems as open as Mercy Brook. Could she be sent to town with Dame Edria and Sister Julianna?"

"To what end, dame?"

"She could follow Julianna to see what she does."

The abbess looked up at Averilla, her eyes steely, her mind calculating. "It does not seem quite, um, candid, does it?"

"No, my lady." Averilla felt as she had as a child when she had stolen her father's war-horse.

"And I like not so well to send another novice out on this business. It might seem a betrayal to the bond they have woven among themselves." She paused, absentmindedly drawing her spoon through the congealing porridge. "Be that as it may, dame, I begin to see the merit of your suggestion. However, I will give Sister Helewise leave to refuse."

They were silent for a moment before the abbess continued, taking another sip of wine from the goblet. "It was difficult for you this morning?"

"Mother, it was. I mislike Dame Joan's meddling." A telltale red started on Averilla's neck and slowly scaled her cheeks.

90

"She thwarts me. She judges my motives."

The abbess raised an eyebrow and let the silence rest on Averilla's anger before responding. "The sub-prioress is entrusted with the job of disciplining our bodies; keeping us from straying. It is not an easy job. Our Lord spoke true when he likened us to sheep, willful and often adrift. Or, as St. Paul said, 'I often do what I would not do.' Joan has even cautioned me. With good reason, I must add."

"Then you think I should not seek Dame Agnes?"

"I think two things: I think we should allow the bailiff to perform the duties with which he has been entrusted; I think that if he fails, it would be well for you to seek the good dame. I know of the bond that has grown between you."

"And?"

"And," the abbess looked straight at Averilla, her hands calm in her lap, the meal before her finished. "I would have you lay this matter at the feet of our God. I fear that you may have forgotten, as you fling yourself against the wall of sickness, that you do not need to save everybody. He has already done so. In giving the problem to Him, He accomplishes it for us."

"And, Mother, there is one thing more."

"Yes." The abbess looked weary.

"The *Laece Book* is gone from its place in the officina."

CHAPTER ELEVEN

On Saturday the sky was clear above the abbey. Sun-fingers crabbed up the side of the church, warming the night coolness. During the afternoon, the shadows lengthened along the western wall and meandered across the garden where the novices took their exercise.

The abbess, sometime in the afternoon before Vespers, summoned Helewise to her office. The younger woman listened quietly then smiled her wide delighted smile.

"My lady abbess, how I would welcome such a respite," Helewise said, her cheeks flushing with excitement. "The enclosure should not chaff. I know that, but it does. Like a brace of oxen where the yoke is misaligned." Helewise risked raising her eyes to her superior. "Is that all right? Knowing that is how I feel, may I still go?"

"She smiled at her own frailty," the abbess later confided to old Dame Aethwulfa. "I have happy expectations of one so young who can take herself with so little seriousness."

"The constraints of the enclosure fret and gall even the most dedicated," the abbess responded. "There is a wearying tyranny of sameness here, and an irritating friction from the closeness of our fellows. Our eyes long for bright colors and our hands for smooth and soft wools. Have you not noticed how so many of our number spend time in the Brode Hall, even when they have no duties there? They hunger for color. That is why Dame Anne grows so many flowers in the garths and the gardens. All the same, beware as you venture into town. You think you remember how it is, but your senses will be ravished by the masses of color and sound. You will," and here again the abbess smiled with her eyes, the dimple showing on one side of her mouth, "be assaulted by the smells. You may find that you have forgotten the nastiness that accompanies our fellow humans. Our abbey is very clean."

Sunday followed Saturday in the round of the church, and the abbey was very solemn. "Not only Sunday, but the feast of Alfred the Great." Dame Alburga's close-set eyes had sparkled at the thought of the midday dinner awaiting them. "We have such plain fare," Dame Petronella always reminded the novices, "that it is easy to become over-attached to feast days." Alburga, in this case, was not disappointed. The baked mutton, a gift from one of the manors, was sprinkled liberally with saffron. The accompanying vertsauce was "neither too sweet, nor too sour." Dame Maura was heard to delicately belch after a second helping of letberry, custard made from milk and eggs. Each nun had at her place a pittance of dried fruit and nuts, and for dessert there was a russeaulx — something like a fried mince pie.

"It always makes my stomach rumble." Dame Petronella was obviously regretting it already.

"Then perhaps, dame, you should have been content with one portion," Dame Joan had said in passing, her hands bundled primly within her wide sleeves.

If on Monday, Market Day in the village of Shaftesbury, Sister Julianna suspected the addition of the younger novice to the small party that was assigned to purchase for the abbey the few necessities they themselves did not provide, she gave no sign.

Dame Edria, as assistant to the cellarer, had seemed a good mentor for Julianna. She had a bubbling forthrightness that the abbess had hoped would wear off on the younger nun. Edria loved the abbey with a fierce joy, but her Norman soul required some intercourse with the stuffs of the world. If this involvement could be had within the context of her vocation, then there could not be found a happier woman this side of paradise. In addition, Edria had a head for numbers and accounts. The tradespeople were delighted with this nun, who had mastered their tongue and could barter and banter as well as the best of them. She even managed to know their names and the names of their children.

Dame Edria did not now question the addition of the another novice. "Glad I would be indeed," she had told the abbess when the plan was explained to her, "if we could find where it is Sister Julianna goes. If it is to be done thus, then I am in accord. To think that we are given time to talk every week, and yet all Julianna can do is look out from Gold Hill over the view of the downs and the chase. Happiness, Lady, is never in the distance. No it is not. It is here, here at our feet to be taken up gladly or trod upon," and Edria had then bustled off, leaving that enigmatic smile dimpling the abbess' face.

The day had turned bitter even before the little party left the east gate. The summer that had drifted through the countryside on Saturday and Sunday had disappeared. A bitter wind hissed up Gold Hill from the south, carrying with it a dragging mist that caused dampened skirts to cling to weary legs.

The streets surrounding the market were narrow, dark and crowded. Thatched houses of wattle and daub with overhanging upper stories blocked what light there was. Crowded buildings tumbled shoulder to shoulder along the curves of the hill. Like water, the buildings ran and spread into every available space. Small huts even crowded and leaned into the alleys, making passage through the narrow ways yet more difficult. The market itself was held in a relatively flat open area not far from, and to the east of, the abbey, where Bleke and Bell Streets flowed into High Street.

Like a young thug throwing himself into a street battle, Dame Edria, lithe and petite, pushed and jostled her way through the Market Day crowd. Following her, the bundle of nuns passed like a knife through butter, respect for the habit moving people when Edria's well-aimed elbows could not.

Helewise was engulfed by the smells. Slops ran in a foul stream down the center of Bleke Street and into the market. The animal smells of dung and urine and the overripe, sickly odor of hanging meat eddied around her. She took in three deep breaths and put her hand to her mouth to avoid gagging.

Despite the damp, the market was like a recently disturbed anthill. The abbess was right. Helewise had forgotten how piercing the color — even the muted autumnal rusts, dirty blues and burnt yellows — were to an eye used to the monotony of black and white. She stood, mouth agape, until Edria nudged her.

The stalls had been set up since early morning. On sturdy cantilevered boards hung tanned hides, cloth, or hooks for pots and pans. Honey and spices stood in waxed jars, while needles and mirrors of polished metal lay in glistening rows. Hawkers jeered and sang of their apples and wine and ale. Dogs barked, and tethered oxen, frightened by the activity, bellowed their terror. A shepherd with a flock of matted, dirty sheep tried in vain to keep them from running down Cop Street and only succeeded in herding them, bleating and maddened, into an open alley. At the fishmonger's stall, near the church, a housewife wrinkled her hairy nose at the fish, both fresh and salt, while the wiry little fishmonger hastily wrapped up the least offensive in thick leaves. Children and dogs scuttled among the stalls, avoiding lusty blows and bellowed curses.

"'Tis enough, this standing and gawking," Dame Edria said crisply. "The sacrist needs a new brass thurible, though I doubt one will be found at this market. Have to wait until Martinmas, I warrant. And Dame Averilla needs more clay pots." Edria sighed. "She breaks them, Dame Averilla does, as fast as they are delivered to her." Edria looked around them vaguely. "There is a woman from Cann who comes up sometimes. Dame Averilla says that those pots last longer because they are local clay." Dame Edria, "like a hawk looking for a mouse," Sister Helewise would relate to the novitiate, moved her head this way and that, "until she spied the pottery stall a little uphill. I don't know how she managed to spot it through all the bustle."

Dame Edria sailed over and started haggling vigorously with the potter, whose stall was crowded with generations of pots, both wheel and hand. Four unglazed, bar-lipped cooking pots were suspended over a tri-legged cauldron meant to stand directly in the fire. Huge unglazed jars used for storing corn and water, decorated with thumb imprints like those on a piecrust, stood all around the stall. The more delicate, glazed pots, in hues of green and brown, were stacked upon the boards. Sister Julianna bit at the lower edge of her lip, and then tugged at her superior's sleeve.

"Dame Maura entrusted me this morn with yet another errand. It seems that there is needed a new bridle for the abbess' palfrey. It would be as well, I think, if I went to the tanner now, so … so that all the errands can be finished in time," she broke off somewhat lamely.

Dame Edria looked up from the pots at Sister Julianna, her eyes unfocused, her mind apparently still on her haggling.

"Um, … no, not that one. But, sister, the tanner is here, see, in the market. We need go no further. No, mistress, the one with the three legs; I know she particularly wanted one with three legs. Sister, the tannery is so far, all the way around the park."

Sister Julianna backed up, threatening adjoining stalls in her haste. Her face was taut. "But it is far better to select at the tannery, and I have naught else to do, and Dame Maura is so particular. It won't take me long and I shall be back here to you … in no time." The last words were spoken over her shoulder as she retreated into the jostling crowd.

Helewise stood and watched Julianna slot herself into the midmorning throng of the Salisbury Road. She barely even raised her skirts against the filth underfoot. She turned right onto High Street, and Dame Edria, head down, still ostensibly engaged with the Cann potter, hissed, "Wait a bit. She will turn to see what we are doing. Come over here. Search with me through these pots. She will turn to make certain none are watching."

Helewise fumbled with the crockery while trying to keep an eye on the hastily retreating black form. "Now, go. Not as if you are following her, not chasing after, but as if you have an errand. I know something of the way. She goes the same way every time. Turn right onto High Street as she did. There is an alley nearby, off the corner of the metalworker's shop. It is there that I lose her. See if you can untangle it."

Sister Helewise tried to slip through the bustling figures as Edria had done earlier. Her height made it difficult, and she was swimming upstream. All the traffic was headed into the market. She rounded the bend at High Street. The metalworkers had already converted their shutters into counters for the business of the day. People milled about, haggling and pointing. Two young men, a hint of beard smudging their cheeks, hungrily fondled a sword. One held it at arm's length and spied down

97

the blade to check its trueness. Stirrups and chains and daggers dangled from the ceiling. Spears were pinioned against the far wall, as were pincers and belt buckles — anything fashioned from metal.

The alley was smaller than the others and ran straight downhill. Helewise could see no sign of Julianna in the fog that seemed to hover just below the edge of the hill. From the hub of the busy intersection, some alleys turned into courtyards, and others were blocked behind the bulk of usurping hovels.

"She went down the miller's alley. There, dame. I canna' think what her duty might 'a been. There she went, though. Not a bit since. If you hurry you can catch her." Helewise looked down into the forthright gaze of Odo, a bundled load bending him over.

"Not s'posed to wander alone, are they?" Odo later asked Father Merowald, whose eyes deepened in speculation.

Thanking Odo, Helewise stumbled along, searching doorways, looking into open windows, wondering if Julianna had already entered one of the houses. At a bend in the alley, two children stood squealing and spitting at each other like furious cats, crowding the middle of the alley, blocking her view. Past them, the alley flowed into Gold Hill and there were no more turnings. If Odo was right, Julianna had gone down Gold Hill. Gold Hill. Goldsmiths? Silversmiths? What could Julianna...?

At the bottom of the hill on St. James Street, a black figure glided ahead of her in the mist. Julianna? Helewise hurried to catch her. "My legs are very long in this horse-like frame of mine," Sister Helewise would explain to the abbess. "She was partway along the road, after the laundry yet before the church of St. James. The houses there are larger houses, perhaps those of merchants?"

"I know the place," the abbess would reply dryly.

"She walked up to one of the houses and knocked on the door, just as if she knew where she was going and who lived there."

"I imagine she did. Does."

"I was at her elbow by then, and said, 'Sister Julianna'. She turned. You could see that she was surprised, but not startled. She raised an eyebrow at me and said, in a superior sort of way, as if explaining to a child, 'Am I late? Dame Averilla mentioned a need of borage. I didn't want to bother Dame Edria. A small matter. Easily accomplished on the way to the tanners.' She smiled. It didn't seem wrong, somehow. She made it sound as if Dame Edria was the novice, and a little dim at that. I am sorry, Lady, that I have not more charity toward her, but I like not to be talked down to."

"No, none of us do."

"Well, anyway, Julianna said, 'It is a small matter, and the wise woman seems not at home.' She turned toward the tanners then, without glancing back. Neither at the tanners, nor the whole way back made she excuse." Helewise hesitated and squirmed against the chair. The abbess waited, hands quiet in her lap. "I know not why, but I am uncomfortable in her company. As if there is some secret and just we two are privy to it." After a moment of further thought, Helewise asked, "And does your palfrey need a new bridle?"

"Not that I am aware of. It would not be something that Dame Maura would have knowledge of in any case." The abbess smiled somewhat ruefully. "It is true that I take much pleasure in that horse; too much, probably, for my soul's good. And if given my preferences would decorate it like a bride of a May morning. I shall send an ostler to countermand the order."

Chapter Twelve

I.

"Helewise said that Julianna had been told to inquire of the woman Galiena," the abbess told Averilla late Monday afternoon, "for borage." Abbess Emma prowled the length of her quiet office, from window to door, from door to window, the heavy black gown bruising the rushes beneath her feet. She turned again, now toward Averilla. "Julianna has no remorse, no apology. There is a hunger about her, a hunger that more rightly ought to be reserved for our Lord. Perversely, with Him she seems indifferent."

Averilla watched the abbess pace back and forth across the room, and listened with half an ear to the puzzled plaint. The other half of her mind reached delicately toward her aching loss. She probed it gingerly, like a tongue on the tenderness of a sore tooth. Agnes was still missing. Four days. Four long days. The hue and cry of the first day had elicited nothing but a repetitive and irritating disturbance. Whenever the bailiff had come to see her, his shoulders had been slumped. He was brusque to abruptness, trying to blunt her disappointment with a string of short, pithy words. If there was aught to be found, he had not found it. He and his men had traversed the woods from Gillingham to the chase. They had circled wide on the gleaned fields from manor to farm. It was as if Agnes had melted into the mist.

"Sister Helewise was quite open in her distaste." The abbess was still speaking. Averilla forced herself to concentrate on the problem of Julianna. I understand Galiena is recently back from Gloucester at the death of her father. And husband. There seems to be no help for it but to assume that Julianna visits Galiena for some reason ... unknown to us."

Neither Helewise nor Edria know enough about the village, thought Averilla. Friendships, family links, obvious to me, are opaque to them. As infirmaress, Averilla had been called to tend the ill of the town. Though not so often of late? She put that question to the back of her mind. She knew the families. Intimately. She had seen how they cared for their sick. She had been invited into their homes. When she had acted as assistant cellarer, she had dealt with them in business. She knew who had been diddled by whom, and where there was soreness and bad blood over a bolt of cloth cut short or a missing ewe. As assistant guest mistress, she had learned which wives watered their beer, and which maids could be relied on as steady workers. She knew them. Well. She, Averilla, might be able to decipher it, or come close enough to hazard a shrewd guess. She knew them.

"Mother, may I?" Averilla spoke now as the wisp of thought coalesced. "I know many of the villagers. They might, perchance, give to me information they would withhold from the might of the bailiff or from those less known to them. They hold me in some regard ... because of my office ... and services I have done for them. They do neither fear me nor honor me overly. On this and the other matter, the matter of Dame Agnes, as well, I might gain some purchase."

"You would seek to find out why Julianna goes to the house of the witch?" The abbess asked, tranquilly, her hands still.

101

The abbess saw this solution all along, Averilla thought.

"Think thou that the door will be opened to one of our habit? Think thou that she will easily tell that which Julianna refuses to relinquish?

"I know Galiena somewhat. We circle one another, preferring not to know too much of the other. I would first seek information from others."

Averilla's mind was busy under her measured words. Dame Joan. That's why the abbess does not encourage me to speak of Dame Agnes. It's Dame Joan. The quest for Agnes must be my own. She but gives me opportunity. Does she think that Agnes might have something to do with Galiena?

"I will not send the two of you alone." The abbess fondled the cross hanging on her breast.

"There is Dumb Will. He is unable to bear tales."

It was settled. They set out after Sext the following day. "It has been some months since I have been out into the town," Averilla mused as she, Helewise and Will stood awkwardly in the middle of the market, near the stairs to the abbey guest hall. Stripped of the swags and the hawking voices of Monday's bustle, the market seemed deserted. There were few about, and these hurried on various errands. Averilla put aside the fleeting thought that they were being avoided, that eyes sought them out and then evaded a meeting. 'Tis naught but the clinging air, she said to herself, the chance again of rain, rain and the thunder of a storm. It was getting colder, and the poor who took refuge from the night under the eaves of the porch were just starting to gather. Like a long, rumpled mole tunnel, faces peeked out from under worn and tattered clothes. The three of them lingered, chatting in a desultory way. "Before we go to the house, I am in hopes that some child or goodwife will happen by," Averilla had explained to them on the way out of the east gate of the abbey. "Someone who is eager for a bit of gossip and will impart some word that will help us in our quest."

Only pigeons, languidly strutting and pecking amidst the debris, displaying their fluffed necks to each other, seemed to have time for idle chatter. Averilla had hoped to find someone in passing. To question at one of the open shops would be too obvious. If someone knew something, surely he would have come forward. Either no one knew anything or all of them knew too much. She brushed the hissing idea from her mind.

"It is strange, but there are none that I feel easy enough to ask."

"Perhaps that lad who helped me the other day," Helewise looked at the square blankly. "Or Father Merowald."

"Both Odo and the parson would have come forward before now if they knew anything. No, I had hoped to encounter an acquaintance rather less known."

As Averilla turned, she felt a soft, tentative brushing at her sleeve. Mistress Alice, the wife of John the mason, stood beside her. She had in her eyes something like fear. In addition, Alice had had from birth an angry purple mark on her temple. The other children had taunted her and thrown rocks when she was small. The mark would have left her an old maid, though a beauty in every other respect, had not the strong young mason found in her a quiet refuge from the tittering maids who sought his favor.

"I, I had meant to hasten to you, the very next day, Friday it was, to tell you of my thanks. John does well, and many indeed are the words I would tell you, and of course the good parson, of my thanks. He — he does well." A tear slid down her cheek. Averilla said nothing. "I — I had so feared. There are five babes now." She brightened and held up a bundle, tightly swaddled. "The youngest ... " and smiled down as she pulled back a lappet

103

of cloth from a scrunched red face. The scent of thyme drifted from the opened bundle. Averilla smiled, knowing that thyme oil had been carefully massaged onto the baby's crown. She knew of no good it did, but of no harm either.

The baby gave a soft whimper at the cold, and Alice gave her a freshly plucked goose feather to suck on. She smiled and looked up at the two women bending hungrily over the child she held. "She is an easy baby. And so we have named her Agnes," she continued almost defensively, "after the good dame."

"Agnes?" Averilla was surprised beyond speech.

"Oh, aye. Kind, the dame was, to everyone, but especially to children. She would have loved — " Alice broke off as if she was saying things that might offend the two before her.

"She loved children?"

"That she did. Would hold my babes as if, as if, well, begging your pardon, but as if she missed having them."

"We all do that, of course, but, was Dame Agnes more ... ?"

"Aye. She was."

"I am glad," Averilla said, looking into the fiercely closed eyes and tucking her long finger into a tiny fist raised against the light, touched despite herself, "that John does well and that this babe does also. Your husband is well beloved of all who have seen him work and listened to him with his men."

"But nay." Alice replaced her confusion with a stubborn fixity. "More thanks are due to you than you will take for yerself. I wot well these wounds of the head. The wives of masons do. It oft happens. Because it oft happens, I wot that it does not oft end thus. They die, dame. As did Corla's man. Or are deprived of their soundness. No, it was your prayers. Yours and the parson's. Special they were. Our Lord healed that way, as we all know. So I am that beholden to you. Would be glad, that I would, of doing you some service in return."

104

Averilla started to say, "The gift is the Lord's," then stopped and sighed and said, "Perhaps, if you so will ..." She explained their quest.

Alice's eyes darted from one face to the other. "No, I, I cannot tell you aught that you will not be knowing of yourself, dame." She paused as if deciding what to say. Her eyes, so open earlier, now seemed guarded. Then, "Mistress Galiena came back from the North. It was after Hogmanay, er, after the Mass of Christ. Mayhap ... I do remember now, seeing the mad one, Dame Agnes as was, with Galiena. In the market. They spoke. As if they knew each other. It was soon after Galiena returned." Alice nervously glanced at Averilla, pulled the cloth over the baby's face, curtseyed once more and, without again meeting Averilla's eye, hurried off and across the square.

Averilla watched after her for a moment, her lips set in a line of exasperation.

"Mistress Alice does know of it," Helewise said, not turning her eyes from the retreating figure. "And what Mistress Alice knows frightens her. Did you see it there behind her eyes, when first you asked? Do you still wish to go, dame?"

"More than ever, sister. There is something ... there. But I am perplexed. Father Merowald must know of it. By the look on the face of Mistress Alice, the whole village does. So, why did not Father Merowald tell us of Galiena? Something is trembling at the back of my mind."

Helewise, sure of her way, strode purposefully down Gold Hill.

More and more curious, Averilla thought. Julianna with Galiena? Dame Agnes with Galiena? When? How? Why? Something links them, all three of them. It makes less and less sense.

The house of Galiena consisted of several wooden buildings around a yard. The door, in the half-light of the lowering day, was stout, stout and old; the public face of a house Averilla had known something of in the past, though she had never been inside. It was bigger than the usual merchant house, with two stories toward the back against the hill, a stable for the horses and a courtyard between. The house had belonged to Thomas, a wool merchant and very rich. Many were the long years he had lain there, a bitter old man. None of his family had come to him in his frailty. The son was in the Holy Land, it was said. The daughter, Galiena, the apple of the old man's eye, had married much beyond her station, Averilla thought she remembered, and had gone to live with her husband in Gloucester. Recently widowed, Galiena had come back after her husband's death, bitter at having been rejected by her stepson (why was that?), to find her inheritance reduced and poverty near. That was all Averilla had heard.

The wide planks of the door had been hewn from a huge oak. It was well aged, a deep mellow brown with much oiling. Heavy iron bands and an intricate scrollwork in a pattern of tendrils embellished the surface. Averilla knocked, using the gold band of her ring.

She knew Dumb Will was not far away. He has probably, she thought to herself, obscured himself in a doorway or within the alley between the houses. A mountain of a man, Will stood well over six feet. He was the only person for miles around to tower over the bailiff. His strength rivaled his height, with arms as big around as Averilla's waist. A knot bent his nose a bit to one side of high cheekbones. Around his mouth the skin was shiny and burled with scar tissue, which he now tried to hide under a bush of beard and red curly hair. He had appeared at the abbey, seeking sanctuary in the conventual church. His bones had shown through the tightly drawn skin. Dried blood stained his tunic. "His tongue was pulled out. Lying, I imagine," Dame Maud had speculated. At the beginning, he had tried to tell them by means of signs and strange wounded sounds. They had not understood the signs, only the betrayed innocence behind them. "I think," Abbess Cecily had said, "that we need a protector." Dame Joan had been appalled. "A man of his kind to protect us? I think not." Cecily's eyes had shown a fired steel as she looked at her subordinate. "Mind your tongue, dame, and remember to whom you speak."

It took more than two years for him to be comfortable with them and with their God. But Abbess Cecily had persevered, and finally penetrated his fear and shame, talking to him and gentling him, and, by dint of persistent kindness, bringing his tortured soul some peace. He had considered himself a servant of the abbey ever since, acting as a one-man escort for any of the nuns who needed to travel outside the enclosure. Only once had any dared attack. Abbess Cecily and the cellarer had been traveling to Fontmell Magna, the oldest of the abbey's manors, said to be in much need of repair. Her mount alone would have seemed a rich and easy prize to a band of outlaws. Will had taken them with such fury, one by one, six of them in all, and had broken them like twigs before a howling wind. Since then the nuns had been left alone when they traveled. They would never know of the horrors that had maimed him. They knew only of his humility, his faithfulness and his immense strength.

2.

IT WOULD BE A FINE THING, ODO TOLD HIMSELF, as the rest of the gleaners started back to the town, to find Agnes. Besides the honor due nuns for their sanctity, Dame Agnes had been kind to him. Not just that time with the boys, either. And she had helped his mother. If she had, by some chance stumbled into the forest...? He hoped she hadn't. It wasn't the place it had been when he and his father had played there, before the foresters had fled. He hadn't his father to ask, about the paths and such, to remind himself.

Agnes had been on his mind all afternoon. He had been unaware of the rhythmic movement of his body, or of the golden, drifting leaves of the late autumn. Instead, he had imagined rescuing the grateful nun. He would hold out a rolled leaf, from which a crystal bead of water would drip onto her parched tongue. She would be tied to a tree when he came upon her, bound with cords of some fine silken stuff. As he untied her, a stream of scalding steam would hiss from the darkness of a cave. The hairy legs of a spider ... or was it the gnarled and slimy-skinned toes, (clawed, of course,) of a dragon? Dragon was better. But where would a dragon get silken cords? Or he would find Dame Agnes in the cave, under the gnarled claw of the dragon. He would go into the cave seeking her, not expecting a dragon, when suddenly...

The sun had already started its descent to the horizon and his stomach was growling. He looked longingly one last time at the town perched above him and shrugged off the coarse sack of gleanings. There was no avoiding it. He had to go search for Dame Agnes. It was up to him. Otherwise he wouldn't have overheard Dame Averilla talking. He knew that when God showed you the opportunity, it was your responsibility to take it. He picked up his jerkin. Just in case. Setting his jaw, he trudged across the golden-brown stubble and onto the turf where the grasses bowed into sad tussocks. The beech leaves had already yellowed and dropped. Though the migratory birds had wheeled and headed south, the jays and magpies in the bare branches complained loudly at him. At the edge of the trees he paused. Mayhap he should think some more. He reached into his scrip, broke off a hunk of the maslin bread his mother had given him and bit into it. Staring across the stubble, he pulled out an onion, peeled the crackly outer skin, and cut it into wedges, using a stump as a table.

Where could a mad nun have taken herself? Anywhere, he supposed. She was mad. That was the point, wasn't it? God knew there were paths enough beaten through these woods. He shuddered to think of what went on here. Dreadful place. He didn't blame the wealthy travelers who stayed on the gravelly sand of the high road. However, since there was little chance that Agnes had taken the high road, if he wanted to find her, he had to go into the forest. He rose, sheathed his eating knife, and started into the trees along a well-worn path.

Whenever the path divided, he chose, by looking at the moss on the bark, the northern fork. As he trudged deeper and deeper, his feet soft on the path, the autumn shiftings began to crowd him, pushing at him like the eerie, soundless prodding of some amorphous force. Even the comforting nagging of the jays and the secret rustlings of small beasts were now absent. When he paused, he could hear only an autumn wind through the treetops. Here and there he passed a little ring of stones or a pile of berries and nuts. He didn't believe that little people scurried and scampered and feasted on these little bits, but if not, he asked himself, why were there no birds?

Dutifully, he peered underneath overgrown vines and into padded glades, parting the wispy foliage, crackly and dry with the decay of autumn. He went as fast as he could, eager to be done with it. The forest was becoming increasingly foreign to him; seemed to be webbing itself more and more tightly around him and narrowing. Branches and brush constricted his sight lines and obscured the trail. Boulders, half seen, crouched in the shadows or coalesced into silent beasts, half-glimpsed, on the fringes of the path. As he gaped at a misshapen hump that

109

had looked for a moment like a body tied against a branch, he caught his foot and stumbled, slamming his hand into a huge boulder. For a moment he lay silent and still, his whole being focused on the crimson vortex of pain that seemed to be consuming him. He groaned. When the grinding waves of shock had receded, he spat out a twig and, rolling onto his back, held his injured arm above his head to look at it. Already the flesh had started to swell, bulging like an oak ball, obscene and unnatural, above his wrist, but the arm was still straight and didn't hang at some odd angle. He flexed his fingers, trying to urge them into a fist. He wasn't able to curl them very tightly, and the pain was excruciating, but he guessed the hand still worked. He'd show the wrist to Dame Averilla. If he ever got back. He looked back at the path, hoping to see what had tripped him. A root? There was no root. A rock protruding? Nothing seemed to be there. The hair on his arm rose.

Avoiding his left side, he put his right hand on the boulder and levered himself up. This was not the only boulder in the clearing. There were at least three others, jutting naked and upright, pockmarked, and pitted with thumbnail-sized holes and dirty gray lichen. A mound, enormous, dominated the center of the clearing. Like a dog with a strange object, he crept closer. A huge flat rock lay on top of it. Both the rock and the mound were free of debris and moss. Strange. He had seen, and avoided, such mounds before. They had always been covered with duff, hardly visible for the debris of the forest. His father had taught him to give such mounds a cautious respect. It wasn't hard. They gave Odo a feeling on the back of his neck, a creeping coldness, as if something was under them or was lurking nearby, or as if the stones themselves might waken and trip him.

Now more eager than before to be out of the forest, he looked around to try to retrace his steps. He had no idea where he was. He looked to the sky for his bearings and found that it was night or the borders of night, and the trees were losing their distinction. He had been so interested in the mound that he couldn't remember which way he had entered the clearing. Was it by the oak or the beech? He didn't know. Hadn't watched. His father had once told him to let his feet feel for the path if he was ever lost in the forest. Seemed like a stupid idea, now that he really needed to find his way out. Even if his feet found a path, he wouldn't know what path it was or which way it was going. His near panic and the throbbing pain in his wrist confused him, and he was increasingly aware, by the hair on his arms, of being watched. He probably was being watched. Boars and wolves hunted at night. They could slink, unseen and noiseless, and then ... Or hags or harpies. He had heard of them. Shroud-bound in sulphur and hate, they hovered, just out of sight on the edge of the vision, and then —

As if summoned, something huge crashed through the forest behind him. The sound slammed and reverberated against the silent trees. Odo ran. Briars and thistles ripped at his skin and the coarse weave of his tunic. Gasping breaths tore at his throat. The image of an open maw, black, and ragged with teeth, pursued him as he stumbled through a darkening mist. An upended branch at the edge of a small gorge slit the bottom of his foot, and he overbalanced and stumbled, slid on a slippery carpet of dead oak leaves, and rolled to the bottom.

He lay stunned. Again. Motionless. Gasping for breath, he waited for the pain to recede. Finally, he lifted his head and looked at the damaged wrist. More swollen. What was that? Over there. A light? He brushed the debris from his eyes. Over toward the west. A fire. Who? Outlaws? Images of crow-pecked corpses, beaten and mutilated, slithered into his mind. Outlaws did attack unwary travelers. But ... it could be

111

the bailiff or someone. Traveling. The bailiff would know the way home.

He rolled onto his right elbow. Shielded by the trees and the gorge, moving on elbows and knees, bottom in the air, wrist held aside, Odo inched up the slope toward the light.

He parted the brush and peered through. Above the gorge was a boggy clearing surrounded by a wall of saplings and bushes, stunted oaks and holly. Sparks swirled from a ragged flame and shone on the glassy surface of a small stream. Men with faces darkened from the open air stood talking and laughing together, with the gruff, too-loud voices of ale. Others, nearer the blaze, sat cross-legged, cracking nuts with their teeth. Scraggly beards fringed dark faces. Jerkins, open at the neck, were ragged and grease-stained. A few scrawny animals nosed at their withey pens. One man turned a spitted pig over the fire. It hadn't been seared, and Odo could smell the stench of burning hair. As the pounding of his heart and his gorged breathing slowed, he heard it: a drawn-out moan. It was soft at first; just incoherent words mewed into the muffling night.

The men heard it too. One man — a man with strange, flat, gray eyes and a scar that puckered the width of his cheek — pushed himself from the oak on which he had been leaning. He spat, then flicked a harsh movement of disgust, his fist striking the naked air. As if ordered, two others scurried toward the far cliff, moved a boulder and dragged something from a cave, which had been cleverly hidden behind nested twigs and branches.

The cave. It looked familiar.

Odo's eyes followed the progress of a figure while his mind probed the image of that gaping black hole. The cave. The feet — her feet, for it was a woman — thudded limply as they dragged her over the rocky forest floor.

112

This was the cave that he and his father had used. The very same. He could find his way back. He had been just a child, but —

A woman. It was a woman. In a smock. A very plain smock without any stitching, just a cord loop at the neck. It must be Agnes! His eyes widened. They dropped her in front of the man who must be the leader, back leaning against the oak. Not just any oak, *the oak,* scary in its magnitude, and sacred.

His father — yes, now he remembered the oak — his father had told him it was sacred. Not sacred to them, of course. And not now. But he had heard, of late, that some of the village came here. At least, he thought that was what he had heard. Came for the old gods, and those that whispered in the night. Odo's father had told Odo not to listen to such as was whispered, to leave it behind. Had told him that the oak was the reason for the clearing. Not the gods. The canopy was so deep and thick that nothing else could grow under it.

But the villagers didn't know that, and neither, it seemed, did the woman. Her eyes were white with fear.

The man with the scar towered huge above the others, and in those flat eyes nothing seemed to move. His voice rumbled sharply.

Like the cry of a hawk, but continuous and piercing and distraught, the woman started again to wail, and the sound went on and on. The man barked something, and two of his men grabbed her and held her arms. Quick as an adder, a small, gnome-like man, long-armed and crooked, crabbed toward the fire. He reached into the flame and drew forth a brand. Gleefully, he thrust the glowing stick toward the woman's eyes. A trickle of drool slicked her chin. The men laughed. The little man, on tiptoe, pushed the stick closer and closer, until the heat forced her to turn her head and shut her eyes. The leader snorted disgustedly, pushed the dwarf out of the way and held a vial to the woman. She drank greedily.

Odo slid backward into the gorge and slithered through the encircling hazel bushes on the opposite rim. Fearing sentries, convinced that eyes followed him, he sneaked from tree to tree. When there was no more hint of the blaze, he ran, crashing through the shrubbery, crawling, falling and running again until, finally, he could see the abbey, high above the fields, the white-green walls startling in the day-end darkness.

3.

AVERILLA KNOCKED AGAIN ON THE DOOR TO THE HOUSE, actually pounded with her fist on the door.

"Dame?" Helewise stuttered. "Ought you? So bold?"

"Galiena, child, has visited me. It is no more than a return visit." In mid-pound they heard the sound of the bolt scraping against its housing.

The door cracked open. Galiena's eyes registered momentary surprise, followed by a flicker of amusement. Wordlessly, she let the door swing wide and stepped aside to allow them to pass into the house.

Averilla hesitated just the briefest moment and then stepped across the threshold. Helewise slid in behind her. They stood, blinking like owls, in the shuttered hall of the house. Galiena firmly shut and bolted the door behind them.

With eyes black as flint, she regarded her two callers coldly. As she turned from the door, both nuns were mesmerized by her dress.

"We can't help it," Helewise had once moaned after being chastised for her fascination with the clothes of an abbey guest. "We may be nuns, but the beauty of what we have abandoned still beguiles." Then she had grinned at Dame

114

Petronella. "Surely we are just marveling at the beauty of the Lord's creation."

Galiena's bliaut, or underdress, with long trailing sleeves, was in the current fashion, having myriad tiny folds. When the nuns had first seen one of these crinkled bliauts, for it had been the fashion for some time, they had been stymied as to its fabrication, until someone's sister had informed them that the crinkles were produced by winding on a broomstick. The bliaut was molded to Galiena's body by a quilted, hip-length sleeveless vest called a corsage. Her plaited belt, or girdle, curved high under her breasts, then crossed in the back and was knotted below the curving lower edge of the corsage, the ends dangling as far as the hem of the bliaut. Galiena's hair was a dull raven black, and hung in thick plaits that had been intertwined with ribbons. She was slender to the point of thinness, and her arms seemed very long. Both nuns noticed the frayed softness of the fabric, the rich embroidered borders at hem and sleeves, and the filth and odor that clung to it.

"To what do I owe this honor, my ladies? It is not so often, I think, that you easily relinquish the ... joys of your enclosure." Galiena then looked vaguely toward the closed door. "Knew I no better, I might fear that you were ill." The look on her face attempted kind concern. "But I would not imagine two ill together, would I?" She left her question hanging.

Receiving no answer, she continued on. "Nor would I imagine that there be any illness you, Dame Averilla, would be unable to find a corrective for." Galiena was leading them further into the hall as she spoke. Averilla and Helewise had no choice but to follow. "I had, not long since, an opportunity to admire your officina. You were in the Oratory, I believe. You are at prayer so often it quite confuses me. I had immediate need of some simple and thus did not wait to greet you. Your assistant," she cocked a questioning eye at Helewise, "er, not this one, was very helpful." Then, as if the thought had just occurred to her, she continued, "Perhaps you have come to view my workroom; to exchange knowledge with me? I, indeed, have long desired to ask your opinion. I was known in the north to posses some small talent in ... 'healing.'"

"I am flattered that you would think to consult me," Averilla's courteous answer covered a gnawing curiosity. "Fewer of the townsfolk have sought my skill of late ... "

"Ah. Yes. Well. 'Tis not long since I returned, but I have tried," Galiena said, gesturing to benches beside the table, an invitation to sit, "to help the villagers with their ailments when it is ... too trivial for your learning." Averilla and Helewise seated themselves gingerly on the edges of the benches.

"This house," Galiena continued, "belonged to my father. He wished to shelter, away from any hint of theft, those most precious of his wares." Bending down, she shifted the chest that stood against the back wall of the room. "So he had dug within the hill, but connected to this house, a room. Come. There should be nothing hidden between we two." She fiddled behind a hanging, and pulled open a door, carefully concealed within the beams. "Not long after they started, the men who dug for him broke through into a cave." She preceded them into a large, windowless room. After a momentary hesitation, the two nuns rose and followed. The space was airless and there was a smell, an odor to it, which did not come from the herbs, for Averilla would have recognized those. It was a dead smell, like rancid fat. She shuddered.

"He thought, my father did," Galiena continued, moving farther into what began to look more and more like a cave, "that this part, within the hill, is very old and of some ancient sanctity. At any rate, it had long been used, for smoke stains blackened the walls, and strange symbols were carved through the smoke and into the greensand. Perhaps there was ...

116

something about it, but you need not fear the place, for it has never done me any harm. This room, this cave, always fascinated me, even after my father had had it cleaned and had some shelves and coffers placed here. But I was rarely allowed to explore it, as it was here that he kept his gold and his finest wools securely ironbound and locked. His place."

The two nuns came only as far into the room as they had to for the sake of courtesy. It was as if there was a strong hand pushing them away. "I felt … unwelcome," Helewise would try to put it into words later to the abbess, "more than unwelcome, spurned."

The walls were lined with shelves, and here and there an iron corbel was affixed to hold a fire basket or cresset. Pots and bowls, mortars and implements were abandoned on a large trestle table, which stood toward the back wall in front of a closed cupboard. Averilla allowed her eyes to scan the shelves. Tiny skulls of bats or shrews, with spiked pinpoints of teeth, the bones transparent, were strewn higgledy-piggledy throughout the room, interspersed with horse jaws and other large bones she could not put a name to. Each seemed to hold the essence of the animal, and did not seem dead to her, but strangely inert, as if awaiting further transformation. Rocks and stones had been relegated to a shelf of their own, and the torchlight glinted from the facets of a purplish crystal. A yellowish nodule that Averilla thought to be sulphur stood by itself. Long twigs entwined with a strange feathery lichen were stuck into a pitcher on the floor and seemed to faintly glow. As quickly as the thought occurred to Averilla, she dismissed it as illusory, and continued to observe the room. Near the far cabinet hung a long piece of hide with dead toads and frogs tied upon it, their leathery shapes dried in agony. "We," Galiena circled her hand linking herself to Averilla. "You and I. Our work has a kinship. There are some needs, perchance, that you cannot,

117

or will not, meet. Someone must tend to these needs." She paused. "I cannot be so dainty as you are. I do not have the luxury of refusing those who come to me. But that is bye the bye. How can I be of help to you now?"

"We came," Averilla said, dragging her eyes from the shelves, "because one of our community has been seen here. Sister Julianna it is. She refuses to say what her business is. Such double disobedience is worrisome in one of our calling. The abbess thought that we might be of more assistance to her if we knew why she slips away from her companion to seek you in secrecy."

Galiena raised an eyebrow. "Perhaps we should not inquire too deeply into another's reasons. I am loath to reveal something that someone who seeks my counsel would keep hidden. However, between us there need be nothing hidden. The young sister has come here, has come to me, because she feared for her future. Her 'vocation,' I believe she called it. She asked me to tell her fortune."

There was a hiss from Helewise, an indrawn breath quickly stifled.

"And did you?" It seemed to Averilla that Galiena might think she had said enough.

Galiena looked at Averilla, seemingly deciding something. "No. No, I told her not her fortune, for that was not her real aim in searching me out. She knew it. As did I. She wanted more. I could see it in her eyes. She didn't need a fortune, that one. She is of the breed that bends fortune to her will."

"Did she then tell you what she really wanted."

"Aye. Indeed, that she did."

"Can you tell me of it?"

"I would rather not."

Galiena fiddled with a beaker on the bench beside which she stood. "Knowing that what she wanted would be forbidden by your 'Rule,' I told her that such things bear a high cost, as indeed they do. I assumed that she had nothing with which to pay me." Galiena raised an eyebrow. "Nuns are not known for their worldly possessions."

"She was rather bolder than I had anticipated. She drew out a brooch of finely wrought gold and said in something of a haughty voice, 'Think you that I would be so imprudent as to leave my home without some provision for necessities?'" Galiena took it from a small casket and turned it over in her long fingers, holding it gingerly, almost with contempt.

Averilla's brow furrowed. "But what did she desire from you?"

"Two wortcunnings." Galiena's eyes were innocent.

"Which were?"

"Ah, yes. Well, that I will not tell you. By the nature of having been paid for my 'work,' the nature of it must remain between the girl and myself." She held up her hand seeing that Averilla meant to speak. "You and I may have our 'differences,' but within my own realm I am true to my word. I think it should be enough for your purposes to know that one of your own puts her faith in another power, a power different from your God."

Averilla was speechless at the audacity of Galiena, the magnitude of Julianna's trespass and the depth of Galiena's knowledge of the monastic life.

As if answering Averilla's thoughts, Galiena continued blandly, "You may not know that I was educated within your very walls. I know much of your 'Rule.'"

For want of anything else to say, Averilla asked, "How heard she of you? She comes not from Shaftesbury, if I remember aright."

Galiena idly picked up a bottle from the worktable and pushed on the wax seal, testing it. "She may have heard, in the town, that I have certain arts … How she came to know of me is really not my business."

Averilla stood, eyes locked on those of the other woman. There was a brief flicker of something behind Galiena's eyes.

"We are the same," Galiena said at length, "except that I must give to people—in this case one of your flock—that which they want. You and your … church can choose to 'know' what is good for those who seek its succor. It was what she wanted. I choose to tend to those you, for one reason or another, refuse. Where a child is not wanted, where a young woman wants a suitor, where a grandame is too old. I, too, am just helping where I am wanted, or needed."

The fire under the brazier crackled.

"So that," the light in Galiena's eyes smoldered, "there may be no misunderstanding between us," she turned to the cupboard behind her and fiddled with a twisted lock, "here is where I work." A cold smile twisted the corner of her mouth.

"I have some things here in my cupboard that you do not use." The lock scraped open, and she unfolded the doors. The cabinet was huge and of a workmanship and art rarely seen since the Norman Conquest. The interiors of the doors were painted with odd signs, tailed and whorled pentagons and circles, symbols that meant nothing to Averilla. Galiena pressed a hidden latch and another series of inner shelves was revealed. She stood back. Her eyes were hooded, but a smile played at one corner of her mouth.

Averilla's eyes roved the shelves, thirsting to know what this woman knew, hungry to add to her own store of knowledge. "I didn't want to be stopped." Averilla would confess to the abbess. "Helewise whispered … something. I heard her and was angry with her. I threw reasons to myself. I told myself that mayhap Galiena knew something. Maybe she had a skill, a potion, that I could use for the good of ... of others. I told myself it would be a sin not to look and learn. So I looked. I fed my craving. But, really, I think I wanted the knowledge for ... me." Averilla would pause in her recital, then would add. "I moved closer. Pots and jars like mine, but smeared through use and not wiped clean. And cluttered. There was no rosemary, lavender or mint geranium, and no rue. The occult things were there. In plenty. I saw henbane and hemlock, mandrake and nightshade, foxglove or witchs' bells, and wolfsbane. I too have those, but high on the upper shelf where the curious can not come upon them by chance. Here it was different. Just looking at them I felt a heavy drowsiness. There was a basket that held nail parings, and, and bits of hair. Helewise plucked at my sleeve. I almost slid as I tried to move away."

"You have no rue, or lavender, or mint geranium?" Averilla said finally, her own voice slurred and seeming to come from afar.

"Those are common," Galiena said. "They have them in every cottage garden. I need them not, nor have call for them."

"Her eyes. I could not break away. They beckoned me; promised knowledge, something wonderful ... She had such strength," Averilla would stutter weakly, to the growing fear of the abbess. At length Galiena chose to look away, sure of herself. "There is nothing that should alarm you here," she said, her voice soothing, caressing. "We are one and the same in our art."

She led them out, briskly, as if nothing unusual had happened except, perhaps, a difference of opinion, of little importance, between equals.

In the front room, Galiena stood with her back to the door, seemingly showing courtesy to well-respected guests. They could not leave without her permission. They would not go back to that room. Amiably, she again sought Averilla's eyes and held them, her hands behind her back firmly on the bolt. "We know much, we two. It is a knowledge from within. A gift. To very few is it granted, this ... power. Meet it. Allow your authority to be honored."

Fascinated, mesmerized, Averilla allowed her gaze to be held. She heard and ignored a despairing hiss from Helewise. Clouded images transfixed her sight, then cleared. She saw thickly clad figures flitting through a deep wood, figures with a mirthless laughter, mouths agape. Cold tightened a vise of pain around her mind, pierced her heart with a sadness and misery and helplessness, a lack of all hope and all belief —

"You see something." Galiena caressed her hand. "You see. What? You fear it." Averilla felt a bottomlessness of self. "Go further in. Give yourself up to it." Averilla felt weightless, a weakness of the knees. "You have the power from within." The words came from far off. "Allow it to bloom. Nurture it."

Averilla sought Galiena's voracious eyes and allowed her mind to be led into a maelstrom of swirling images. She needed, wanted, clamored for, such certitude. The figures reappeared, snarling and bloodthirsty, elongated heads jerking and writhing in front of her eyes. A huge gray stone gyrated behind them, swelled like the rotting corpse of a long-dead badger and erupted into a blasting cauldron of flame. She sought Agnes. Was she in the flame? That dark, formless center? Yes. She was there. Somewhere. Averilla couldn't find her.

Deep within, but very faint, as if from far away, she heard the piercing sound of the nuns' voices chanting the psalms.

"I, I want...to know — "

"Averilla! Averilla! Dame!" she felt a shaking, far away, within another person.

A fierce banging echoed through the house and jolted the

122

door behind Galiena. The sharp blade of an ax splinted through the door between two planks, and a splinter flew and lodged itself in Averilla's hand. She started to bleed. The pain. Finally, when nothing else could, pain managed to pierce the numbing fog that enshrouded her. Dully, she raised her hand and looked at the oozing blood as if it were something entirely foreign.

Galiena ignored both the ax and the splinter. She watched Averilla hungrily. Slowly, Averilla's eyes refocused. Galiena smiled with one side of her mouth, raised an eyebrow and placidly turned and drew the bolt. "Honor your oneness," she said coolly, as if nothing was happening. "The young sister needs to be allowed to grow. Perhaps this is not the right avenue. And permit your authority to be acknowledged."

Galiena opened the door so quickly that Dumb Will stumbled across the threshold, his ax raised for another blow. One of the door planks was shattered. It looked gnawed, like a dog's bone. The iron had been shredded. He saw only the two nuns in polite conversation with a beautiful woman, rumored to be a witch. He glowered at her. She made him the shadow of a curtsy. If he thought she mocked him, the thought was quickly dismissed.

4.

SHUTTING THE MANGLED DOOR BEHIND the two nuns, Galiena leaned against it for a moment. Then, as if something had been decided, she strode swiftly into the middle room. A reading desk, a high slanted board on a pedestal, stood near a small window. The shutters were thrown back to admit the remaining daylight, and the water-light from the pond beside the house danced in shards across the ceiling. She pushed an embroidered cloth off an opened book and quickly scanned the page. When she had found the passage she wanted, she read over it two or three times and then looked up, thoughtfully fingering the runes that marched across the vellum as if they had shape and substance. The runes were angular, sharp in shape, much like tiny bones, but all that her sensitive fingers could feel was a subtle trace of the ink with which they had been so meticulously penned.

A lonely croak sounded from the pond beside the house. She looked out the window, thinking, absently listening to the voice. It was a new sound, not one that she knew. A new frog? Perhaps. Leaning her arms on the sill, she gazed at the pond and the great hill of earth that rose steeply behind it. The rock of the hill glowed even greener tonight than usual with the autumn light and the coming storm. A sand-charged draft swirled down from the heights and spat against the house. Finally it was changing, she thought. No, she had changed it. In the few months she had been here, she had used the forces around her, and it was grinding to her chosen conclusion.

It was her brother who had started her. Though he would never know that, she supposed. In her mind's eye she could still see him as he was that year he had come from the Holy Land, standing next to the pond and showing her about the frogs.

She had only had ten winters upon her then, and this older, sun-bronzed man had been powerful and somewhat frightening. She had listened wide-eyed for days to the stories of his travels, the strange trees and spicy smells. He had been wounded in battle, he told her, and foreign healers had been hired to tend to him. They had used flower seeds to ease his pain. If the visions of the foreign places had fascinated her, the descriptions of these foreign healers held her spellbound. Sensing this, he took a store of the seeds that had been given him to soften the continuing pain of the wounds. She had watched, eagerly, as he ground the seeds, watched how, when he mixed them in wine, they calmed the shaking of his hands. And then he had shown her the frogs; told her how the healers had used frogs, yes and toads even, to cure the festering of his wounds. Laughing at the horror in her black eyes, he had dragged her outside and forced her to slit open the new-moon-shaped lumps that lie behind a frog's eyes. The creature squirming in his hands, he had pressed down on her wrist, forcing her to milk the thick, white liquid stored in the lumps. Then he had shown her the secrets to its use.

Then. She had felt in her then the first stirring of the gnawing hunger that now consumed her. It was just a glimmer, at that young age, but forceful and full of awe all the same. She remembered how, on the last night before he was to leave, she had surprised herself, creeping to his snoring body near the fire, telling herself that he wouldn't mind, that he had intended it all along, and noiselessly slipping from his scrip the leather bag of seeds. As if in a dream she saw herself pour at least half of the seeds into a flask and hide it in a secret place between two beams. She hadn't known she would do such a thing, didn't know why she did it, wouldn't then admit to her need.

Three years later, however, on the way to her wedding, she had solidified the mystical union twixt herself and this realm of true knowledge. She remembered she had fought against it, not recognizing even then what gift was being vouchsafed her. It made her shiver now to think on it. In her mind she saw it all as if it had been yesterday. They, she and her father, had started north after Easter, as weddings were never solemnized during Lent. They made a rich band, they did, with the many and sundry accoutrements and retainers that were needed to do her honor, for she was to marry above her station.

At Fairfew, or right before, the surface of the road had trembled strangely, like the skin of a dog when you scratch

125

his side. Closer, the very mud writhed and teemed with a multitude of creatures, like maggots in a corpse. Closer still, they could see that it was frogs, masses of bulbous, wet, wart-encrusted creatures, knotted and maddened, pushing against and crushing one another. A plague of frogs. She had screamed. Her horse had shied. She would have fallen had not someone grabbed her bridle. It was a sign. Obviously. But she had not understood the nature of her initiation. Perversely, she had begged her father to forego the marriage. Moses, she had pleaded, and the plague of frogs. Luckily, her father would have none of it. "Ah," he had said, 'tis just the madness of male lust. You may as well learn of it now, lass." She remembered how she had staggered to the side of the road and vomited.

By the time they had reached Gloucester, the spring rain had turned into a gale that blasted around them and tore at their cloaks. She had been helped off her horse and taken to the solar where she could change out of the wet clothes. Only then had she preceded her maid into the warmth and glare of the great hall. Orange flames flashed across the faces of the men as they turned to examine her, this their future mistress. She had worn, for this first meeting with her betrothed, her finest Flanders wool, lady blue for her virginity, tight fitted across her new-swollen bust, and embroidered with gold and pearls at neck and hem. Admiration and awe for her youth and beauty smoothed the crest of babel sounds. The head table, separate and oblivious, had continued in its carousing. She had looked toward the sound, seeking her first glimpse of her betrothed. There were two younger men seated there. Surely one of them. The handsomer and better clothed smiled. She gave him a melting look and abruptly his smile vanished as he turned nervously to the older man beside him. No. It couldn't be. The older man at the head of the table, next to her father and of her father's age if not older — forty winters or more — was

126

to be her husband? Florid, he was, with face and lips fleshy and glistening from the fat leg of goose he had been gnawing. He was her betrothed.

Rising when he finally noticed her, he came around the table, stumbling slightly, his clothes still steaming from the wet. A grin lifted one side of his mouth. He wiped his lips on his forearm, said something over his shoulder, laughed and grasped her hand. She had almost swooned with disgust at the thought of what she would have to endure; hadn't then understood that such abuse would enhance the glint of her power.

For a short time at the beginning, her beauty had so enthralled the old man who was her husband that he had been unable to function, and had pounded the air in frustration, saying she had hexed him. He would storm off into the countryside and force any woman he came upon who took his fancy. Their screams, he said, hardened his cock. Soon after, he took to beating her. The first blow was to her nose. One night, after a particularly savage beating, her eyes swollen against sight, something broke in her, a fragile thing like the wishbone of a fowl. Her initiation was complete. From then on she was no longer a child, and began to understand the nature of her gift.

Her maid, bathing her bruises, must have sensed the change. "You can fight, you wot," the woman had said, and the blackheads in the creases of her eyes had crinkled together. "There be ways."

Galiena had learned everything the old woman knew of plants and of men and the getting of one's own way. She became wily when she was with Roger; would pretend to give in to him, to delight in his beatings. It maddened him.

Before the beatings had started, she had tried to win the affection of Miles, her stepson; the one she had first dared hope was designated for her. He was her elder by some years, the son of her husband's first marriage. Miles unequivocally rebuffed her advances, and so Miles, the man who rejected her, became her first victim. Since the thing inside her had broken, she found a squeaky kind of pleasure in tormenting him, slyly, discreetly, never openly confronting him. She would place herbs and such in his food. He would vomit, or sleep, or suffer strange pains. It didn't take him long to catch on. After a time, he took to serving himself, tending his own meat on the spit, ladling his portion from the great pot.

With Miles no longer a challenge, she turned her attentions to others in the castle who had displeased her. They didn't connect it at first. She needed them to know, or at least to suspect, and so she had taken to wandering up and down the long trestles as people ate, pausing to straighten a dish here, to lift and sniff at a trencher there, and subtly, softly, she would add something. They would have symptoms the next day. More or less, depending on her displeasure. As the years progressed, they too shrank from her. All the while she experimented and slowly began to learn the nature of her gift. She even went so far as to have the great toad that inhabited the dungeon at Kingsholm skinned and brought to her so she could salt the rolled skin and collect the precious liquor in oyster shells.

Strangely, Roger never suspected. Too sotted with ale or wine. He even relied on her to ease the pains that her art had so efficaciously inflicted upon him. He had blubbered and cringed from pain, any pain, wanting the effects of the poppy or that other, better drug, her own power, that she gave or withheld according to her whim. She took pleasure in letting him experience an exquisite torment before doling out relief.

The frogs outside the window where she now stood had settled into a calm croaking, listening to themselves, the new voice oddly at one with them. The silken fingers of light on the water were like the gossamer strands of pale hair. The watery gray beneath it reminded her of the wiry hair on her husband's chest. In her own solar, it had been. Roger, in a last desperate bid for freedom, had taken a wench to her bed! Gold hair across his chest. In her own room! He had barred her out for days as he sated his lust. More importantly, for days she was unable to administer her 'elixir.'

Finally he had summoned her. "Ah, Galiena," he had said with an ironic twinkle, a contempt and disdain. The wench had had the audacity to grin; had turned over, flaunting her flat belly and her protruding hipbones above the soft mount of yellow fuzz. "I need your 'medicine' no more, it seems. All I needed was one who *liked* to share my bed," and he had looked down meaningfully at the tousled blond hair on his chest.

Galiena now shivered at the memory and pulled the shutter closed with the latch. Thoughtfully, she crossed to the hearth and removed the curfew. The coals the little clay pot had sheltered glowed white on the brown tiles. She flung on tinder-dry twigs, crisscrossing them absently.

A frail mistiness, she remembered, had gilded the midnight sky by the time she left the humiliating scene. It took her all night to finish her preparations, but she was infused with a blue-white hate, which gave her an uncanny energy. She had appeared in the hall as usual, at cockcrow, her tunic neat, her still-raven hair firmly bound into the two plaits that hung down her back. She had not even turned when Hawise, Roger's whore, had giggled and swayed down from the solar.

Agnson, her daughter-in-law and Miles's wife, was busy over the pot. Several lads staggered in, their fingers blue, the wood faggots they carried still icy from the cold.

Galiena had peered into the great pot. Oats and barley bubbled with a sluggish, moist popping. She had removed a round of cheese from the well and placed it before Roger with a jug of ale and his horn. He had glowered up at her before stabbing his knife into the cheese and savagely slicing off a huge hunk. He would soon, she knew, figure out how to replace her at his board. She was still his wife, despite being out of his bed. His people expected her to retain the right to serve him.

She sat beside him, broke the wheaten loaf and smiled at him. "Slept you well my lord?"

That night Galiena continued the appearance of the dutiful wife, helping Agnson with the dinner preparations. They had some rabbits, and the thin stew would have barely sufficed to feed the household.

"I shall fetch some mushrooms," Galiena spoke absently with no undue interest.

"It would help, my lady. And if you had put some turnips by …" Agnson was thin with the winter, and hunger flickered behind her eyes.

Galiena returned with a basket of mushrooms and a string of turnips, cold from the wind. Agnson looked at them, suspiciously at first, but was reassured by the familiar oyster shape. She added the whole basket to the pot.

Galiena busied herself until it was time to serve her husband. She took a loaf and placed it on the table, cutting it lengthwise into two trenchers. She passed her hand over the platter of stewed rabbit and mushrooms. "Not too hot, I warrant, for my lord's tongue."

Agnson had watched the whole thing. She looked long at the platter, but the same number of mushrooms floated atop as had before. He had died, of course. Not at first. Not that

130

day. The next day he had had diarrhea. "Perhaps the wine, my lord?" It had passed, and he seemed well. A week later, blood had oozed from his skin like sweat, and he died in a dreadful agony. Although he could prove nothing, Miles had not even waited a day after the funeral to pack her off to the house of her father.

Yes. Knowledge had done her bidding. She had used it. For what she now had planned, though, she needed something different, more lasting, with a longer effect. Somewhere in this book she had taken such trouble to acquire, something would be mentioned that she could use. That croaking again. Strange. It was not any frog she had ever heard, and though the window was now shuttered, the sound seemed louder.

CHAPTER THIRTEEN

I.

Dame Avis, the sacrist, was readying the church for Vespers when she noticed the abbess kneeling. Blushing at the thought of intruding on the abbess' sanctuary, Avis quickly averted her eyes.

I can't imagine why, Dame Avis thought to herself, Mother seeks healing. With her back firmly to the kneeling abbess, she lifted one of the heavy silver vases from the altar and bustled across to the sacristy, engrossed in this tidbit of speculation. Probably Dame Joan again. That woman. And the abbess had to deal with her and who knew what else. I wouldn't be abbess, for all the pomp and the separate kitchen. No calm. No precision. No certainty. No cold, quiet peace. At least when I put the cross just so, on the altar, it stays there. Where it belongs. When I fill the thurible, it burns as it should. People, though, they wiggle and turn. Always have to redo and change, a little here and a little there. No, not the job for me, and she gave a final swipe to the processional cross, erasing an imaginary speck of dust from the dignified brilliance of the gold.

The abbess was unaware of the pattering noises that came from the sacrist. She had closed her eyes some fifteen minutes

132

earlier, and had then tumbled gratefully into the canyons of her soul like a lark soaring through the vastness of piled clouds. Soon her body had quieted. Long breaths, far apart, stilled her mind. She wandered behind the red that held her eyelids, sliding, slipping, deep into the peace of the tunnel within her where she felt a pervasive sense of oneness, a rapturous billowing over her throat and down her body, a wealth of silence. After this gift of preparation, then she listened.

After a long while, as the mist thinned, the thought came to her that there was much that she did not understand; of which she was unaware. Perhaps, somehow, Averilla did indeed stumble into the veiled places; places which she, the abbess, was not permitted to go. It had happened to others: King Edward, called "The Confessor," certainly. It was possible. But the evil there was so near. The temptation was so enormous. Did Averilla have the strength? Father Merowald. An image of the little man sidled into her mind. The image smiled the gentle, questioning smile he had when he was seeking to understand. He was both wise and insightful. He would give, when asked, sound counsel. He was not like those two popinjays they had for chaplains, who rummaged in their souls with salacious fervor. A certainty came to her about Averilla's quest of Agnes. It was good. And proper. She folded the thought into her consciousness, and climbed back into her body and onto the cold stone under her knees.

Sometimes after prayer, the abbess found her knees so stiff that she needed to place both hands on the rail to bring her body upright. She paused, allowing the circulation to ease the ache. In the dimness near the altar, Dame Avis was busily polishing and arranging. Dame Joan had complained that Avis made an inordinate amount of noise when others were trying to pray. "We know the sacrist works hard," Joan had said. "She need not prove it to us." The abbess now smiled to herself. She knew that Avis' noise was an effort to place a barrier between her and the person at prayer; to give to them the peace they sought.

The abbess walked over to the other woman. "Dame."

"My lady?"

"The flowers are lovely. I thank you."

Avis' face, round and smooth as a baby's, flushed crimson. "Thank you, my lady. But the gift is God's."

"Indeed. But he has used your hands and that special gift you have not withheld to return to Him."

Avis said nothing.

"I wonder," the abbess mused, picking up a leaf from the fair linen. "Think you that the English damp breeds a life of vision? Or is it something in the soil?"

Avis smiled. "I know not, milady." There was a pause. "Dame Agnes?" she asked at length.

"Well, yes. Of course. But Dame Averilla has also had a vision. It disturbs her."

"I cannot, er, do not ... milady," she finally spat out in a rush. "Such doings are far beyond my knowledge." Avis plucked a stray spider that had come in on the flowers and squished it between thumb and forefinger. Finally, recognizing the abbess' request for counsel, she said, "She, Averilla, too, needs time to pray, I think ... and the wisdom of a confessor. Father Merowald ..." She let the suggestion lie.

2.

ROBERT BRADSHAW STRETCHED HIS ARMS INTO the cold of the October morning and decided that he felt more like himself. What did he think he was doing dragging his men all over the countryside after a mad nun? What was it — five days now?

134

He pulled his tunic over the rough leggings and walked down the steps from the solar, a separate upper room reserved for the bailiff and his family. For a moment, he stood at the bottom of the stairs in the warm main hall of the castle and watched his family.

Mavis had kept her early prettiness. The huge dark eyes that had reminded him of a doe had not diminished with age. She was not fat, just plump enough to snuggle up to in the recesses of a cold winter night. The huge room served the household of the castle as kitchen, dining room and counsel chamber, and was the sleeping area for the men-at-arms, some of whom were still curled up on the benches they slept on to avoid the rats in the rushes. A big copper pot hung over the fire and splashed brightness into the shadows of the dark autumn morning. Smaller, three-legged pots, rounded and spoon-handled, crouched in the embers. Mavis seemed serene in the bustle of the working women and the desultory waking up of the men.

Robert's eldest child, named Clement after Robert's father, sat, legs crosshatched, next to the fire, toes pointed toward the kindling warmth. Mavis had set the child to feeding the fire and using the bellows. The latter lay limply in his hands, for the fire blazed vigorously. Clement's huge blue eyes were entranced by the flames. He was like that, this child, a puzzle to Robert. At the same age, Robert had been out playing in the woods, setting traps for badgers and fishing with nets in the abbey fishponds. Clement took little interest in such pursuits. His eyes were ever in the fire, searching out faces. Often he could be found drawing on a bit of bark that had fallen from a log. He was biddable enough, God knew, and a blessing to his mother. Robert heaved a sigh. Maybe Clement would want to go to the monks at Sarum. He seemed bright enough. Robert would ask Father Merowald. And yet, and yet. Who would willingly send a child away with this wretched war still smoldering; bursting out here, there and everywhere in a vicious lawlessness and evil? Even the king's writ no longer ran throughout the country. And there were those who had seen the ghost of Edward, the boy king, being harried through the streets. Bah!

One of the maids came in from the oven outdoors and handed Mavis a basket of freshly baked loaves. Mavis laid it on the trestle. Robert met her eyes. She had caught him again, doting on Clement. He grinned and there passed between them that look of warm companionship shared by those who have been satisfactorily wed.

Still preoccupied with the completed preparations she came over to Robert and looked up at him. "It is wearying you, this chasing after the mad nun, is it not, Robert? You were that fretful last night. Felt like a herd of pigs, a' snorting and rooting about, you were."

"Aye, wife, so it is," he sighed. "The days blend together as we ride hither and yon with naught to show for it in the end. That first day we came upon a rag of linen, all bloodied, and I felt we had taken the scent of her. Since then it's as if the forest people whisked her away."

At her signal, Robert crossed to the high table and straddled the three-legged chair set there for him, the only one at the high table. Trestles covered in boards for the men-at-arms and their families were set up and taken down at each meal. The high table, Robert's table, was the only one that remained throughout the day to be used for a variety of needs. Resting both arms on the board, Robert folded his hands over the steaming porridge and invoked a short blessing.

Children never sat with their elders for a meal, but stood at the table and ate, silently.

"Father, may I speak?" Clement was shifting from one foot

to the other in anxiety.

Robert nodded, his mouth full.

"Odo went into the wood yesterday. Started in the skirt of the demesne lands. He thinks he saw the lost dame."

"The nun?" Robert asked around the food in his mouth.

"Aye."

"Why told he not me of this? God's blood. Enough know that I seek her."

Reddening, Clement twisted his little finger around the spoon. "Last night, when I went out with the slops for the midden, I went to see him."

"You what?" Robert's fist banged the table with such force that the ale jug tipped over. "By the thorns, you shall not disobey me and not — "

Mavis put her hand on the table, softly. Just a small gesture, but Robert saw it and swallowed.

Clement spoke quickly into the momentary lapse. "He couldn't leave. His mother would not let him. We have a sign, he and I, for I can see his house over the edge of the cliff — "

"We will deal with that later. What said he?"

"Just that. We had no time for more. He had seen something there. In the forest. It scared him. He wanted to talk to you, but she wouldn't let him go. It was well past Compline," Clement finished in a rush.

"I shall ask him of it," Robert said, wiping the beer off his beard with the back of his hand. "You," he said more grimly, I shall attend to later."

Lifting his gloves, Robert rose, his emotions so mixed that he needed the outlet of action. He was glad to have a real trail to follow, furious that Clement had defied — no, disobeyed — him, and delighted that Clement had found the guts to do so. Like as not, Odo had seen something. There were places aplenty in the wood to harbor such a stray; places only boys could manage to find.

Allowing Warin to pull the door to behind him, Robert strode across the bailey, through the fortified gate and out onto the Bimport, unconsciously checking the bracing of the sharpened wooden pikes that made up a low defense at the brow of the hill. He sidestepped the ditch in the center of the Bimport and headed down toward St. James Street and the lower town. It was there, across from the tannery and the laundry, that the town's mischief hunkered, hiding in the huts and hovels of Tinter's Lane. Discontent bred there, and in the cold creeping mists of December, it would fester and then, like as not, in January it would burst and ooze its rancor up into the town.

Robert did not think that the coming winter would be peaceful. The harvest had not been good, as a June rain had hurt the hay. There would have been enough fodder for both man and beast, despite the August hail, had they not been forced to send oats and barley to feed Gloucester's army. But the ones without — the outlaws and masterless men — wicked strength from the town, lurked like so many sly weasels in the forest, waiting to take the little from those who had, leading those on the edge even further astray. This searching about for the mad nun had at least given him a reason to probe into their coverts, and he hadn't liked what he had seen.

A near door slammed as Robert stepped onto St. James Street; slammed into the dull thud of a blow, fist against bone and the delayed whimper of a woman. The tired mew of a hungry baby trickled between the cracks of a shattered shutter and mingled with the screeching howl of an older child enraged. Slops squelched under a thin oily layer of straw flecked with bits of offal and a torn cabbage leaf. Because of who he was, Robert knew the place well. The houses were mere shells built

138

too close to the ground-hugging damp. Like wicker baskets, they collected the wind that swept across the downs. Again, like baskets, the straw of the thatch was never hale. The wet dripped through, dampening the skimpy fires. At least there was enough wood to be had. Anyone who had a will and a strong back could gather in the woods. Bless the abbess for that. She had the right to gather for the abbey fires, but she allowed the people to gather, too.

Odo lived here in this miserable place with his mother. Odo's father had been a man of Robert's sort, and one of Robert's closest friends. When Stephen of Blois had grabbed the throne from his cousin, Matilda, Odo's father had followed Robert of Gloucester to fight against Stephen. He had never returned. His comely wife, Meredith, and their red-haired son had been thrown out of the fine house in Bleke Street by her husband's brother. The abbess had taken pity on Meredith and had given her this hovel on Tinter's Lane, where she tried to scratch out a living clinging strongly to the belief that her husband would return. The child of six Odo had been when his father left, had grown into a sapling of ten. He was to be seen everywhere in the village, helpful, doing whatever he could to earn something to help his mother. For her part, Meredith spun and weeded for the abbey, tended the small plot behind the house and made ale. Robert never needed to check her ale. As long as it lasted, it was considered the best in town. One could only hope that some strong man would come along and woo her. But that was not Robert's problem. Hard to remember, that. Always wanted to keep on helping.

He pounded his fist against the door. He liked people to know that it was an official visit, not just the rap of a neighbor, before they opened the door.

"Mistress Meredith," he inclined his head with slow and courteous warmth. She smiled and moved back from the door. Her face was glowing red: from bending over the fire, he presumed, but he noticed, too, that new wisps of lines had etched themselves around her mouth and eyes. "It's Odo I need to see. Is he about?"

"Aye, Sir." The lad came forward. "I am here." His mat of red hair seemed dampened by the dimness of the cottage.

"You are a good lad to your mother, I know. Your father would be proud of you. I've come to ask your...counsel." Robert chose his words carefully, not wanting to frighten the boy from a clear and candid answer.

"Sit by the fire, Master Robert. The two of you can talk. I've work to do." Meredith crossed to the farthest corner of the room and took up her hanging spindle.

"I've been seeking Dame Agnes," Robert said, settling himself on a stool near the open hearth. "I understand that you may have seen something, somewhere in Gillingham Forest, that might be a place of hiding for her. It would help me to know what or if you saw anything?"

Meredith's head came up as she heard his words.

"Clement told me. I have told no other."

"I, er, overheard Dame Averilla talking of Dame Agnes some days ago. I had cut my finger and had gone to her, ..." Odo said finally, taking up a twig and drawing in the white ash that rimmed the fire tiles. "I was helping with the gleaning yesterday and just thought that as I know the forest some'ut that I might just look a bit. It, it frightened me to go in to the forest." Odo kept his eyes studiously down.

"As well it should. Anyone with any sense stays clear of it...now."

"But Dame Agnes had always been kind," Odo flushed, "and somehow it seemed that I should go. So I went in."

There was silence for a moment. Robert waited. A coal fell from a piece of wood. Odo pushed it back with his stick.

"I got lost. Something f-f-fell, I think ... and I thought ... anyway, I ran and then fell. I was near the oak."

"The oak?"

"Aye. You know it, sir. It is so large that two or three men, mayhap half a dozen could hide in the trunk of it and none would be the wiser. My father and I, we used to play there of a Sunday." The boy looked into the shadowed corner where his mother sat, but was seeing his father instead. "We would take our bread and onion on a Sunday and play there, he and I. Such stories he would tell me." Odo turned his face to the fire. The light flickered on the planes of jaw and cheekbone starting to thin and lengthen into manhood. "Yestere'en, though, there were men there; ragged, scary, outlaws, mayhap. I, I, there was someone with them. A woman ... But I couldn't tell if it were her. Dame Agnes I mean. Without the veil or her habit."

"The woman wore?"

"A smock. Tattered it was. And dirty. And, and she wailed."

"I think I know the place, knew it as a child. Remind me of the way you took." The bailiff tried to keep the grimness out of his voice. Probably near the barrow, he thought. Full of the ghosts of long dead Saxons and Danes.

Odo stammered, "I, I wot not. I wasn't sure how I got there, ... and afterwards ... I, I ran home. But, but sir," the panic that had simmered in his eyes reappeared, "it will be known that I have said something. People have watched you come here. There are eyes behind the shutters and your knock is well known. Sir, I, I get what work I can from ... all around here. They will know I told you. Can you but ask another?"

A twig snapped under the flame and fell into the embers. There was a muffled bubble from the porridge as it simmered in a squat pot at the fire's edge.

Robert measured his words. "But surely the whereabouts of a

141

mad nun should be of no consequence to any other."

"Sir, there are things…I think…that happen in the wood."

"What things?" Robert's eyes narrowed.

"Things — things known hereabouts," Odo licked his lips. "Were I to tell, I would…" He paused and his eyes flicked to the gentle form in the corner of the room.

Meredith had been watching her son with tired eyes as she spun. Now she spoke. "Odo," she said, "your father would have you tell the bailiff what you know. You fear for me, but my lad, without honor…Tell the bailiff, son, what you know."

Odo looked from one to the other, hesitated and then said, "I know little, milord, but this I know: Mistress Galiena. She goes into the forest sometimes. Often. Others follow her. From the town. They look over their shoulders when they go. I-I think she does…things."

"What kind of things, lad?" It was all Robert could do to not grip the boy's shoulders in both hands and shake him. "Do you know that these men you saw be in league with her?"

"No, but…" Odo's eyes pleaded across the room at his mother. Robert turned to look at her also, and a look passed between them.

"No." Robert said finally. "But you think so. And you have some reason for so deciding. Tell me no more." Robert stood up. "I can find this out. You say it is not one alone but many who go there?" He shook his head. "This has all transpired under my nose, like the ants in a hill, and I have seen nothing."

"They do not allow you to see them."

"Thank you, lad. They shall not know of you. I can ask blind Mog. He lurks by the west gate with his bowl and hears everything. What he doesn't hear he digs out with threats. He must know of this. Mayhap he can tell me something. I can make it seem that I was here to see your moder, not you. I have done so in the past. None shall remark it." At the door, Robert paused. "Mayhap I needn't say this, but," Robert pointed to Odo with his gauntleted finger, "see that ye remain here, in this house. Protect your moder."

Chapter Fourteen

I.

That same morning, after the Parish Mass was long over and he had gone back to his lodgings, Father Merowald found himself crossing the outer court. The message from the abbess, by way of Wat, had been troubling. "I don't understand it. Doesn't make sense," he mumbled to himself.

The nuns. Not really his responsibility. Had their own priests. Supposed to tend to their souls. Father Merowald sighed. One of the nuns' priests, however, was a bit too eager for the stuffs of this world. It was a pity, but there it was. Often absent. The other priest a mere lad.

Father Merowald loved his abbey with the accepting, familiar love of a child for its family. He knew that he also loved the abbey because, like a well-padded mother hen, it harbored the traveler and soothed the sinner. As well, his spirit loved the abbey as a place of miracles. He could only shake his head in wonder and awe at the power of God. "Not only," he had once said to one of his students in Paris, "did He feel and know what it is like to hurt, but He shares our hurts with us, even now. Our every suffering grieves Him, and because He knows pain, He helps us through our pain and, sometimes, helps us

144

through the use of a miracle." Ultimately, the abbey church had become for him that place where the known existed in the midst of the unknown. He could sense, almost feel the presence of the Holy Spirit, brooding in the dark, high above the rood screen. Above all, he loved the abbey because there, during the brief moments of the Mass, daily, weekly, year in, year out, he shed himself; freed himself from his flesh and gave himself, soul and body, to the needs of his God.

By contrast, for his lodgings, the little hut in the lower town that served his body, Father Merowald felt no affection at all. He tolerated it. After all, his Lord had known no better. It huddled next to another hut, that of one of his flock, with which it shared a side wall of stone. The stone was always cold. Only now was his body beginning to thaw as the thin autumn sun released him from the cold that had imprisoned him through the shuddering stretches of the night. He had wondered, time and again, as the clamminess slithered from that cold wall to coil around his ankles, why any would choose to live in anything built of stone. A snug wooden hut, newly thatched, with a crackling fire. "Now, that I would like," he muttered to himself as he made way for the men who daily carried water from the springs at the bottom of the hill, and who looked at him curiously, thinking he was speaking to them.

"Those who choose stone to live in choose it because they fear for their bodies," he said to himself again.

He had once known such an alarm for the stuff of his body.

A raw fear had usurped his mind like a hound clamping jaws about the neck of a kitten. The fear had snuffed out, with one sharp toss, all his knowledge of himself. Terror-stricken in the midst of his first battle, he had run and hidden under a haystack. Later, when he had crawled trembling out of his haven, he had vowed to give to himself and his body such mortification that his body would become used to pain and accepting of death, and would never, ever, shrink from them or run from them again. To that end he had embraced discipline. The stone lodging, with its clinging drafts, was a welcome penance.

"Yes, but," he muttered to himself, "did I run to the church after the battle, for protection? Is this love for God only self-deception to protect my body?"

He stubbed his bad toe on a half-submerged rock, and his mind as well as his body was jolted into understanding.

"Yes, of course," he said as he hopped and bent to rub the toe. "Of course." His eyes focused on a hawk, just a black mark above the church, hovering over a pigeon. "I do love God. Yes, I do." He resumed his walk. "I worry about Him. Like a parishioner. Just the same. Dear, dear God, giving His glorious love to His stupid, grass-preoccupied sheep. Incredible. And I fear Him. So, if it is acceptable to fear God, then it must be acceptable to fear fear. As long as the fear of battle is not pretending to be a love of God."

"I really don't think it is."

"Then the two fears and the love are, strangely, wonderfully, ultimately compatible. Fear is a symbol, a sign — that's it — an outward and visible sign ... of an inward and spiritual grace. A sign of ... love of God."

A sweet and light sense of freedom released him. He stood there, with those sheep of his flock bustling around the outer court, and he smiled his sweet, bewildered smile at them.

146

2.

Sɪsᴛᴇʀ Tʜᴇᴏᴅᴏsɪᴀ ᴍᴇᴛ Fᴀᴛʜᴇʀ Mᴇʀᴏᴡᴀʟᴅ at the gate to the inner court and took him to the abbess. More and more troubling. Why was he not allowed to find his own way? He was supposed to see Averilla, wasn't he? Surely Averilla should be in the infirmary. There was that new chapel beside the infirmary that they could use.

When they knocked on the door of the abbess' rooms, it was not the voice of the abbess that answered, "Deo Gratis." It was that of Averilla. Father Merowald stumbled into the room from the full light of the melding day and was partly blinded by the dimness. She looked at him — a long meaningful look — that trembled on the dust motes shimmering in the one window's light. She did not rise for him as she should have, would have; merely sat as one large tear rolled down her cheek.

"Come, child, kneel here before me." He took her two hands in his.

"Father, forgive me, for I have sinned."

He waited.

"I, I put myself before God. I wanted me to be God."

There was silence. Averilla had expected either outrage for her blasphemy, or encouragement because he was known to be lenient. Instead there was silence.

She lifted her eyes to his face. In his eyes, instead of the reproof that she feared, there was a heightened awareness. A question furrowed his brow.

He said nothing.

"There ... " she hiccuped, "there is a woman in the town, by name of Galiena. At the end of the tanner's lane. The daughter of Thomas the cloth merchant." Father Merowald nodded. "I was seeking Sister Julianna. Julianna had been visiting

147

Galiena. Slipping from Dame Edria on their errands. Sister Julianna has been strange, and we — the abbess, really — sought the reason. I was to seek it out. Have you been in that house, Father?"

He shook his head.

Nodding, Averilla continued. "She has a room, a cave almost, at the back of the house, where she has herbs and such. She opened a cupboard. Father, she had all the evil herbs, but none of those of compassion. It smelled. She said- she said that I had the power to see things. To find Agnes. That I had the power within myself. Not God, but me." Averilla's voice became so low that he could barely hear. "I have sometimes had, in my mind, the ability to see things. I wanted more of that. I wanted that power even as I knew it was forbidden me. I have sought it before, so I hoped Galiena could give it me. Father, forgive me. It was wrong to so disobey. I fear this yearning. It has an awesome strength. Father, can you forgive me? Knowing that this breast still harbors such evil?"

Father Merowald put a gnarled finger gently under Averilla's chin and lifted her face so he could see her eyes. "That presence in you is unacceptable. It must be rooted out. This basis of all sin, bequeathed from Adam, lurks in every human heart. Most have not the will, or the insight to name it. In them it skulks unknown, and because unknown, unfettered. You must name it, and fight it, and above all remain vigilant, for it will assume other guises. What was it that released you?"

"I- I don't know."

"Were any with you? Surely the abbess sent you not alone."

"Sister Helewise was there."

"She prayed as you battled inside yourself? Prayed for your soul?"

"I imagine so. Yes. She must have done. And then, then

148

Dumb Will pounded on the door."

"Did you pray?"

"I could not — "

"Oh, Averilla, my child, my child." He paused in thought, absently increasing the pressure on her two hands, which lay between his gnarled ones like a knight swearing fealty. "Let this be your penance. Every day, recite these words: 'Jesus Christ remitted my sins.' The words will remind you that He took your sin, this very sin of pride, to Himself, there on the cross on that dismal day. He took your sin so that you would never think that any act of yours is too evil to be forgiven. He feared — " Father Merowald stopped speaking and absently dropped Averilla's hands. "Can God fear? Can God feel? He loves. Yes. He loves." The man's eyes rested unseeing on her face for a moment. "I don't know, of course." He shook his head. "But He loved us. He didn't want us, His sheep, to turn away scared and ashamed in front of him. He wants us near. I cannot imagine why, but He does. So, He took your sin, that very turning from Him in the house of that woman. He took that sin, there on the cross, so that nothing could separate you from His love. As Paul says, neither the depths nor heights. Nothing… "

He paused then, whether to examine the interesting note of theology or to let her understand. After a moment he continued, "I would have you train your body and mind with this penance, so that even from the depths of despair, or in the midst of evil, you will turn to Him for succor. Maybe this rote which now I give you will allow you to call; will force you to remember that your sins have been remitted by your savior Jesus Christ."

"Even this greatest of sins, that of putting myself above …" she trailed off, could not say it.

"Yes even that. It was your despair that forbade you to

149

call Him, and your despair may have been the work of that woman."

"Then you know of her?"

"Know of her? Yes, I know of her." He heaved a sigh. "To my shame," he muttered. "to my sorrow, I, I have done nothing about her. Have allowed this bramble to grow among my sheep. Too frail. Too tired. I have sinned. I shall try now. Somehow."

Father Merowald tried to rise.

"Averilla knew she had lost him. Knew he was unfocused and worried. "Father?"

"Aye, Averilla," he said with a rueful chuckle. "Still here, am I? My body doesn't move as I would like. Pegged I am, here to this chair like the legs of a stool. So you may as well continue."

"Father, I fear something."

His face became hawk-like, again, piercing. "What?"

"I, I don't know. Something evil. I fear that … something else may be the reason for Agnes' disappearance. I can't give it a name. Let me tell you," and here Averilla described for him the peculiar encounter with Mistress Alice in the square. "It was as if everyone were watching us to see what we did, watching and avoiding us, not wanting to be questioned. She feared to tell us what she knew."

Father Merowald's face was blank for a moment as he thought of the days, weeks past, his encounters and conversations. Was there something to what Averilla was saying? Could he catch a whiff of it? Had there been a certain reticence among the flock? Had there been a vagary, a hesitancy in their confessions, over and above the usual plainchant of sins? He thought so. Now that she put a name to it, it had been there, lurking behind the forecourt of his mind.

150

Finally. "I think now that you bring it before these old rheumy eyes, I have seen a difference. So very subtle," he added as if to himself, "but then evil is always so. Never forthright. Think you it touches the lost dame?"

"Were it not connected to Agnes, would they have anything to hide from me?"

"That woman, Galiena. I think, perchance she provides spells and herbs. She casts curses, wortcunnings, I imagine. I have tried not to know. I have tried not to see. But I think she would give a potion to increase a lover's fancy. It may be that they are embarrassed. They know you would not approve. Nor do I. But it sounds like," he lowered his voice, speaking as if to himself, "I should have seen to her before. I should have been there. The poor soul. No branch offered. Drowned in a rushing torrent of evil. She invited it in. But she didn't know how it would overwhelm her; inhabit her husk like a hermit crab. Much ashamed."

The abbess, reentering the office soon after the bowed figure had left, could see that her peaceful lion was back to her. "Are you at peace?" It was a rhetorical question.

"I am, Mother, but, please may I seek her?"

The abbess sighed before answering. "If it is the only way to ease this in you, then you may seek Agnes. You have only the one day while the sun is up. No longer. There is danger there. I will send Dumb Will for protection, and Sister Helewise for propriety. Choose your paths well."

"I shall start tomorrow."

Chapter Fifteen

After Prime the next morning, Averilla rushed to the infirmary. "The abbess allows me to seek Dame Agnes," she whispered as she entered the warm room.

The color drained from Dame Edith's face, "But you mustn't. Outside the enclosure?"

Sister Cadilla clenched her jaw.

"I shall come to no harm. Sister Helewise and Dumb Will shall accompany me," Averillla answered, grabbing two oatcakes from the table, stuffing them into a scrip. Turning, she plucked onions from the string hanging from the ceiling and rummaged for ripe apples in the barrel below the window. "I thank you aforehand for the extra burden this will be to you," she said as she spigoted ale from the barrel into a leather flask.

"With Dame Agnes gone, naught will trouble me," and Dame Edith turned back to the steaming water she was pouring onto a wad of linen for an infusion.

Sister Helewise was waiting for her superior outside the infirmary and the two hurried to join Dumb Will in the outer court. The long ears of Will's mule twitched as late flies probed the delicate hairs.

"I am sorry Will," Averilla made a moue, "but we shan't need the mule today, I expect. I mean to take only shallow paths. She might be too high. And I shall not need to ride. And

I promise that we shall be fleet of foot. But thank you for the thought. Such care you take of us, your black ladies."

He grunted in assent, and the mule brayed in anguish as he handed the reins to a passing ostler. Irritated hee-haws pursued them out of the main gate. Will grinned.

To Averilla, Gillingham Forest was a familiar luxury. Certain herbs and mushrooms could be found only there, nestled under the beech mast or peeping between the tumbled rocks near the brooks. Most of what she knew about herbs she had learned from her nurse. As a child she had trotted behind the older woman, probably prattling incessantly, but also observing, with the keen eyes of childhood, which leaves and buds were to be plucked and squirreled into the voluminous scrip, and which left to bloom beside the path. Later, Dame Maud, the previous infirmaress, had showed Averilla the plants and herbs native to the downs and forests around Shaftesbury. It was these that drew Averilla frequently into the fields and woods.

Averilla and Will, with Helewise following in bewildered delight, walked northwest from Shaftesbury and pushed their way through the furry hazel leaves at the edge of the road to reach the thread of path Averilla intended to follow. The crimson rust and burnished gold of the autumn leaves were scattered among the oaks and beeches. Willow shoots lined the brook, their shafts golden in the dappled sunlight. Even the brambles were gemmed with ruby leaves. Mosses and lichens of saffron and jade carpeted the rocks, muffling the pattering and stirring of small feet in the undergrowth. Above, hidden in the fast-drying leaves, birds chatted in the desultory conversation of a sleepy midmorning.

They crossed a brook. Purple loosestrife with its lance-shaped leaves, and waxy-leafed myrtle fringed the shallow banks, as did bright, feathery clumps of fern. The water was amber in the sunlight, red-brown in the shade, with striped pebbles glinting along the bottom. At the foot of a weathered oak, Averilla came upon a patch of rue. She paused. "Some herbs, like rosemary and rue, are valuable for the growth of the soul," Dame Maud had told her. The smell of rue counteracts the work of poisons in the body; counteracts the work of pride in the soul."

Averilla stared at the low-growing herb. What had the abbess said? About Dame Joan? Helping them to see themselves? She, Averilla, had stumbled across the rue. Was the rue, then, for her? Was it she and not Joan who had the pride? She saw the face of Father Merowald as he had looked yesterday. Healing was unimportant if it led her to pride.

Will passed her as she bent over it and continued to follow what seemed to be the more worn of the paths trickling beneath the trees. They passed a badger's holt, and Will, grunting, pointed to it. Eventually, the path sloped downhill, where it meandered across a moss-carpeted hollow, bent to the left on the other side, and disappeared within a twisted thicket of briars and brambles. Averilla looked at the prickled rampart in dismay. There seemed no way through, and yet the path was as well worn as if some had indeed passed through the tangled thicket. Will examined the wall of briar for a moment; then, with a growl of satisfaction, he bent a large branch inward to reveal a gap through which Averilla and Helewise could just squeeze. He followed, pushing aside the briars by brute force.

As Will extricated himself from the last of the clinging vines and bent his head to pull a thorn from his finger, Averilla stood still, looking. Before them stretched another sward of grass, green, lush and velvety, not even brown from the lateness of the year. She was in time to see a pair of pheasants herding their young and nibbling at insects and drinking water from the leaves. Sensing their presence, the chicks scurried for refuge under their father's wings, while the female tossed herself into the air, feigning a broken wing. Will crooned some soothing sounds and, as the birds scurried into the wall of holly, he directed Averilla's gaze to a small stone hut on the far side of the clearing. Some of the stones had worked loose, and the windows no longer had shutters.

"The old hermit's hut," Averilla whispered. "An anchorite she was. Took care of the animals, listened to people. I never met her. She has been dead many years, and it has fallen into disrepair."

Will strode over and put his shoulder to the door, which was propped partway open by the fallen debris and loose hinges. The interior was bare, save that the earthen floor was spangled with the lacy skeletons of dried oak leaves and the varied waste of the forest and its small creatures.

Will had moved aside to allow the women to enter, but Averilla hesitated, so Will peered over her shoulder, his eyes scanning the walls, the ceiling and the hard-packed floor. With a grunt, he pushed past the women and crossed to the far right corner, stooped over, and scrabbled among the bits piled up against the dressed stone. With an indrawn breath of satisfaction, he turned to them. A cross and chain dangled from his massive fingers. It was as familiar to Averilla as the sight of her own hand. Each of the nuns at Shaftesbury was given such a cross at her clothing. They were the most treasured part of a nun's habit. The silver of this one was still bright, not dulled with tarnish, and Averilla turned over the intricately wrought symbol, the man on the cross, to find the initials she sought. The M. A., meaning Mary Agnes, was there inscribed below other initials. The crosses were handed down from one generation to the next. It was believed the current wearer received support in her trials from those

155

who had worn it before.

"She would never give it up willingly. You think she intended it to be found?"

Will shook his head and pointed to the broken chain.

"But how, how did they?" she mused. "Why do I think it is they? Think you also that it was 'they?'" He nodded.

Will looked around, his blue eyes probing the dripping cobwebs and chinks between smooth stones. A sliver of the morning sun trembled on the floor. He again grunted, and pointed to a slight furrow, a mere crease in the layer of dust and debris that the shaft of sunlight had revealed. It looked as if someone had been dragged.

"They dragged her?"

He nodded, and then yanked at his chest and pretended to throw something into the far corner.

"They pulled the cross off her and threw it into the far corner? But why? Who could have done it?"

Solemnly, he crossed himself.

"They thought the cross would save her? They feared it?"

He held her eyes with his for a moment, unseeing. Bending on one knee, he knelt, smoothed a patch of dirt, and started to draw using a twig. The dirt was hard packed. There on the floor he drew crude images of the sun, a tree, and the unmistakable features of the green man.

Averilla creased her face into a questioning unbelief. "You think so. The old gods?"

He nodded.

"Oh, Will, no! That was so long ago… " She trailed off, remembering the looks people had given them in the marketplace.

"If that is so, she is in … danger?"

He nodded. Averilla turned and started out of the hut. Helewise trundled after, giving a wondering last look to the ancient ruin. Will followed, brushing away their footprints with a branchlet of dried leaves and drawing the door firmly behind him.

Outside, when he caught up with her on the near side of the clearing, and with a hint of deference, Will pulled Averilla from the path she would have taken, and pushed her behind him. She surprised even herself by waiting docilely behind him until he had satisfied himself of something; seen some sign he was unable to tell her of. He led her ninety degrees away from their place of entry. The exit from the glade, like the entrance, was hidden in prickly foliage and intertwined thorn-bearing canes.

On the other side of the hedge he continued north, but bearing a little toward the west. As he strode before them, moving quickly and quietly, Averilla looked around and was overcome by the oldness of the forest they had now penetrated. She had never before been this deep, and she felt as if she were underwater, so thick was the canopy overhead. She had always loved forests, though where she came from they were neither as dense nor as omnipresent as here in the south. She had, in her childhood, been accustomed to the windswept hills and deep dells. This was like the conventual church, overarching and with an eerie listening quiet.

Will glanced repeatedly over his shoulder, testing the whereabouts of Averilla and Helewise, uncomfortable in front, where he could neither see where they were nor ascertain whether they needed his assistance. After a long while of the fast pace, as Averilla had fallen farther and farther behind, he stopped to let them catch up. When they had done so, with a half-bow he motioned with his right hand toward a moss-covered rock, and then stood expectantly waiting for them. Averilla looked at him quizzically. He chewed the tips of his fingers and smacked his lips. Eyes crinkling in a shared joke, Averilla said, "I'm hungry too, and sat down on the little tuffet.

Helewise clambered up beside her and sat.

"Food tastes better in the open," Averilla said, breaking the oatcake she had doled out to herself and crunching into its dry nuttiness. She alternated bites of cake with some from the apple, mopping in a desultory way at the juice running down her chin. The warm ale slipped bitter and solid against her throat. She was surprised at her thirst. Almost grudgingly she handed the bladder over to Helewise and Will. At the next stream she would let the cold, rippling water run over her fingers and scoop it up.

Since the hut, a slight wind had pricked at them, drawing clouds from the south. It was becoming cold and somewhat misty as the wind prowled through the trees and sent dry leaves eddying to the earth. Averilla groaned as she rose. Will placed the flask back in the scrip, hefted its negligible weight to his shoulder, picked up his staff and waited for them. "I am getting too old for this," she said to him as much as to herself. She spoke aloud when she was with Will.

"I get very little exercise anymore," she complained in an almost querulous voice. "Do you know where you are taking us? I long ago lost the path, if path there was."

He smiled his sweet smile, recognizing her words as mere words. They had gone less than half a mile when they came to a rivulet where they stooped to drink. On the other side the forest was, if possible, even denser, the duff thick and spongy with age. Averilla noticed Will's lightness of foot, his deliberate sneakiness, "as if," she would tell the abbess, "he suspected we were being watched and yet still hoped to keep our presence from them. It scared me."

Averilla, matching her pace to his, placed her foot where his had just been, where no hidden twig could snap underfoot. When he suddenly stopped, Averilla, intent on her feet, almost ran into him. He stayed still. Cautiously, she peered around

158

him and saw it. In front of them, out of a thick patch of yew and oak and hazel, peered a face, old beyond time, and wrinkled. Little rock-black eyes, half hidden beneath craggy brows, stared out at them. Averilla held her breath waiting for the face to change. Nothing happened. No arm was raised. Nor did shouts or arrows rain down on them. Nothing.

Before Averilla could grasp his intention, Will hunched his shoulders and rushed across the small glade. Grinning over his shoulder at her, he grabbed the bulbous nose between thumb and forefinger and twisted it. No snarl of anguish, or gnash of teeth, or blow from a club to Will's knees. The nose remained firmly where Will held it. The face did not change. Averilla approached slowly, hand outstretched. It was just an intricate, clever carving on the bole of an oak, with a branchlet covering it.

Averilla searched her mind. "A green man? I've never seen a real one. Only those carved in the church. It's supposed to scare us, I suppose." She searched her mind for more. "It says where they live?" she whispered to his answering quiet.

Will nodded grimly.

"So if we go in there, behind it we will be in their lands?" Again he nodded.

"But, Will, these lands belong to the king or the empress, the crown, and the abbess has rights on them."

He raised an eyebrow and shrugged.

"You are saying that the foresters have fled and it has gone back to the old people? If we go in there, we will be in danger."

He held up the cross.

"Yes. Well. And Agnes is in there?"

He nodded.

"Somewhere?"

Again he nodded.

159

They edged aside the lowering branches. The forest protected by the green man was park-like. Shafts of cloudy light slanted down like columns to the spongy, leaf-carpeted forest floor. The undergrowth was sparse, cold and sodden; the tree trunks rose black from the perpetual damp or were pewter-speckled with moss. Occasionally, an acrid green lichen shone against the trunks. Even that brilliance was dimmed by the bright yellow, russet and near green of the fallen leaves. Now and again, where a behemoth had fallen, the forest was rife with new life; small plants pushed through the duff, providing home and feast for the scurrying, whispering little beasts that lived there.

Will stopped at such a place where seemingly a windstorm had toppled numbers of trees. "This is different," Averilla whispered to Helewise.

"How? I can't — " Helewise looked more closely.

"Will sees something. I know he does. He is waiting for us to see it. Ah! Look, Helewise! The downed trees have not fallen. They have been cut. There are ax marks on the stumps. And the trees don't lie all higgledy-piggledy."

In their place, a belt of beeches glowed a muted gilt, the last leaves still clinging to the slender wrought iron forms.

Will edged backwards, turned, and they struggled on through the brush and briars and thistles.

They followed a stream that eventually seemed to disappear, falling over a mossy cliff into a basin and lapping out into a wide, shallow pool. Overhanging and possessing the entire bowl was an enormous oak with a trunk larger than a stout oxcart. Will helped the women scramble down the waterfall, and they stood, cloaked by the shrubbery, looking up. The trunk of the oak was gnarled by the passage of time, and striped like a badger's pelt. The evenly balanced canopy sheltered the clearing so thickly that rain would rarely touch the ground. The more massive of the branches, each the width of a normal

160

tree, extended wide across the pool and, overwhelmed by their own enormous weight, leaned briefly against the ground and then climbed again skyward. The oak and its stream were nestled in the crook of a valley; embraced on three sides by a hill. At some time in the distant past, the valley floor must have been soggy, like the nearby meres that threatened the unwary traveler through Gillingham Forest, making it a good place to hide.

Averilla expected Will to circle around the bare openness, but he had melted into the leaves and become nearly invisible. For a moment, even knowing where to look, she couldn't distinguish his green and brown form from the thick underbrush.

She searched the crannies of the glade. Whatever he saw, she couldn't find it. All was eerily quiet. It was the quiet itself that was peculiar. No everyday chat of forest noises. It was as if some unseen predator crouched out of sight and all the animals knew it.

She allowed her eye to rove. The moss beneath the oak seemed untrammeled. There were no flowers. That was as it should be. They would have all withered. There were no animals or birds, no creatures. Will waited. She tried again. There must be more. Something that Will had already seen; something he wanted her to see. He waited for her to recognize it. She looked again, scanning to find whatever it was that had disturbed him.

Tall stringy trees fought each other for the light, and for footing on the opposite cliff. Here and there a bark-clad root elbowed its way into the ground. Ferns littered the hillside; their spent fronds dry, listless and dangling. She searched the floor of the clearing again. There was no one there. That was not what he wanted her to find. There was no one *now*. Had there been someone? There in the center? A fire, yes? Yes. The gritty look of spent ashes, swept aside and hidden. And

161

those twigs — there on the bank — had been disturbed. Not by animals. Someone well versed in woodland lore had tried to cover the residue of movement and life. Alone, she would not have seen it.

Averilla looked over at him again, questioning.

Will grunted, and then with the slowest possible movement, inches at a time, he lifted his hand. There is no one there to see us, Averilla wanted to scream. They have been here, I see that, but there is no one now. Why this discipline? His outstretched index finger pointed at the tree, at the oak.

Averilla looked again. There is no one in the oak, is there? She reached out in her mind, feeling the clearing. It had been her experience that you could always tell if you listened inside. If you paid attention to the hairs on your arms, you could always tell if there was someone in an empty room. There was nothing in that tree. Nothing but clumps of the gray-green, leathery leaves of mistletoe. That was it. Did he want her to see the mistletoe? Surely not. Those superstitions went long ago. She had heard of them. Because mistletoe appeared from nowhere, it had been considered sacred, a gift from those long-ago gods. No one knew where it came from or how it stayed growing without water or soil, even now. But as a medicine, it produced a grateful sleep to creep upon the eyes and dampen their too-vivid wanderings. She herself had used it — with Dame Agnes for one. But it was good for nothing more that she knew of. She didn't even know how the ancients had used it.

She looked again at Will. She mouthed the word "mistletoe." He nodded and drew back from the glade. When they were some distance from it, she tapped his back to stop him.

"There was no one there, was there?" she whispered. "I saw no sign." Will shook his head from side to side. "There was someone there?" He nodded. "Where?" In answer he stooped over and drew a crude picture of the tree on the ground. "And I thought I could tell. Did they see us?"

Will shrugged and started off, heading northeast, following a thread of path that had sprung up as if from nowhere. This path was well trod, and recently. The dead leaves had been shattered, their slivered bits blown off the path by the passage of many feet. They moved more quickly now. Averilla could see that the tired sun was half through its afternoon course. There was much forest to traverse before they could return to the abbey. Suddenly, Will stopped. "Mother," she would confess later to the abbess, "I was sorely tried by these sudden stops and starts of his. That time I barked my nose in his back and couldn't focus for a moment, the pain was so great."

Will stooped down, fingering the bowed twigs beside the path and the fronds of fern and thistle. There was a faint tracery of a less used path, one Averilla had noted but dismissed as used by deer and wild boar. Will grunted his satisfaction and started to follow it, going more slowly, unsure of the track. He had to stoop now and again for a low-hanging branch or for the bushes that grew close. Finally he elbowed his way through a stand of holly, the berries already starting to redden. Holly, Averilla said to herself. Another dubious plant.

With branches pricking their faces, they peered into a clearing. Bushes and trees had been hacked to widen and lengthen the natural contours of a small, open dell. Tree stumps dotted the perimeter of the expanse of cultivated garden.

Averilla pushed past the cumbersome holly, curiosity overtaking caution, and noticed that the tilled rows had been covered with thorn and bramble twigs to protect the plants from the foraging deer.

"Tended." she whispered. "A tended plot in the middle of the forest. Masterless men?" She looked back at Will, still standing within the embrace of the trees. "With the foresters gone,

163

they could plant and till and create for themselves ..." She stooped over the first row of leaves, fingering them with dawning comprehension, and gave a deep, sorrowing sigh. "No," she whispered, "this is not food." She looked around. "None of it."

Will furrowed his brow, confused.

"This? Looks innocent enough. But it isn't. It's devil's eye. Some call it Jupiter bean. And if I am not mistaken," she moved briskly down the row, "this is mandrake. I have seen only pictures in the laece books, but it is enough like. This is thorn apple. They are all here. Even those that mask themselves in dainty dress, like monkshood, larkspur and lily of the valley."

Averilla bent motionless, touching the yellowish green leaves of the nightshade. She cast a practiced eye over the untidy roots of other plants. Will had moved to stand over her as she crouched on the hillocks, and he cast nervous glances over his shoulders, vulnerable in the open clearing. Prudently, Helewise stood with her back against a tree.

"This is a witch's garden," Averilla whispered to Will. "These. All of these. Poisonous ... or fell in use. I like it not." She thought to herself of Galiena and sighed. "We have to go. It is getting dark. I didn't find what I sought, but what I found portends naught but evil for Dame Agnes. Alone in this forest, and no cross to protect her."

Uneasily, they made their way back to the abbey in the silent gloaming, presuming that their presence was noticed and known, the thumb pricking of many eyes watching. Fear caused them to move swiftly. Will's reputation protected them.

"Mother!" Averilla blurted out, bursting into the abbess' chamber and hurriedly kissing the abatial ring. "We must summon the bailiff."

CHAPTER SIXTEEN

I.

t was after Vespers and already dark when Robert joined Averilla and the abbess in the parlour. He listened to Averilla's tale with growing apprehension. It fit together. Finally. The slain and missing animals; the sudden rash of unexplained illnesses; the expedient deaths of the very old; the fortunate miscarriages.

"I felt as if we were being watched the whole way out of the forest," Averilla's clear gaze did not waver as she spoke, "and yet, I could see no one lurking, just a sense of presence ... somewhere, following us."

"You are acquainted, I think," Robert said, "with a young lad of the village, name of Odo — he is known by everyone, for he is everywhere. He is of the same age as my own son, Clement. He told me just this morn of this place. I had not time to look today, but Dame Averilla and Will have somehow stumbled upon it." As Robert made his case, he deliberately spoke only to the abbess, not giving Averilla the discourtesy of his back, but effectively excluding her from the conversation.

He later explained to Averilla, "I wanted the argument strong to her critical eye."

165

"Odo," the bailiff continued to the abbess, "says he saw the mad nun, wailing and speaking in her madness. I like this not. Tonight is Allhallows Eve. I think I must ask Will to lead me into the forest tonight. If aught is to happen, it will happen then. They have seen you, Dame Averilla. Though you saw them not, you can be certain that they saw you. I must act now before they decamp to another place. We can have a surety that they will move, but probably not before whatever is planned for tonight."

"I would come with you." Averilla's words were for the bailiff, but her beseeching face sought that of the abbess.

"Dame! You are enclosed." The abbess was appalled.

"Would be in my way," Robert's voice was equally firm. "Probably in danger. In the forest the outlaws have no fear. To them life has no meaning. Think you that I would put you, the friend of many years, into such peril?" He turned back to the abbess. "My lady, will you grant me the services of Dumb Will to lead us? I shall leave you one of my men in exchange."

The abbess nodded and inwardly breathed a sign of relief. Averilla bowed her head in an unusual display of meekness. There was no point in offering the argument that she, as infirmaress, was the only one who could calm Dame Agnes. That was no longer presumably the problem. However, the bailiff's blunt refusal had forestalled the abbess from the dreaded words, "I command you in full obedience ..." Her conventual oath did not lie between them, there in the tension-filled air of the abbatial office. There was a chance. Meekly she kissed the abbatial ring, bowed and followed the bailiff out of the door.

At the door, as if struck by the thought, Averilla turned, "Mother, I will be late to the frater ..." She left the meaning hanging.

They left together. Averilla, with customary courtesy, accompanied Robert to the main gate, already locked against the coming night.

"Can you arrange for Dumb Will to meet me? The question was a formality against any hidden ears. "Meet me, er, have Will meet me an hour hence, when the tower bell calls for Compline, at that spot where this trail of yours meets the main road."

"He will be there. God be with you on your journey."

2.

When Averilla reached the infirmary, Sister Cadilla and Dame Edith both looked up, questioning. She shook her head mournfully, and each returned to what she was doing. She saw at a glance that there were no new patients. That was good. These two could easily watch the night through. Another night without her. Couldn't be helped.

The infirmary was already well settled into its nightly routine. Rush lights winked from their niches. In the center of the room, the fire snapped on wood a little too green. Drowsy corners were half illumined, half shadowed by the mingled flames of wood and rush. Sister Cadilla, down the short wall by the kitchen, cradled Dame Isobel's head as she spooned broth into the bird-like mouth. Dame Edith, at the far end of the room, crooned the psalms of the day to Dame Jeanne, too infirm to hobble even as far as the infirmary chapel.

Averilla passed through the vaulted room, looking to each patient, smoothing a blanket here, pushing sweaty hair off a forehead there, holding a parchment-thin hand, the veins like worms beneath the skin. Then, as Sister Cadilla mopped at a dribble of broth on Dame Isobel's chin, Averilla slipped into the kitchen as if to see to the stores there. Quickly, she bundled two plump pasties from the low shelf into her scrip, and then bent down to remove from the well some cheese and two rather bug-spotted apples. Will would not complain at the sparseness of the fare, but just the same, she hoped he had already eaten something more. It had been a very long day.

Trying to look officious, she picked up an almost empty saucer of borage, strode into the larger room, and nodded to Dame Edith, who gently withdrew her arm from under the now sleeping form of Dame Jeanne and tiptoed over.

"You didn't find her?" she questioned, wanting verbal confirmation.

"No... No." Averilla paused, trying to focus on the conversation. "But Odo may have. Yester'een. He says so. The bailiff goes back tonight." Averilla stopped trying to look thoughtful, painfully aware of her need for speed. "It being Allhallows," she continued slowly, "I shall abide the night in the officina. I have some concern for my wares." She tried to look rueful. "But I shall not be idle. My presence there has been scant of late, so there is much that needs tending to. I know we need more salve for Dame Aethwulfa. Is there aught else?"

"That — that infusion of borage needs mending." Dame Edith nodded at the saucer still in Averilla's left hand, obviously relieved that Averilla would be the one isolated in the herbarium on Allhallows Eve.

"Yes, yes of course."

With eyes half-lidded, Sister Cadilla gently laid the bowl of broth she had been holding onto the wooden stool near the bed, gave one final tuck to the blanket over Dame Isobel's frame, barely a wrinkle under the coarse wool, and stood up.

As she watched her superior flee out the door, she fingered her elf bolt. A furrow creased her brow. Averilla means no more to stay in the officina tonight than I do, she thought, pursing her lips. Bah! Knows little of what she is about. Fears not this stuff of blackness, nor does she understand its power. A shiver ran up Cadilla's back as she thought of her superior alone in the forest. Even with the bailiff.

After a moment, she turned toward the door and motioned to the low chinking embers on the hearth. Dame Edith nodded. Sister Cadilla pulled the infirmary door to, and crunched noisily down the side path to the neat pile of wood stacked against the building. She jerked at a log in the middle of the pile, jostled it against its neighbors, and bumped it convincingly against the stone of the building's wall. With a loud imprecation, she pushed at the regimented pile, forcing it to tumble helter-skelter to the ground. Grumbling loudly in the broadly accented English Edith would not understand, she pulled two or three smaller logs from the jumbled heap, and picked her way back up the path to the door. She stomped across the floor and dumped the logs onto the fire, raising a cloud of ash and sparks.

"Well, you had best mend the wood pile," Edith said, flapping her hand against the flying ash. "As well now as any other time. It needn't have happened if you had been more careful," she added, allowing herself to be spiteful, certain that Cadilla did not understand.

Cadilla glared at the other woman and, with feigned reluctance, grabbed her cloak from one of the wooden pegs and trudged back outside. She noisily restacked the wood against the wall and then crept to the near hedge where she had a view of the workroom.

THE OFFICINA WAS DANK AND COLD. The fire had long ago lost its luster to the invading afternoon shadows. Averilla was tossing a handful of fir cones onto the embers as Cadilla watched. She then knelt and more purposefully fed dry kindling to the sparking yellow flames. "It needs," Averilla mumbled loudly enough for Cadilla to hear, "to present a light to the outside,..." The cat, nested against the straw in a hamper of walnuts, stretched forepaws against the grain of the wicker, extended its claws in a halfhearted scratch and leapt delicately to the center of the floor. Twining its tail against Averilla's skirts, it paced with her, rumbling loudly, as she dragged three short oak branches from the pile beside the door and settled them wide apart on the smoldering twigs. "Big enough to show through the cracks, at least until after Lauds," she muttered half-aloud. "Any who might wonder need to believe me to be here" She raked the near rushes with her foot, pushing them away from the fire.

As the flames snaked around the logs, Averilla pulled off her habit, then knelt on the floor and, careful not to spill the piled herbs and leaves, scooped the stacked baskets and clay pots from the bottom shelf. When enough had been removed, she wiggled her fingers down to the bottom layer, wormed her hand among the baskets, and jerked at the heavy, felted weight of homespun wool. It was a tunic, roomy enough for a man, and slipped easily over her smock.

She yanked two long rawhide laces from the side of the cupboard and pulled on thigh-high wool leggings, weaving the laces over and around her legs.

Taking off her veil, she scratched at her cropped hair. She then buckled a belt around her waist, blousing the top of the tunic, and fitted her well-worn sling into a strap on the side. Then she put her wimple back on, draped her mantle over the tunic and leggings. With a last look to see that all was in order and that the fire was controlled, she held the cat in with the tip of her boot and slid into the night, quenching the door-light with her shadow.

4.

CADILLA WATCHED HER SUPERIOR HEAD THROUGH the orchard toward the court, nodded to herself, and turned back to shove halfheartedly at the woodpile. Back inside, she hung her mantle on its peg and pushed her stool against the wall by the door to watch and wait. Red sparks flared on a twig and skittered up the blackness of a log, ticking as embers settled. A gentle snore grated against a shutter. One of the nuns coughed in her sleep. It was only a matter of time before Edith's head would fall to her chest, and then Cadilla could slip away. She needn't follow Averilla. *She* knew where they would end up.

Outside the infirmary Cadilla could hear the wind mooning around the outer walls and could feel the draft around her ankles. Averilla shouldn't be in the forest, Cadilla told herself again. Will or no Will. Averilla didn't understand. At all.

Galiena. Even though she'd been gone these past years, Galiena had been known in the village since their childhood. Everything about Galiena had scared Cadilla, but Cadilla had followed her anyway; had gone where Galiena led. They all had. Cadilla remembered one time in the abbey fishponds. Galiena had been standing, legs bared, spearing frogs. She had seemed strangely excited as she pricked into the mud. A secret smile had flickered on the edges of her lips as she watched the frogs' struggle, flailing scrawny limbs on the end of the pointed stick. The memory, even now, made Cadilla shudder.

171

What was going on between Galiena and Dame Joan? Cadilla herself had seen them together, hadn't she? That day when Galiena had come looking for the borage. Strange that was. She remembered now the look the two had given one another. How Dame Joan had come over and they had spoken. All cordiality. In French. Too far away to overhear.

No, Averilla had no idea what lurked in the depths of Gillingham Forest. Not the foggiest.

There was no other movement in the night-calm room. Edith was asleep, chin resting on her chest. Cadilla rose and backed to the door, watching Edith's face for any flicker of awareness. The door creaked silently inward, but Edith didn't stir. Cadilla slipped into the cold misty air of the night. She knew the forest far better than anyone suspected. They thought she had always gone into the abbey when they couldn't find her as a child, but sometimes she had hidden in the forest. In the trees.

5.

THE SMELL OF THE NIGHT WAS COLD on the inside of Averilla's nostrils. There was the comfortable sliver of light oozing out of and around the edges of the stable door in the forecourt. As she entered the stable, she could see only the rump of the nearest horse; the abbess' palfrey, she guessed, by the color. A voice, just on the other side of the stall wall, was droning on drearily into the half-light, droning and hacking with a cough, and cackling now and then at its own wit. She could hear the spittle caught in the breath and knew that Old Winan had got into more ale than he needed. That meant Dumb Will was trapped. She slipped back outside and fumbled around her feet for a rock, about the size and shape of a newly baked bun. Hefting it, she drew back her arm and tossed the stone toward the shutter, hoping to splinter the wood and clatter against the tools. It bounced off the boards and fell to the ground.

"Dam'ee. Hear that? There be things abroad this night." She could hear Winan shift on his stool to rise.

There was no voice from Will, of course, just the scraping of the stool and the vibration of his tread as he ambled over.

When he unbolted the shutter, her face shone bright in the flickering light of his lantern, a half moon as she looked up to him. She hissed out the bailiff's message. A grid of wrinkles scored his forehead. When full comprehension registered, he bolted the shutter and strolled back to Winan to shrug his shoulders and motion goodnight to the mellow old man.

Averilla slipped mantle and wimple off and rolled them into a ball, which she tucked into the shadow of the wall. When Will appeared, she followed him at a distance into the courtyard. He strode unconcernedly, a man going about his business. She tried to match her stride to his. On second thought, she changed her gait into Winan's stooping shuffle and followed a bit behind.

Wat, the night gatekeeper, made no demur as Will casually pulled the bolt on the slot door beside the gate. It was not unusual for some of the servants of the abbey to meander down to one or another of the alehouses in the town after the hour of Compline, and Wat remarked them little.

There were few about, and those few staggered purposefully toward some blurry destination. Will sauntered down the Bimport, with Averilla a number of paces quietly behind. He turned toward Tout Hill, and ducked into one of the thistle-lined paths that twisted between the huts on the brow of the hill. Hefting three of the pikes of the palisade out of their holes, he crawled beneath them. After a moment, Averilla followed, squirming and slithering against the heavy, loamy earth until she had enough momentum to roll down the steep sides of the hill. She emerged close to the road. The grasses here were ruffled by the down-valley winds, and rumpled with the subtle night whispering of small creatures. She stood and watched Will as he ambled down the road, melding his huge form, where he could, into the shadows of the trees, and where not, blending his gait with the waving movement of the grasses. The night felt like water to Averilla, caressing her face and hands with the thick, murmurous decay of autumn. Near the vines, the air seemed warmer, liquid, sly and slightly fruity with the spoiled death of the grapes.

When she reached the path, Averilla melted her body into a towering oak, becoming a part of its girth. Will had already taken a stance, back straight, knees loose, in the middle of the road, his wide hands clutched around the center of his staff.

After some moments of eerie quiet, the rustlings and whifflings of the small creatures resumed, slowly at first, then louder with returning ease. Dead leaves rattled in a backwash of a prowling wind. Averilla felt a claw of fear slash down her spine. An owl crooned above her, half beckoning, half warning its prey. A cuckoo uttered three sharp cries and then stopped. She felt her skin enveloped in wildness as the night flowed into her pores.

Chapter Seventeen

A trembling agitation stirred amongst the dank and dark hovels of Tinter's Lane. The cold air vibrated with apprehension and a clammy, stalking fear. Turgold slowly closed the shutter that barred the one window of his cottage. It would have been completely dark inside had it not been for the glow from the fire's embers safely caged under the curfew. His mother made a loud hacking noise in the corner where she huddled day and night in the pile of rags, her mouth still gumming away at the remembered gruel of the noon meal. Her hands had become so knotted and curled with the crippling rheumatics that he could barely trace through to the young woman who had raised him. He scuffed at the dirt of the floor and pushed past the scrawny pig that rooted in the embers, cuffing it with his foot. There wasn't room to pace in the small area of the hut, nor had there been enough food for a long, long while now. His bones ached from the heavy work on his own meager strip of land and that which was forced from him to keep up his serf's payments of food to the manor and to feed the voracious armies to the south. What there was of life left to him promised to be savage and short except that, when he was old, there would be no one to feed him from a bowl as he did for that fumbling figure drooling to herself in the disfiguring shadows. Yes, it was probably time. He thought he could hear the soft pattering of feet in the lane as people moved with the early night wind. Best to get out there with them. Best to be there in time, or before time. Mayhap there was something to what was whispered, some hope against this overriding fatigue and helplessness and hunger. Maybe Galiena could … Turgold pulled on his hood and picked up his heavy wooden staff. He pulled back the hide door and stepped out into the shadowed street. There were no lights, no lights and no noise except for the thin puling of a fretful child. And there would be no lights in the forest, but others would be there, companions against the night and its dark spawn.

2.

THE MASON'S HOUSE, BIG FOR THE TIME, with two windows to the street, was on Bleke Street. "Above themselves, they are. And her withal." The gossips had been livid. The house had the one large room, a smaller one and a loft overhead, though that was barely enough for the tumble of children that Alice produced with impressive regularity. John didn't mind. He was respected, and well paid. Were it not for a nagging sense of not-rightness about the world, he would be quite content. It was that not-rightness, that sadness that ate at him. His mother had been that way too. And she had given herself up to it, sitting for days in sorrow. That had done no good. Best to get on with the job and do what you could when the time came.

The shadows had lengthened in the room as the light from the fire probed the darker corners and gilded the heads of the children as they lifted their bowls to drink the last of their pottage. Standing abruptly, John cracked the shuttered window and peeped out.

"Samhain. They are starting to leave."

Alice lifted her hands in distress. To peek through a shutter was not a gesture she associated with this man. It was as if a beast outside their door were pounding to get in.

"There'll be mayhem tonight."

"Aye."

He kicked at a piece of wood that had tumbled from the carefully constructed pile on the hearth.

"And I should be there."

"Why, John? Why should you go? You have naught to do with it."

"They will not know," he said, "but she will."

"She will? Knows she even who you are?"

"Aye, she knows. And has a score to settle. To bring me into line. To see that I do not stay her hand."

"Why would you oppose her?"

He couldn't say, 'For you, my love. She sees you as the runt of the litter to be destroyed.' He wouldn't say 'Because, to her, the great bruise that shadows your face is anathema.' He couldn't say those words. Nor would he tell Alice that when he went out in the morning, there had been blood, cock's blood, probably, on the doorstep. He said instead, "I saw her one time when she would rather that I had not. With Dame Joan."

"So?"

"So, I need to have her believe that I will do her no harm."

There was a quiet between them. Alice looked troubled. "Would you have me come with you?"

John's head shot up. "Nay. Nay, Alice. You must stay here. You must not leave. For anything. Do you obey me in this?"

A crease lined Alice's brow at the ferocious response.

"Aye, John. Always."

177

"The babes," he rationalized. "You cannot take them."

When the children had gone peacefully up the ladder to the loft, he took his mason's leather bib from the peg on which he was accustomed to hang it. Alice watched without comment as he hefted the weight of his hammer against the other hand. With a look to her, not even a kiss, he strode toward the door, his face grim. "Bolt it."

He never commanded her. Not ever. Wide-eyed, she watched him leave, and with trembling hands, slid the bolt into its housing and checked the latches on the shutters.

3.

FATHER MEROWALD HAD HAD A DIFFICULT DAY. With the war, the amount he had to eat had become distressingly meager and it made him tired. He wasn't alone in this. Many, nay most, in his parish suffered. He smiled ruefully to himself. Averilla believed he wouldn't eat if his parishioners went hungry. That may have been true when there was plenty, but now, whenever anything was offered, he took it, and gladly. He knew his old cassock hung limp on his back. His bones rubbed against his skin. He was so tired. He didn't like being tired, nor did he like these feelings of confusion that overcame him more and more frequently. He knew that Christ was near, but he was desperately afraid that he would become so confused that he would forget there was a Christ. He rarely prayed for anything for himself, but for a memory of Christ to the last he prayed with a humble tenacity.

He was battling with himself just now. Had he the energy to go out tonight? He was so tired. Usually he walked, after the men had come in from work, past the cottages of the town. He liked to see them close in upon themselves, the chinks of light from fire and rush lights glowing cozily through the cracks in the shutters. Beside each cot he would pause and pray for those within. That they would survive. That each cottage would uphold its part, would be a brick in the wall against … against what? The fear of the Norsemen? The rapacity of lawless men? The ebb tide of the world's pain and anger? The sea of trouble? The old man shook his head. They needed protection and he was so old. He patted the Psalter that lay open on his knees, letting his hand caress the soft vellum. Slowly, creaking, he rose. They needed him. Ineffectual as he was, still he was all they had. He took his cloak from its peg beside the door, flung it over his shoulder and, blowing out the rush light, edged down the hill toward Tinter's Lane. He squinted at the houses he passed. Strange, all of them were dark. No fires showed through the all-too-wide chinks in the daub. Why was that? What was today? They were past the feast of Alfred. He knew that. He had had a plump duck. Allhallows Eve! That was it! Oh, Lord, help them! They did foolish things on Allhallows.

No. He was wrong. There was one light still showing through the chinks. He breathed a sigh of relief. Whose was it? Of course. Odo. Odo and his mother, Meredith.

He knocked. It sounded more like a twig brushing on the door. But Meredith knew the knock. Too quickly, as if she had been expecting him — someone — she unbolted and tugged open the door. Too quickly. Father Merowald, surprised, stumbled across the threshold, almost fell, but caught the lintel.

"Father Merowald."

"God bless you, Mistress Meredith."

Odo appeared behind his mother, the light from the fire glinting from his eyes.

"I hate to disturb the tranquility of your evening," the old man continued, and then he peered dimly at her and at the room again. "You are not yet abed then? I have not awakened you?"

"No. It is not so late. Come in," and she drew him into the room. Odo pulled a stool to the still-burning fire. Burning, Meredith would have admitted, to keep away the ghosts and harpies and to make sure that Odo stayed away from whatever was going to happen in the forest tonight. "Sit, sir, and warm yourself." She put her hand on his back to lift off his cloak and blurted without thought, "Why, sir, you are too thin. You must take some porridge. With a wooden spoon she ladled some of the pease porridge from a three-legged pot onto a round slab of bread. Carefully he spooned up a bit of the thick soup.

After a moment of thoroughly chewing his porridge, he said, "Mistress Meredith, few were the fires peeping through the shutters as I came down from the abbey. Know you aught where they have gone, the townsfolk?"

She had turned her back to him at his first words, allowing a lappet of cloth to hide her face. She fidgeted with the pot.

"Please."

She sighed. "I - I know very little." She turned back toward him. "It has, though, to do with Galiena. She has been much among us since her return. Her name brings garbled sentences and a hush on gossip. I heard the people leave. Their tread was quiet, the quiet that comes when you fear to wake a sleeper. So it was the more obvious. They went like the hush of the wind on a summer's fine day, and then they were gone. I peeked out the door and there were no lights left. That is what I know."

"And the woman. Know you no more?"

There was a pause. "Indeed. I know that she will- will see to ailments that Dame Averilla has no spirit for. A maid with an unwanted babe will be heard. I-I myself went once to her. To know what had happened to my husband. To have her tell me

180

Odo's future." This last was said very softly, whispered. She didn't look up as she spoke.

"To look into the future?"

She nodded.

"What did she say, lass?"

"That he would be safe."

"You know such things are — "

"I know."

"So. That is why I knew nothing of her. No one wanted to tell me of the paths they were taking toward their desires."

There was quiet for the moment in the cottage.

As Meredith waited for her penance, Father Merowald asked, "Know you which way they went? Did the bailiff say anything?"

"The bailiff fears for Dame Agnes. She ran off. From the abbey. Out of her head, like as not. He, the bailiff, thinks it is something to do with Galiena. Or that is my guess. Came here to ask Odo what he saw in the forest. Odo went yesterday to look for Agnes."

"It's the path that takes off from the northern road, toward Gillingham Forest," Odo blurted before he was asked. Father Merowald nodded and rose, stiffly. His joints had again had time to solidify.

"You mean to go after them? No. No, you mustn't. You are too — "

"Blind is the word our Lord would have you use. I chose to be blind to it. So now I must try." He again wrapped his cloak around him. "It could be that there is something, some way that I am meant to help. If that is to be, the Lord will help me get there. He can't help me if I don't try. If I am not meant to be there,' he shrugged, "I shall wallow around in the dark woods. I probably shall anyway."

"But there are boar, and ... and wolves."

181

"There is not enough skin," he said as he fumbled with the bolt, "on these bones to make a meal for even the most famished of wolves," and he went out into the night.

4.

BELOW THE WALLS OF THE CASTLE, on the road past the northern fishponds, Robert approached a large shadow that loomed in the middle of the road. "I thank you, Will," Robert whispered, "for coming. I need for you to guide us to the clearing you came upon with Dame Averilla. And if you can, to where the giant oak has planted her feet within the rushing of the stream? I saw the oak, I know, but so long ago it was, I could not be sure of the way now. Been blundering around trying to find it all day. The lad, Odo, believes he saw Dame Agnes there yestere'en. He was there only the once, and had lost himself so ... "

They started, single file behind Will, feet feeling for what the eyes could not see. The land undulated, swelled away from the swath of the flat valley floor, climbed as on the waves of the wind-darkened sea. Even the moon little pierced the roof of the forest that son closed around them.

After the last in line had pushed through the brush, Averilla detached herself from the oak where she had been hidden. She kept her distance so that if she stumbled or tripped, no one would hear her.

She saw the path the men took from the road, and entered the forest. But she felt alone. The fear, which had receded when the bailiff arrived with his men, knotted itself against the back of her throat. There were others here. Not men, not the bailiff's men. Others. She could feel them. In the crowding of the bushes. She turned. A sardonic face stared back, winked. It was a woman, like a dryad, her dress green streaked with black. Averilla's hair stood up, and her eye sockets expanded as

182

her eyeballs seemed to contract. No. It was a tree. Just a tree. But ... they were here. They had been here today when she was with Will, and were still here now: fleeting presences, trailing, watching, hovering — fingers of blackness flitting from tree to tree. No twig snapped. There was only the ruffle of the wind and the pricking on the outside of her skin. Her nurse had told her about them. Hallows. "Clinging mists," she had said, her eyes wide, "to tear at the flesh; wraiths with skeletal maws and an enormous power of evil." Averilla hadn't believed about them. Then.

They had been there. Were here. She knew it. A leaden weariness dragged at her brain. "Christ be with me," she whispered. Her knees felt as if they might very suddenly give way. "Christ within me." She wanted more than anything to lie down. "Christ beside me." Her hands trembled. All her energy was draining from her like blood from an opened vein. "Christ before me." She stumbled over a root, her ankle turned and she fell headlong onto the path. She gasped as arcs of pain stabbed up her leg and tore through her. She lay there for long moments, giving her whole being to the pain, existing only for the currents of red that flashed through her. After some time, she couldn't say how long, the forms slithered into the night, like a flock of blackbirds at the approach of the hunter. There was a sudden flurry, a blurring of the underbrush, and they were gone. After they had gone, like the grain on a piece of wood, the pain started to ebb. She felt her ankle. It had already swelled. She lifted her tunic, tore a four-inch strip from the hem, and bound the ankle as tightly as she could.

Silence crept back into the forest. A late cricket scratched his song into the autumn gloom. High above her, a branch rasped against another in the wind. Averilla could smell the moist coldness of the mud. In disgust she pushed herself up onto her hands and knees and managed to stand.

But now there was no longer any trace of the men. Blood started again to pound in her ears. She tried to hear a sound, any sound that would betray their whereabouts. They were no longer here. The forest was quiet. Eerie. She was alone. And she had lost the path. Even the snaking trickle between the trees had gone. Where did they go? Which way?

Fie on Robert! Fie on all men! 'No, Averilla may not go! Just a woman! Too dangerous for a woman.' Well, who was fighting this war anyway? Stephen took the credit, but it was Matilda, his wife, who fought the battles. Matilda the Queen against Matilda the Empress! The Normans. Bah! Wouldn't allow girls to fight. Confined them to solars! Took away their weapons; said women were the weaker sex. Of course they were weak! They had not been trained. Pent-up rage and frustration coursed through her veins.

As she stood, the presence of another behind her usurped all other thought. Another being. There. Behind her. Almost touching. All she had to do was turn. Her eyes started to water. Fear and awe seized her soul and, like a dog with a mangy cat, shook her. She knew the essence of the calm reality that stood with her, behind her, all around her. It was not tame, but wild and elemental, awesome and reassuring. All powerful. Omnipotent. To grovel wouldn't be enough. She wanted to hide.

With sudden clarity she saw her own sinfulness. Even then the Presence didn't leave. He waited. Her nakedness was acknowledged, as were her sins. But clearly, as if the words had been spoken. Rung into her soul. Meant for her, he said, "Enough. Your anger wastes an opportunity. If you do not act for me, you act against me. Help me or get out of my way."

She felt as she had felt as a child when the arms master knocked her down with a blow to her head, and she had risen not knowing which way the castle stood or where the stable lay. She stood, chastened.

Then, surprisingly, like salmon heading upstream, three new figures swam out of the blackness, real people this time, pushing their way into the wood. Had the bailiff come for her? Averilla would call to him. She cut off the sound with a strangled gurgle. The nearest figure was a woman.

Chapter Eighteen

I.

As the bailiff and his men pushed through the under-growth, it seemed to Robert that Will felt his bearings with his skin, the slant of the path, the whisper of the wind. Something. Will's sense of direction, his sense of the wood, was truly amazing. As if he was … Robert didn't finish the thought.

Robert, however, had not Will's forest sense. As they trudged along, Robert would blunder too close to the shrubbery, and nettles would sear fire into his skin, or a branchlet would whap him in the face. The sliver of moon that trickled down among the leaves didn't help either. It made the going harder, created huge leaf shadows in the moving patches of light.

They came first to the glade of the oak. Will stopped. The sound of the waterfall was loud against the night, and insistent, roaring white. Robert felt, more than saw the great oak as it hulked over them, shadowing the silver glint of the moon.

Nothing but moon shadows moved in the glade. Though there was not now the great bonfire Odo had said he'd seen, or any band of men, the place was coldly eerie. Will sniffed. Loudly. That was it. The astringent smell of old ashes. Seemed that this glade was the place Odo had mentioned. Certainly someone had recently had a fire here, anyway. Robert scanned the vale. Finally he saw the darker blot, halfway up the far hillside, that he had needed to see. The cave. Right.

If whoever had been was not here now, like as not they were nearby. Odo had spoken of a mound; had said it was near the oak somewhere. Allhallows. Damn. Robert glanced at Will and whispered. "We'll look to the mound. There's naught to be seen here. From the smell of the fire though, it was not long ago that they left."

Will looked at him for a moment, and then nodded and turned.

Robert insisted that they move with agonizing caution. He had learned to be wary of the hysteria and frenzy that swirled around Allhallows and the other festivals sacred to the old religion. The forest was much too quiet. There was no comforting questioning from hunting owls, or the sharp bark of a fox. He bade his men squeeze through the forest, "inch by bloody inch," away from the hollow of the oak and up the hill to the barrow. Had them hide themselves behind trees, dart between trees, or stand immobile next to the damp moss on the north side of yet more trees. They took exaggerated steps. Except for their own labored breathing, the night around them remained deathly silent.

When it seemed to them that they were climbing into an eternity of black, slow nothingness, some of them, the first in line, started to feel, on the skin of their arms and in the blood coursing through their veins, a sort of throbbing vibration. Robert thought at first that it was some kind of bird, or beaver, or rabbit, mayhap thumping; some strange night beast that could sound a hollow knocking.

Will stopped so suddenly that Robert ran into him. Their trickle of path had flowed abruptly into a wider track.

187

"Holy blood!" The whispered exclamation was drawn from Robert with an outrush of breath. The path ahead of them was lit with a verdant pallor. A strange greenish glow hung from the trees, creasing the bark of the wide trunks as if some inner woodland fire lit each tree. A harsh muttering whispered around him as men motioned toward the greenish light.

Something like this was enough to scare the bravest man. And these men knew what it meant. Probably better than Robert did. He clenched his jaw and whispered, loud enough for them all to hear, hoping they would follow, "We take this path."

Hearing the reluctance of all the men behind him, Will turned, a momentary flicker of disgust on his lips, and started on the hazy path. Robert and Tom followed. The rest seemed paralyzed, their fear trapping their strength like quicksand, or a shroud, binding and hampering them. After some moments, when Tom and Robert and Will had disappeared around a bend in the path, the rest of the men looked at one another and, with a common mind followed, panting and stumbling, chased by the enormity of the forest and their vulnerable meagerness.

The throbbing ebbed and flowed around them with a stronger beat. Sometimes it was no more than a hint of sound in the wind, but it seemed that as they moved along the path, the rhythm grew louder — louder and faster. Insistent. They seemed to be heading inexorably toward it. Despite himself, Robert felt it draw him, excite him. It promised something. I want to run to it, he thought, surprised. The men, too, had increased their pace. Caution was forgotten.

Soon, it was no longer a mortal rhythm, but had become menacing, syncopated, and frenzied, galloping faster and faster into their blood, swirling into a dizzying maelstrom of beat, goading them into it, urging them on, separating self from reality.

Robert stopped and held up his hand, and the man behind him trod on his heel. "Slow, now," he whispered, measuring his voice away from the beat. "From tree to tree. To arms. 'Ware of sentries. We don't know..."

2.

AVERILLA CROUCHED IN THE DUFF, TRYING TO SEEM as much like a tree as she could. She felt the sweat trickle between her breasts. She could smell the fear of those she followed. All her senses were heightened. Except sight. She could see very little. She still followed the three figures as they struggled through the wood. She would keep after them. She was no longer eager to find whatever it was. But these were other humans and she was afraid.

There was a thrumming, which became deeper as they straggled forward, a rhythm of wildness, pulsing and insistent. Averilla felt a frenzy blaze within her; felt her body flame. Something real and foreign and pagan lurked in these woods, something wild and beckoning, carnal in its need.

The two men and the woman increased their pace, panting with the wildness, the savage vibration, the unrelenting beat. They pushed past another oak, this one bent and stooped with age. A flicker. In the darkness. Suddenly they were upon it. Distorted silhouettes of revelers twisted against the yellow-eyed flame. The wind soughed and caught the flame and eddied it, sending it sprawling skyward.

An Allhallows bonfire. Of course. Pagan, but ... Averilla's panting slowed. She was far enough back that she couldn't see it as those before her could. But she could see the glow and knew what it was — just a bonfire.

A drawn-out wail sliced through the gloom and reverberated

from tree to tree, flung skyward on the wavy gusts of heated air. For one moment all sound hung suspended. Then, like sheet ice breaking, the crowd growled a single response. The many were individuals no longer.

Averilla froze. Her quickened pulse throbbed against the coarse stuff of the tunic. She leaned against a trunk, dug her nails into the spongy bark, and forced herself to stay there. Softly there drifted into her mind, quiet at first, but in the same pulsing savage rhythm, "*Kyrie, Kyrie, Kyrie eleison.* Lord, have Mercy." Then stronger, mimicking the beat, using it and transforming it. "*Christos, Christos, Christos eleison.* Christ have mercy upon us."

This was more than an Allhallows bonfire. What could elicit that harrowing roar? She didn't know. What did she do now? There was still no sign of Robert or his men. She was all alone. She thought she heard the wail of a small baby. No — surely a nighthawk.

3.

FATHER MEROWALD FALTERED. His knees had started to ache. He eased himself onto a moss-covered stump and started to pray aloud.

"Here I am, Lord. Take me. That's what Samuel said, didn't he? Made rather a mess of this Lord, haven't I?" His voice was a dry rustling wind over leaves. "Been preoccupied with things that were none of my sheepfold, and not tending to those who knew my voice. There is a woman, Lord. Trapped, I suppose, by her longings. Don't know, really. I never sought her out, though she was my charge. She rarely came to Mass, barely took the Lord's Supper; never but that once when I thought she took the bread out again from her mouth. I knew of her but … ignored her. I went not to put it right. A sheep of my own fold. *Mea culpa, mea culpa.* How little you ask of me ... all the worse." He bent his head and listened.

He heard, in the stillness of his mind, by some easy trick of the wind, or the new cloudlessness of the night, the distant thrumming. His heart struggled against the bones of his chest as if caged. It was hard for him to rise. "I don't want to face it, do I?" he mumbled to himself. "Legs ... don't want ... to obey."

Grasping at a leafless branch, he pulled himself upright, steadied himself and headed for the sound, little minding the absence of the path, heedless of the terrain. He splashed through the tumbling creek after it left the valley of the oak, missing the path by mere inches, focused on the fear within him. There was a frenzy to the music that felt ... evil. In spite of his fear, because of it, he hastened toward the sound with all the speed and courage his frail body could muster, and because of his haste, stumbled into the bramble.

Near the path, where a streamlet had pooled into a marshy bog, over time had grown a lush, fragrant patch of blackberries. The maids were used, in the summer months, to pluck the ripe berries for tarts and fools. And, greedy for more and more of the fruit, had convinced their swains to cut a path through the canes so that they could harvest every last sun-suckled berry. Like the interior of a snail shell, the path wound inward to a center where now only shriveled black husks hung amid the dried leaves and thorns.

On the outskirts of this bramble, Father Merowald searched with his hands until he came upon what he thought to be a path. Path it was, but it led nowhere. He followed it to the center of the tangle. Blinded by the dark, hands bruised, hem of his cassock torn, he felt around the trailing and usurping vines until he stood, bewildered, like a trapped calf penned away from its mother. The thumping he had heard before was becoming more and more frenzied. A tear trickled down his face. "My job is to tell people about you, Lord. That's all. And I don't seem to be able to complete even that small task."

Somehow, the path was now obvious, illuminated by a silver shaft of moonlight. He took it and shuffled slowly on.

Chapter Nineteen

The red pulsed and pulled at her eyelids. The familiar red. The nimbus was brighter now. It splashed upon the soothing blackness and devoured its fringes. Sound. Sound, too, around her, rising to an angry roar and then, snake-like, slithering into a mumble. Black descended and trampled on the nimbus. But the nimbus defied the black, devoured in gulps its dusky lengths; surrounded them, and then engulfed them into her fiery womb. The black violated her, yet the violation was her will and she took it into her and sucked the life from it.

Hurt. Her ankle. Could the fire be hurting her? She thought about that. Her. Screeching hurt. Her ankle. She knew that word. Her ankle burned. She opened her eyes and brushed at an ember burning her leg. A fire was beside her. It spat, glutting itself on sinews of oak and beech. Beyond the fire, the night wood was entangled in the stars. She was lying, curled up. She tried to rise. Too hard. To stretch, mayhap? Or crawl? Ah, Galiena. What was Galiena doing in the wood? At night? Galiena might have some draught about her. There was her face, Galiena's, close now, saying something. The words came from afar, deepened like the sound of a voice in the crypt.

She could feel her tongue try to curl around words. Ah, words. The Word. They spewed forth then, in a torrent; tumbled over themselves. Some of them satisfied something in her, righteous words, well spun. Others made her eyes squint and her lips curl. Powerful words. Words of might and control.

She was tired now. No more words. She didn't care. She wanted to lie down. The rumble was attacking her. The landslide was overwhelming her, crashing against her oneness in groans and shouts. Voices. Eyes. From every direction. She could see their eyes. Cat's eyes glinting in the firelight, ready to pounce. The goblet. Ah. Galiena had the goblet. There. Agnes grabbed it and drank deeply. Then she sank down onto the welcoming cold and curled tightly into a ball around the goblet. Contentedly, she slid deep into the fathomless canyons of nepenthe.

2.

STONES. ROBERT PEERED THROUGH THE UNDERGROWTH in foreboding. Everyone knew of the stones. Even the abbess. Could be found everywhere, all over the countryside. Some had designs, carved deep. Others were barren, pockmarked by time. Strange, aura-ridden groups they were, standing or lying according to some long-forgotten plan. Some said the stones could draw you in and devour you. Others said the old ones cut out people's hearts there. The stones were revered, venerated and avoided.

Robert felt leaden, already defeated and overwhelmed, battling an amorphous foe bigger and stronger than he was. The stones were symbolic. The biggest stone, that on which the fire was built, rose four or five feet above the duff, and was more than eight feet long and weather-beaten, like worm-eaten wood. Not a stone at all, his age told him, but a barrow. It was hollow, he remembered. Had explored it as a boy. Found it full of dung — dung, small bones and sometimes snakes.

Robert checked the clearing for other stones. Two smaller ones leaned like frail old men among the shadowy figures on the far side of the fire.

Trees picketed the margins of the glade behind the people, caging them in, making of the stones and the barrow something sacrosanct, a place apart.

The throbbing stopped abruptly, leaving echoing beats to reverberate through the forest. A child wailed. Robert scanned the crowd.

"Used their staffs, I warrant. Banged 'em together. To make the beat," Tom, Robert's deputy, whispered. These people had come with purpose. What was going on?

"Bit of strange, even for Allhallows, eh, sir? The fire and all is traditional, but..."

But this was more. Even the quiet waited, expected. What? It was ominous. Taken altogether it was more than ominous. It was sinister. "Could 'a used a few more lads, eh, sir?"

Just searching for a lost nun, was he? Right. How could he have been so stupid? Robert breathed in the acrid odor of his own sweat.

An emaciated woman of more than middle age huddled atop the barrow in front of the forked blaze. Her light eyes gazed blankly through a curtain of short matted hair. She wore a white smock, tattered and filthy. Agnes. They both noticed her at the same time. Neither knot nor cord bound her. Bits of briar and crushed, dead leaves clung to her smock. Her jaw sagged. After a moment, her toes and hands started to quiver, curling in and out like a dog on a mat before a winter's fire. Her body jerked. With a piercing shriek she shredded

195

the precarious silence.

"You den of thieves." Agnes' words were those of the Bible, those of the psalms and gospels, but strangely mixed. "It is no wonder that you have no surety. No. Nor any help. There is no help in you. But I, I can part the waves and deal with the whirlwind. Thus says wind and fire and beasts of the air."

"Your transgressions. I know them. I know them well and they pierce me. Bring to my gates your thanksgivings and give to me the lives I crave."

Robert rested his hand on his dagger. The crowd murmured and muttered among themselves as if something had been unleashed and set free. He wished he'd brought more men.

"Draw the lads close," Robert whispered over his shoulder.

"This war ... " a voice floated from the crowd. "Our crops, our houses and our kin. Taken."

"Aye. And raped; killed. Murdering bastards." a new voice growled.

"Gudred's house. Burned. In the night. King's men, they said. Bah! Old King Henry wouldna 'ave stood for it. And this king, Stephen of Blois. Made a pact with the church. With his brother, Bishop Henry of Winchester. The devil, more like."

"Last year. Crops south of the Stour. Trampled. Just before harvest."

"Rid us of this war." The voice was desperate and tired, on the verge of exhaustion, no longer able to mind its tongue.

The answer growled from deep within Agnes, spewed out from her very gut. "Ask her. Plead. The putrid canker festers. Among you. You it is that bleeds corruption. Not the king." Agnes' voice continued to deepen and change. Her eyes slitted; her lips curled into a mask of hate. "Submit. Justice is mine. I am fire." There was a long pause. Then, she hissed. "Bring them to me."

196

As if they knew what was coming next, the people closest to the bailiff and his men started to push, crowding and bunching, shoving each other closer to the fire like a herd of cattle. Robert calculated the men he had. No more than a score. He turned. Each man had hidden himself as well as he could. Not Will, though. Robert looked closer. Will didn't seem to be there. But ... Will had a forester's sense for the woods. Could remain unseen.

"Will?" Robert whispered to Tom. Tom examined the forest.

"Dunno, sir." Then after a moment. "Mind of his own." Neither man worried about Will. "Can look after hisself."

The fire suddenly flared white and glass-bright, momentarily blinding the men. As the brightness receded, a shadow emerged, then became the fullness of a form, standing above Agnes, tall, and shrouded in a deep flowing purple.

"Has to be Galiena."

She ignored the woman at her feet and, after a pause, stretched out one arm and pointed far back toward the edge of the clearing.

Agnes continued to mumble and sift. Galiena strode toward her and bent to speak. Her lips moved, but none could hear. The dell was hushed as each, fearing the words, tried to catch them.

"Agnes says," Galiena's voice gained in strength, "that she speaks for Helias." At the name, Galiena bowed.

"Yes, Helias. Have you forgotten, you lowly worms, the Earth Mother of us all?" The witch's voice had risen to a screech. "Bow your miserable bodies, lest she hear of your disregard and give to you that which you well deserve."

Like wind moving the billowing wheat on a summer day, they bowed.

"Your mothers and their mothers bowed low to Helias," Galiena continued. "Worshiped her. It is Helias alone who brings forth the sprouted sheaf or withers it with her flame. It is Helias who named the plants, and she alone who can will them to do her bidding. You who have come to me in the night, you who have lost a babe or who have needed someone by your side in the long watches of cold. You who have ailed and sickened unto quivering fever. It was to Helias that you then prayed. It was her potions and cordials; her plants that tranquiled your sorrow and healed your wounds. These mysteries come from her loins; the bounty of the woodlands, the lore of the wild, handed down from dame to daughter."

"Remember you to thank her for her bounty? Honor you her with sacrifices? No. You go to that other with His gold and His wretched cross. To Him you give your bounty. And then when you sicken, you come again puling to Helias for succor. Wonder you that this war rages when you honor Helias not?"

Suddenly Galiena dropped her staff and strode toward the edge of the barrow, propelled seemingly by the venom of her words. Agnes groaned and toppled to the side, her eyes turning to whites, and yellow drool tricking to pool on the pockmarked rock below her head.

"See this." Galiena ignored Agnes, leaving her to twitch there on the mound. From the depths of her cloak she extracted a book.

"It was the *Laece Book*," Averilla would tell the abbess. "I knew it at once."

"This," Galiena held the book high, flashing the firelight against it, "they took from Helias with their pointed helmets and bloody spurs; took it from her rightful followers. They harbored it for years in their sterile wombs, keeping it from us. The secrets of Helias. These are for her followers alone. How dare they use her secrets for their God?"

Galiena paused, looked to her left and scanned the crowd.

The fire hissed over the silence. Then she continued. "You have angered her. Helias will not be trifled with. She has fed you. She has healed your wounds from the womb of her earth. Little do you fear her. No more sacrifices do you bring. Expect you all from her and give nothing in return? She has spoken through Agnes. Heard you her? Helias requires ... blood. Not just any blood. No. She wants those that befoul her; those that are as anathema to her; whose very existence is a stench to her; a defilement. She alone is creation. She alone is perfection. Imperfection saps the strength of her womb. It must be ripped from her body. Burned. Here. As was done of old. Theeeeeeere." Galiena swirled and pointed. Her garments and loosened hair clouded around her. "There. On the corner of the crowd. One of them ... He who defiles her purity."

"It came so suddenly. She had been ranting but I had little expected this to be her aim. I had expected a band of marauders, a raid on the barns of the abbey, the burning of the castle. That I had expected."

Instead, fingers fanged like an adder, she turned and pointed into the crowd. Her voice shimmied into a howl of inhuman timbre, like a hawk seeing its prey. "There. There stands the impure one, protected by the whimpering celibacy of the sterile wombs, defiling our existence with his deformity."

"I couldn't see whom she was pointing at, but the crowd did. They swarmed like hounds quarreling a stag to bay. A vicious tumbling of bodies, it was, the hard thunking of wood against bone. They fought and trampled each other eager to rip and tear."

"They grabbed him. Someone. Red hair. I saw his red hair. It was Will. I didn't want to believe it. My heart tore."

Galiena's voice gained in strength over the swelling rumble of the bloodlust that gripped them. "Wonder you that the harvest is puny? We have strayed from her ways. Helias, too,

199

craves a bigger harvest. Her blood harvest." They threw him into the air. The hands made a platter for their blows. The now limp form lay lifeless like so many pecks of wheat.

"Does a ewe suckle the blasphemy of deformity? No. She kills it. Casts out the impure. Leaves it to die. The runt of the litter. Casts it from her teats. Denies it her rich, sustaining liquor. That is the way of Helias. We will not have impurity in our midst to sicken our flocks or put our world out of her ways."

They carried Will to her and tossed him at her feet. She looked down for the briefest moment. Looked down in satisfaction.

3.

JOHN THE MASON WATCHED IN HORROR as the crowd turned. Galiena was fanning their fear into flame. He watched Will flail against the savage force of them, and then, with the corner of his eye, he noticed near the edge of the crowd a boy whose grace and cleanliness and whole carriage were foreign to his clothes. Reminded him of someone. John combed one side of his brain, while with the other he watched appalled as the ferocity grew. It wasn't a boy. It was Dame Averilla. No. It couldn't be. His head swiveled and he looked again at the slight boyish figure. Now that he suspected, there could be no mistaking. He watched her as she moved tentatively into the crowd.

CHAPTER TWENTY

I.

"W are," Robert's voice was hoarse, croaked out of parched lips. His warning came too late. The men had already unsheathed daggers and swords. Bithric planted his back next to the rough silver bark of an old oak and pulled a tightly fletched arrow from the quiver at his belt. Two of the men elbowed the nearest bystanders out of their way and started to shoulder a path toward Will's limp body. The nearest of those watching whirled angrily at being jostled and shoved, at having any interruption to the slaking of his bloody thirst. Others turned, sensing the stir. Their anger turned to a numbing shock as they recognized the bailiff.

Robert's cry, "To arms. They are — " was drowned by a rumbled howl as shame turned to angry self-justification, and like the bay of some ravenous beast, lusting, thirsting after blood, their voracious, visceral roars mingled with the rekindled flames of the witch's fire. Robert felt a driblet of sweat trickle down his ribs within the leather jerkin, tasted the dryness of his lips. He knew the fierce and mindless rapacity of hatred when it was united against a scapegoat.

The mob attacked like a swarm of locusts on a field of golden wheat, staffs raised and teeth bared. Panicked, Robert's men fought hard, and the bitter tingle of fear tinged the smoky air. They were not easily overwhelmed. Robert kicked and hacked, his unsheathed knife in one hand, sword in the other, trying to ward off the grappling arms and bone-crunching blows. Suddenly, someone picked him up from behind and flung him to the ground where another, a wiry, toothless man, started methodically kicking him in the groin and kidneys. He curled up like a centipede. His ribs were pummeled. They took their staffs to his head. His last memory was of a leer and of fetid breath through cragged teeth.

2.

AVERILLA STOOD PARALYZED. She felt the fire of the mob. They jerked and writhed like an injured snake. Then, when they saw the bailiff, the grunts and howls erupted into the fiercer fighting born of shame. She felt rise within her the uncanny ability she had used before, an ability to sense the feelings of those around her. Images flooded her mind, unbidden and revolting. Her fingers felt the globs of torn skin under ragged nails. Her shoulders shuddered with wood cracking against bone. Her palm knew the curve of the hand-polished ax haft. She tasted on her tongue the mineral-sweet blood. An oozing, blood red, shrouded her sight; she felt a sense of childish elation, and a memory overwhelmed her.

> The night is lit as if with the morning sun but red and shaking. I rub my eyes. Yells echo from the hall. My father grabs his sword. I hear the bolt on the outside of the door shoved home. My nurse. Where is my nurse?
> Screams and gurgles, sounds of breaking, and a low crackling of fire reverberate through the wood of the door. I cry and scream and pound on the door. It opens. I tiptoe

down the stairs. Cold on my bare feet. The hall roils with thrashing bodies and redness and fire and mouths agape. I stand near the high table and scream and scream and hear no sound. My father is nowhere. Yes. He stands there, near the hearth. His sword flashes. Men writhe around him, all around him. Others stand near the cauldron, stuffing their mouths with food. They look like skeletons. "The cattle are sick," my father has said. "There is not enough food for the people." Is this what they want? But...

My nurse heads toward me, her elbows flailing. Two men grab her. One throws her down, holds her by the shoulders. The other lifts her skirts and lies on top of her. Jerky spasms like a fit. I scream. Someone comes toward me. I must get to my nurse.

I grab my father's goblet from the table. It is not heavy, somehow, and comes easily to my grasp. I stumble down the last few stairs from the high table. My tunic makes me trip, but I do not fall. Everything seems to follow me in a dream. I can see her because I am small and there are only legs between us now. She is screaming, her mouth open like that of the geese, but not a hiss, a sound, comes out. I raise the goblet with both hands and bring the heavy weight down on the man as hard as I can. The blow strikes his shoulder and he pauses just for a moment, just a moment. As if bothered by a fly, he brushes at the place I have hit. Yells sound. My father's voice. He strides across the bodies. He takes nurse's hand, gently cupping her elbow, and helps her rise. With his other hand he lofts me over his shoulders, like a bag of wool.

"I, I must have dreamed," she would later tell the abbess. "A ... a cold fear ... I stumbled around the edge of the crowd, to be closer, to get nearer, to hide myself ... I wanted to help Will."

203

At the time, the gnarled burlwood of her walking staff seemed enormously heavy. Averilla curled both hands around it and held it forward, thumbs under, knuckles out, as she had seen the arms master teach her brothers. With a rage born of memory, she hacked at the nearest man and jabbed the end of the stick into the back of his waist. "That is for Will." As he tumbled sideways, away from her, the staff swept across his falling body. The blow caught a second man in the ribs. His arm was upraised over Tom, Robert's deputy, and the second man fell on Tom's unsheathed blade. She heard the outrushing breath and saw him fall, saw, with part of her mind, Tom turn and wipe his blade on the recumbent form. Not pausing, appalled at what she had done, mind still on Will, she stumbled on, but caught her foot in a leather jerkin. For the fraction of a moment she was alone in the swirling mass. She couldn't see for the tears. Tears? Her detached position was like a magnet to the surrounding mob. Another man, his mouth stretched in a grimace of fury, came at her, a bloody knife clutched at the ready. She turned her body, instinctively raised the long staff and caught the man on his Adam's apple. He gagged and, clutching at his throat, fell sideways. She stared at him in horror. Another came at her as she bent over the man she had just killed. With an upward heft, he twisted the burlwood out of her grasp. Not pausing, he raised it over her head and slammed it down. As his arm swung down, he was pushed "by a woman, the woman I had seen in the forest. She ran into his arm so his blow was less severe than it might have been." A fiery pain shrieked through Averilla as she fell. Blood gushed from under the fluffy curls of her scalp.

204

3.

CADILLA HAD THOUGHT SHE HAD PREPARED HERSELF for what she would find when she and her two brothers finally reached the clearing. She had expected an Allhallows frenzy; had seen one before, when she was small. The numbing madness and hysteria had terrorized her. It was why she had so fervently embraced the kindness of Jesus and His God. She knew that He, too, must abhor the mindless horror that crept into people and changed them into contorted, hate-centered fiends.

When Cadilla finally reached the edge of the light, she scanned the glade frantically. She couldn't find Averilla. The maelstrom of tumbling humanity scared her. She started to tremble, tried to remember Averilla, tried to keep herself from running. She stumbled behind a tree and stood there trembling, feeling the indentations of bark on her face. After a moment the trembling ceased and she forced herself to turn back to the glade. There. A profile. That nose. But it was a lad. No. The stance. It was Averilla. Hands held over her ears, like a child afraid of taunting voices, Cadilla scuttled through the hazel and briars. Trying to ignore Galiena's seductive invective, she hummed the *Kyrie*. Over and over under her breath. Muttered the *Pater Noster*. "Thy kingdom come ... deliver us from evil. Trespasses ... "

When Cadilla finally reached the spot on which Averilla had stood, Averilla was forging her way through the molten mass of thrashing bodies. Hands over her head to ward off blows, ducking with a quickness she thought she had relinquished to childhood, Cadilla doggedly pushed through the crowd to where, momentarily, Averilla stood alone. Seeing the upraised staff, Cadilla dove across the intervening space and lunged into the arm, deflecting, just enough, the brunt of the blow.

Single-mindedly, not even bothering to look at Averilla's

bloody scalp, Cadilla lifted the limp woman under the armpits. She was too heavy. There was no way. From quite close came a maddened bellow of anger. John the mason had just seen what was happening. The witch looked up at him, caught him in her slanted eyes, and smiled — more of a grimace. John thrashed through the crowd like a wounded bear, clubbing with his hammer right and left. Those around him scrambled aside. He hoisted Averilla's body over his shoulder like a peck of wheat, and muscled his way through the crowd. Cadilla followed meekly behind.

4.

ON THE BARROW, THE WITCH GRABBED A HUNK of Agnes' hair and yanked back her head. With the other hand she ripped the modest tunic from neck to hem. Agnes screamed and writhed, but could do nothing against hands dipped in hate. "Who," Galiena yelled, "which of you, my good men, would like to taste her fear. Helias would have a child from the womb of this slut, conceived in hate and loathing."

5.

FATHER MEROWALD, FUMBLING THROUGH THE FOREST, had heard the savage howl, the answering maddened rumble, and had known it for what it was. Panicked — knowing that here at last he was needed; here at last, there was something for him to do — he pushed his old body onward. He ignored the gritty pain as his swollen rheumatic bones grated one against another. Evil was slithering through the forest and coiling its blackness into men's souls. Not far now. Just around the next bend. He could hear the growling, the loud breathing, as evil fed on men's fear and hunger and exhaustion. He tried to run and stubbed his toe. It was the one with the corn, and the pain was fierce. Limping, his weight on the other foot, he barked his knee against a stone. He pawed wildly at a protruding branch; managed to grab it and right himself. Chastened, Father Merowald slowed down to a hurrying shuffle. His feet molded themselves to the ground and he floundered on toward the clearing.

When he turned the final bend, the fierce blaze momentarily blinded him to the night. He saw the woman. Eager hands thrust wood, twigs, and even huge stumps, into the yellow-blue maw of the fire. A body was being hoisted toward her, its legs and arms at unnatural angles.

He limped into the maelstrom. Knees shoved. A man, eyes whiting, pumped blood onto the parson's face. The smell was sweet, iron-rich. The splintered end of a broken staff, aimed at someone's groin, gashed his shoulder, tearing the fabric of his cassock and his gray, chicken-neck skin. He careened into a man rhythmically hacking, in an obscene parody of love, at a bloodied mass of hair and gore. Above the deep thunk of wood against bone, and the harsh curses, Galiena shrieked and keened like a maddened crow.

Father Merowald focused the full power of prayer on those around him: men whom he had known since infancy, men whose confessions he had heard, men he had fed from his meager allotment, men he had comforted in distress, men whose sanity he had saved with his absolutions and concern.

"Alcheferd, my lad. Lord? Bless Alcheferd," and the priest put his hand on the man nearest him, a man whose father had been killed by the casual flick of de Redvers's crop. The feather-light touch of his hand and the peace of his voice sent a trembling quiver up the man, bringing to him the memory of his own name.

"Will," not Dumb Will but another of the same name. "Lord,

take Will to your heart." The man turned, swift as an adder, his club raised. Confused, hearing his own name, he peered at the scrawny figure before him. Recognizing the priest, knowing him to be the man who had convinced his friend to marry his pregnant sister, Will banked his eyes and lowered his club.

"Midred?" Midred looked into the age-dimmed blue that he had known as a child, and then looked down, his ax limp.

"John,"

"Simon,"

"Ralph,"

"Eadric,"

"Warin,"

"Bithric,"

"Turold,"

Around Father Merowald as he crabbed forward, the men he had touched hesitated, just for the moment, confused and bewildered as if wakened from a dream. If, after he passed, they continued with their mayhem, they did so with less than the original vigor. Others simply stopped, in shock, looked at their hands and at the scene before them, and drifted backwards into the anonymity of the surrounding forest.

The little man crawled, hands on rock, the last few feet to the top of the barrow. He thought that perhaps he would not make it, thought his body would fail him. Someone gave him a push and he foundered to the crown. He took a tentative step toward what he thought was the witch, black behind the red, only to stumble heavily against Agnes, spread-eagled in a heap at his feet.

He stooped down and tried to rearrange her legs, then he shrugged off his own cloak and covered her. Frantically, she rolled under the cloak, recurling like a scorpion and reaching for a small wooden goblet. He stared down for a moment, uncomprehending. Then, understanding, he uncurled her fingers from the vessel and smelled its contents.

His eye seized the dark vacuum of the witch on the far side of the fire. Unflinching, he held her gaze, lifted the beaker high, and slowly poured its dark contents onto the ground.

Galiena faced him. Her eyes, like shiny orbs of black obsidian, pulsed with coldness. She was unnaturally still. Only the fire-eddied breeze twitched the hem of her skirt. The power that had resided in him, unbidden and unknown, challenged the dark nothingness peering from her eyes. His power was that of tranquility, of memory, of usefulness, and of knowingness of the power of God behind him. She stood, drawing at him, pulling, sucking, trying to match his strength with the strength of hurt, oblivion, and ordinary meanness, trying to suck the creative love from him.

Sensing a threat, not understanding, one of Galiena's followers looked at the two forces and then rushed blindly for the priest. In the end, something, fear perhaps, stymied him. He could not bring himself to kill the old man. He grabbed the front of the cassock and started to lift Father Merowald off the ground. The intricate silver cross the parson wore under his cassock stabbed through the coarse cloth and pierced the man's palm. He squealed and then, enraged, slid a slim, lethal dagger from the sheath at his belt. As he lunged, there was a sudden swishing sound, just the faintest hiss, inaudible to any but Galiena or Agnes. The man's dagger clattered to the rock as he fell forward toward Father Merowald, an arrow protruding from his back. The parson put out a hand to deflect the man's fall, but the man was too heavy, and Father Merowald staggered as he tried to ease the dying man to the ground. He looked for a moment at the arrow, and then raised his eyes to Galiena.

"My child." He reached out to her, his face a mixture of pain and longing. Her image flickered against the forest behind her. She sucked in a hissing breath. With a wide cast, like a woman feeding her chickens, she flung something onto the fire. In the blinding brightness that followed, before any could catch her, like vapor she had disappeared.

Father Merowald squinted at the place she had been and then at the upturned, shocked faces. She had done, had used, something to make her seem powerful. Could he make them understand? His sheep. His stupid sheep. So easily led. Always wanting for themselves, and for their bodies.

"My children," his voice quavered and he coughed to clear it. "Follow not strange gods, strange gods whose purposes you cannot fathom." The fire raged momentarily behind him. "They will reap what they have sown. You would not be with Helias on the last days. She will give to you what she has required of you: hate and evil and pain and fire. Serve only the God of love —"

"Nay, Father," the interruption was swift, with battle-weary boldness. Father Merowald knew the voice. There was an answering mutter from those who could hear. "Why, Father," he continued when the muttering had ebbed, "should we believe that your God is any better than this here Helias? She done stuff for my grandam. That should be enough for me. What's your God done for me? He is asleep, He is, Him and all His saints. We get no help from Him."

As if the question gave him strength, in the nacreous light of the creeping dawn, the gentle man took on a new power of being.

"Eadric," the disarming recognition of person, "there is a difference between a god who seeks to shred and defile a man, and a God who loves that man with such a fierce ardor that He is willing to die a human death of torment for that love."

210

"Nay, Father, that death warn't for me, not where I live, anyroad. That ware for de Redvers and the nuns, them as have a good life and can think of that. What's 'e ever done for me?"

The little man took a deep breath. Did they ever hear him? Probably not. "He's loved you, Eadric. You've seen hate, Eadric. Here tonight. It is easy to hate. It could be turned against you, just as it was against Will. A mere matter of a tongue. That could have been your wife, Eadric, or your grandam. Hate doesn't care what it attacks. To her," and here the little man gestured at the vacancy where Galiena had stood, "evil is the same as good. Helias is in torment. The agony of others gives her company, in the depths and breadth of a bleak eternity." He paused to let it sink in. "You don't want what she has to offer, Eadric. Serve the God of love. Let Him stand with you and comfort you. He gives you love, Eadric, and life with Him. You have seen that love in others around you, Eadric. You have known the sacrifices your mother made for you. That was love. She chose to marry a man much older when your father died, so that you would not starve. You saw him take a younger woman to his bed. And when that woman left him, when he turned back, your dam gave him love. She chose love. For you. Choose, Eadric. They are not the same. Choose love."

6.

"WHEN I AWOKE, THE FIGHTING HAD STOPPED. Like ants around a gravel anthill, those who could dragged bodies, the limp forms of men I knew, toward succor, towards others who could care for them. Someone was bending over me, wiping my brow with a cloth, cradling my head. It felt like a woman," Averilla would later tell the abbess.

"It was."

Averilla started. "It was?"

"Cadilla followed you into the forest. She … knew something of what was going on and felt somehow responsible. She feared to see you go off on your own." The abbess' face was expressionless.

Averilla would continue. "I tried to focus, but I was faint with pain. Colors swirled around in my head. I looked for Galiena. She seemed to have gone. It sounded like Father Merowald was giving a homily."

Painfully, Averilla had rolled to her knees. Bitter juice flooded her gorge. She scrabbled forward and vomited, retching long after her stomach had emptied. She wiped her chin with the back of her hand, and, leaning on the same hand, painfully tried to lever herself to her feet. Dizziness overwhelmed her. Once again oblivion clouded her vision, and Averilla crumpled sideways onto the softness of the duff.

It scared Cadilla, Averilla's second retreat into insensibility. It brought her again to the reality of the scene; suffocated her with it. She tried to pray. It emerged as an agonized bleat at the Almighty, nothing like the disciplined prayers of a quiet mind. Her lips moved as she shut her eyes to her fear of losing this one nun who seemed to understand her; this headstrong woman Cadilla could have stopped from blundering into this inferno of rage. Undisciplined words fought for her mind. Over and over they rolled like pebbles around her brain. "*Kyrie, Kyrie, Kyrie eleison.* Lord, have mercy. Help me, God. Dear Jesus, help this woman. She is yours, Lord. You know this. None can help her now but You." In desperation, she slapped Averilla's cheek.

7.

ATERILLA WAKENED A SECOND TIME to Father Merowald's voice. This, though, was a different voice, loud, confident and full of power. She looked curiously at the hedge of trees surrounding her. Where was she? Before the thought had left her brain she gagged, rolled on her side, and heaved dry heaves onto the duff. Duff. The forest. It came back to her. Will.

Father Merowald had somehow mounted a barrow. Averilla tried to stand, the better to see. Her torn ankle buckled under her. Consciousness again ebbed around her, dizzy in reds and deep yellows.

When she could finally climb to her feet, most of the crowd had melted into the forest. Unaware of Cadilla beside her, she put a hand on a thin hazel twig. It steadied her. She could stand. She made her stumbling way to the barrow. Curses and growls came from it; or from the near vicinity, but there was no one there. Averilla rubbed her eyes and looked around. Hell? She hadn't thought it would come so quickly. Had she died? She pinched her arm. It hurt. So on hands and feet, Averilla inched up the side of the barrow.

Agnes looked beaten and ravaged, but seemed to sleep. Averilla knelt beside her and looked at her dully. Maybe it was over. Her brain tried to tackle what it all meant and wallowed in confusion. Someone would have to help Agnes back to the abbey. Averilla tried again to stand and fell back.

Will? Will. Maybe he had crept away. Maybe it wasn't he she had seen. There were many with red hair. She shook her head to try to think straight. It hurt to shake it, so she stopped. She looked around again, slowly. Crumpled, on the edge of the rock, but close to her, was a pile of old rags. Strange. No, it wasn't rags. Pile was too big for rags. And it was red. No one had red clothes. Blood? Or hair? Hair. Will? Averilla crawled to the pitiful, crumpled pile and pulled at it. It was heavy. A body. The head had red hair. That was what was red. She turned it toward her. The face was leaden, white and peaceful. No grimace marred the strong kind features. It was not Will. No longer. He had gone. Tears ran down her face, her shoulders heaved, and she heard a wail from somewhere, somewhere near.

Later, when she thought about it, Averilla knew she had stayed there for a while, how long she couldn't tell. The forest had quieted by the time she remembered again. The sky had started to lighten. A hand touched her shoulder, light like the wings of a butterfly. Father Merowald stood there beside her. "He was a fine, fine man, child." His voice shook, cracked. He cleared his throat. "We will miss him more than — " The little man never finished. Two large tears glistened down the creases of his cheeks.

8.

AFTER THE BAILIFF HAD BEEN TAKEN, Tom had started toward the barrow. "I knew it was up to me," Tom would tell his grandchildren years later, "with him, the bailiff, being down and all. The priest and her were looking daggers at one another. Black they were, her eyes, just 'a staring with malice. I'd ne'er before seen such deadness. Menacing she was, and awesome, as if something was there pacing around behind her eyes."

Tom had crept between those in the crowd as they watched Galiena and Father Merowald, awed by the deadly conflict. As the fire roared into an inferno, Tom had staggered backward, shielding his eyes. "I'm not proud of that, ye wist, but the fires of hell were rising up from the bowels of the earth. I was afeared."

"As swiftly as the fire had raised itself up, it sank down like a beaten old nag. Galiena had disappeared. Completely. I thought mayhap the devil had taken her. I stood there as stupid as a poleaxed ram, looking at the sparks and the blue flames, but she was not there."

Slowly, Tom had slipped among the packed bodies, careful not to touch those around him, aware of the momentary stupefaction of the crowd. Reaching the base of the mound, Tom mounted it matter-of-factly, nodded to Father Merowald, who was still talking, unsheathed his bloody dagger, and hacked at the tough strands of rawhide with which Robert and the others had been trussed, hung by their wrists, their feet not touching the ground, their strained tendons bulging.

There was a black hole on the side of the barrow, behind the fire. "Like the devil's womb, it was, black and sore and stinking." Steps had been carved into the rock. The stones were moldy with the damp and foul with a black clinging slime. The nothingness of it caught Tom's eye as he hacked down the men. "I knew 'at was where she had gone — to her foul den." He unsheathed his sword and started for it. "Smelled worse than a pigsty; more like a house when someone has died." The stairs were uneven, slanting away from the barrow side, with varied risers. He felt with his toes for the edges.

"She was there when I got to the bottom. Heard the rattling of her breath." Those of the bailiff's men who were able had followed Tom to the mound. While some saw to the bailiff, Robin stumbled down behind Tom. His torch cast elongated shadows that hovered and loomed like birds of prey. "My hand brushed something. I looked down. On the wall beside me, ye wot, were human skulls, brown and greasy with bits of flesh still attached." Galiena, crouched like a badger at the back of the cave, bared her teeth. In her right hand she clutched a curved, stained dagger. "We'd ne'er 'ad gotten her, but two

215

other lads, just then, stumbled down." The sound of their feet encouraged Robin. He poked at Galiena with the torch, feinted closer and closer, danced in and then out again. "Looked like one o' them dogs as you see baiting a bear." He finally hit her hand. The knife clinked on the stones and skittered across the floor. They fell on her. Four of them to her one. "Scared, we were. She clawed at us, at our eyes like a she-cat with kittens." They finally pinned her arms to her sides. Chest heaving, sweat running into his eyes, Robin ripped the hem of her gown and bound her wrists behind her. She spat. It hit Robin's open eye and oozed thickly down his face. He hit her then, hard, with the back of his hand.

She slowly swung her head to face him, and fixed her black motionless, emotionless eyes on Robin's face, "May your bowels crawl with worms and run until you drop like a withered leaf in the fall. May all your babes be born with no arms and but one eye."

Robin hit her again across her mouth and turned his back.

Blood flecked her lips. She ignored it.

Chapter Twenty-One

I.

They marched Galiena up Castle Hill to the castle. The watchmen, having seen the party in the thin dawn light, had the heavy wooden gates open for them. They filed through the gates into the inner keep, and half-pushed, half-dragged Galiena into the wide hall of the building.

While Robin held Galiena, Tom strode across to the far corner, brushed aside the rushes, and lifted a trap door that dropped down to the dungeon. They pulled Galiena down the narrow, dark stairs carved into the rock of the hill. The dungeon was empty, dark and windowless. The air was stale and reeked of mice and urine. The low, cobwebbed room, once a cave, had been enclosed by a wall of dressed stone; the very outer wall of the castle. Iron rings were shackled to the wall. The two men looked at one another and there passed between them an unspoken thought.

Tom thrust the torch into the curled iron corbel, went to the center of the dungeon, and pulled on an iron ring set into another heavy, grated wooden trap door. He hefted the lid of what looked like a tomb carved into the floor of the cave, nothing more than a shallow grave with a lid. Galiena

217

struggled when she saw it, and grunted strangled gasps, but the men were determined. They pulled the gag from her mouth, forced her down and in, and quickly slammed the grate. They listened for a moment, but she neither howled nor wept. Vaguely disquieted, they climbed back out of the dungeon and shut the second trap door behind them.

2.

LATER IN THE WEEK, THE PRIEST FORCED his aching knees to the castle. Mavis looked up from her baking to find him standing beside her. She wiped her hands on a lappet of cloth and silently led him into the hall where Robert was resting. Father Merowald smiled sweetly and blessed her.

"Robert," he said to the bailiff who was sitting in front of the fire, his leg up on a stool as Averilla had insisted, "she must be tried soon. We cannot just let her rot."

"She has food and water," Robert did not take his eyes from the fire.

"Does she?" Robert jerked his head up and searched the priest's face.

"I think that perhaps Tom and Robin may have placed her in the 'cage.'"

Robert's brow furrowed. "I gave no such order."

"No, nor any specific not to. Have you checked on her?"

"By God's blood, she's a witch. Will you berate me for treating her the way she did others?" Robert struggled to his feet and hopped on one foot to the far side of the room. The wound on his foot had festered, and Averilla had made him promise to stay off it.

"Robert, you mustn't." Mavis ran over to her husband and pulled at his arm. He brushed her aside.

Robert struggled to pull tall leather boots over his swollen

218

foot. "The crime took place in a royal forest, but there are no foresters, so she cannot be tried in the Forest Court. It is early for the abbess' court, even if we could get the bishop down to try her, and you know that Robert of Salisbury is somewhat occupied elsewhere. She could as well wait a fortnight. You know that."

"Aye. I would imagine, however, that we can speak to the abbess to convene the Manor Court and I am sure that the steward could be persuaded to preside. Would you have me so do?"

"I would not. This woman has caused no end of trouble. As if there were not trouble enough with King Stephen in Lincoln. Wants men and horses. Robert of Gloucester being teased into a pitched battle, de Redvers on one side and then another, and someone stirring up trouble in the forest. It's not only Galiena, you know. And you want to see if her lodgings are comfortable? To her liking? Bah! He gave one final heave and his boot slipped on. He grunted, and gave Father Merowald a long look. The latter nodded and started to turn. "No. There is no need to ask the abbess. I would as leave forget that damned woman, but you will not let me, will you? Aye. I will do your bidding." He pulled the latchstring and went out, the other following meekly behind, his mission accomplished.

3.

WHEN THEY OPENED THE CAGE, GALIENA was withered from dehydration, and bent from lying in the same cramped position for four days.

"Taught ye some'ut, mayhap. Didn't think ye could be hurt by the likes of us, did ye?" Robin asked the limp form as he pulled open the hatch. "Ach. Gots a body, don't ye, just like the rest of us?"

"Aye, and a soul, my son, do not forget the soul."

"Well, she took no heed of it."

"Nay, nor did I."

Galiena blinked and squinted at the light as if it hurt her eyes. They pulled her out. She was stiff, curled into a fetal position. She had had little water or food for four days. Those who had been detailed to go and check on her had used the grill above her as a urinal, and she smelled of their feces and her own.

They half-carried, half-dragged her from the castle and down the Bimport to the abbey gatehouse. The winter morning was blue with curdled clouds on the horizon. A scathing gust blustered now and again across the hilltop, and the trees in the far distance were bare and pronged like jagged corpses. Bits of limp chard and slops and an odd feather or drift of wool lay trapped in ice in the ruts. Despite the raw day, a crowd had already gathered. The small boys who usually spat and threw dirt at the prisoners were awed, and only a few bits of green gravel spattered around her. Her hair was matted with filth, as was her tunic. Her eyes were carefully hooded. Only occasionally did she raise them to glare with livid hatred at those who lined the road.

The abbey gatehouse was a large building with rooms below and chambers above in the twin towers. In the larger of the lower rooms, both the Abbess' Court and the Manor Court were convened.

The *Curia Legalis Feodorum Baroniae,* or Court Baron, was a domestic court held by the steward within the manor, for redressing misdemeanors and nuisances and settling disputes. It was held every three weeks, and all the bailiffs from the barony manors were required to attend. It was not a court of record, but then, according to Norman law, women were not within the law, so records could be dispensed with.

"The bailiffs are here, anyway," the steward had muttered under his breath. "We may as well get it over with."

There was an uneasy quiet tacked on the crowd, muffling all sound. Galiena's shuffling stumble and the strong booted steps of her warders could be heard as the crowd parted to make way for them.

There was little to be said. Robert, still bruised with purple and black blotches on his face, presented the case. What sun there was had reached that point on the horizon where a sliver came through the narrow lancet windows to catch Father Merowald as he stood watching the proceedings; caught him and he suffered under it, casting down his eyes to the hard-packed earthen floor. He knew all his parishioners were thinking that the sunbeam represented God's favor somehow, pointing him out. "I, who had had many a chance, and did not help her. Much ashamed."

When asked if she had anything to say, Galiena moistened her lips and spoke, her voice rough and cracked from her days of silence. "'Witchcraft,' you call it? And what have I done? Let me remind you that both Margaret of Scotland and Henry the late king were interested in prophesy. Henry even consulted Wulfric of Haselbury. Neither of them was condemned for witchcraft. Geoffrey of Monmouth has recommended baths of water run over the stones on Salisbury Plain."

The verdict of the twelve who were the county was to be expected. If she would not repent and recant, she would suffer an ordeal by hot iron. "Said not a word after that, she didna. Just stared toward the door, as if waiting, expectant like, for some'ut."

4.

"WHY DIDN'T THEY HANG HER?" CLEMENT hung on every word as his father related the events to Mavis later that evening.

Robert had responded, looking thoughtful. "I would guess that they didn't want to hang her because hanging is considered an honor in the old religion. They would know that. Taught it at the teat. But murder or rape, those things as has a penalty of death, the matter is too grave to be left to the imperfect judgement of men. That's why the county went directly to the judgement of God through the ancient trial by ordeal. At anyroad, they asked her to recant, to confess Christ crucified as her savior, and she spat at them like a cat."

"Verily," she had said. "I know that Jesus Christ is the Son of God." She said that, but went no further. Said it quickly, glibly, and refused to kiss the cross.

"It was never said that the prince of darkness didn't know," the abbess had later reflected, "that Christ was the Son of God. He knew that. All too well."

If Galiena wanted to say more, she refrained. Something like triumph glinted in her eyes "as if she had willed them to so judge. As if she had a foreknowledge of what would later happen. Mayhap she did."

5.

THE FOLLOWING MORNING, THE SKY had turned iron gray. Ground fog oozed between the houses and shrouded the trees. The boys of the town were the first to arrive in the market square to watch. It was not often that such a spectacle was provided to slake their blood thirst. Although youngsters were forbidden access to the manor court, everyone could be present for the punishment. One of them, younger than

222

the rest, pissed behind a protruding wall. Another found a stray dog and started to kick at it. His fellows joined in the fun, pelting it with rocks as they waited. The starving animal was cornered for a moment between a cart and the side of the Guest Hall, but in a burst of terrified speed, it ran at the boys and disappeared. Others started to arrive: a gaggle of old women, the fishmonger's wife, and two from Tinters Lane. Many of those who had been present for the trial absented themselves, wishing to have no part in the punishment. Many who had been there for the Allhallows bonfire yelled the worst curses at her.

They marched her swiftly along the Bimport from the castle. She had spent the night in the dungeon, not in the "cage." Perhaps it was her relative comfort, or perhaps the closeness of her adversary, but something more now sparked behind Galiena's eyes, and she no longer staggered. Tom lashed her to the post that had been hastily erected in the middle of the market near the stocks. The rubble and mortar that held it firm were still wet.

They placed the iron in the brazier that had been brought over from the metalworker's shop. When it was red hot, Peter, the metalworker, picked it up with tongs and held the tongs out to Tom. Galiena stilled herself as she watched, retreated to some inner space. Her eyes remained open, fixed on something in the middle distance. She did not blink. Nor did she tense. She allowed her arms to be raised as Tom approached with the heated iron. Father Merowald stepped forward from the crowd, holding a cross. "It is not too late, my child." There was entreaty in his eyes. She gave no response; stood anchored as if she had not heard. At a signal from Robert, Tom touched the tender flesh of her inner arm with the iron.

He then wrapped her arm in linen, winding round and round a length of it. Next, he walked to the steward, who pulled the signet he wore from his pudgy fingers. One of the men dripped wax onto the linen in three places, and Tom pressed down the signet so that no poultice or infusion could be applied to the wound.

When the three days were spent, they hauled Galiena again from the dungeon and slowly, portentously, unwrapped her arm. Not only was it not blistered where the iron had stung, but it was barely red. The crowd let out an audible hiss; some crossed themselves.

The steward, who had sat in judgement in the place of the abbess, was bound by the verdict of the jury. His eyes shifted from face to face and he licked his bottom lip. He knew his duty and hastened to perform it. "Unbind her. She has withstood the ordeal."

Robert glanced at him and motioned to Tom. As the crowd grumbled and murmured in anger, they roughly untied her. She staggered to hold herself upright as Tom and Robin backed off. The black malice resurfaced in her eyes, and a shadow of satisfaction lifted the corners of her mouth.

"Galiena," Master Chapman continued when the crowd had quieted, "you have survived the ordeal, but you are liable for the death of Will, the servant of St. Edward's, the death of Blind Mog, a sometime beggar, and the death of the crippled child of Corla, a widow of this parish. For those crimes, you shall pay wergeld. In lieu of coin, you shall forfeit the house of your father. It shall become the property of Corla and her remaining children, along with all the goods and chattels thereto pertaining. You are hereby sent out of the walls of this town, into which you shall never again venture on pain of death. You shall no more give herbs and medicines as a way of making a living."

A thought passed across her face. "You could see it wrinkle her nose, but whatever it was, she told it not. 'Twas a curse, mayhap, but she held it inside." Galiena turned her back on the crowd, straightened her spine, and limped down Tout Hill toward the forest.

6.

AVERILLA HAD NOT NEEDED TO BE TOLD what had happened. Five days earlier, during the afternoon, as she had tended the sick in the infirmary, she had been engulfed in a clinging sadness. Despair. They would be giving the testimony now. Poor Father Merowald. She felt his melancholy, his lack of confidence in himself, his failure to this one lamb, never counting what he had done in saving the others. Averilla knew that the he would be the only one to question the verdict. A tear trickled down her cheek.

The morning of the ordeal, Averilla was burned. Pain shot into her arm and through her being with the white-hot fury of the iron. She was in chapter, listening to Dame Felda drone on about the new lambs and idly gazing at the marble tablet placed on the chapter house wall by Alfred the Great. A stabbing pain seared the tender flesh of her inner arm and streaked to her shoulder. She gasped aloud, and beads of sweat broke out on her forehead.

The abbess looked up at the infirmaress in barely concealed irritation. She had no more patience for these forays into hysteria, which had rumpled the calm of her abbey. Averilla's lips turned a mottled purple; her face was sapped of all color. Her eyes rolled back into her head. "Dame Edith." The abbess' voice cut rudely through the monotonous catalog of sheep. She needn't have spoken. Edith had already slid over to catch her collapsing superior.

7.

AVERILLA WOKE TO FIND HERSELF ON A PALLET. She was not in the dorter. She looked from the whitewashed walls to a window set high above the floor. The shutters were open to the clear morning light. As she watched, a daddy longlegs scuttled across the ceiling and then hung motionless, descending.

She remembered then. The stabbing pain. The ordeal? Could she have felt Galiena's ordeal? A shudder trembled the length of her body. For the moment she lay and endured it. When her teeth had stopped chattering, she pushed back the sleeves of the coarse homespun to examine the tender skin of her forearm. An angry red blush, blistered and oozing, marred the inside of her arm. She lifted her eyes in thought and met, instead, the direct and steady gaze of the abbess, sitting on a stool, her back not leaning against the wall but straight as the watchman's pike.

"What happened to you, Averilla?"

"I know not, my lady. I had a stabbing pain. On my arm. I think — I know not how — it sounds like witchery, but I think that mayhap I, I suffered with Galiena during her trial."

"How is such possible? And why?"

"I know not how such is possible. But sometimes — I don't know how it is — I feel what others feel. I, I know their thoughts, too. I had thought that it could only happen with those to whom I had an affinity."

"I little understand these things. They are beyond my realm, but we needs must consider them. I would speak of these matters with you. There is water in the basin. Tidy yourself. I have sent Sister Clayetta away. We are alone." The abbess pulled open the plank door to her office and then shut it softly behind her. The cackle of the fire and the comforting aroma of apple logs wafted into the bedchamber from the other room as the abbess opened and closed the heavy door. Averilla limped over to the pottery basin. Her ankle still ached from the fall she had taken. She splashed cold water on her face, lapping a drink of it from her hands. The tears she had suffered from the brambles and thorns of the forest had scabbed over. A thorn that had pierced the other thumb was beginning to fester. She would ask Dame Edith to look to it.

But, but for all that, Agnes was back. Back and sleeping. She sighed. And the *Laece Book* had been found. It shouldn't be so important. It must be very wrong to feel as much satisfaction over the restoration of a stolen book as over the return of a lost sister. It was wrong, but so she felt. She shook her head. St. Paul's words echoed in the abbess' voice, "I do what I would not; I think what I would not."

Standing there in front of the basin, her hands idle, she tried to imagine how the *Laece Book* was found. After the men had dragged Galiena away, cursing and kicking, while she, Averilla, was searching for Will, one of the men, she knew not which, stumbled while ascending the stairs. Something had caught his eyes. He had looked closer, hoping, she supposed, for a witch's horde. It was the *Laece Book.* It lay on the floor near the place where Galiena had been found. He had hurriedly snatched it up, and then, embarrassed by his fear, had run from the crouching malice that wanted him gone. The bailiff had given it to Abbess Emma with little more in the way of explanation.

Now, in the forthright plainness of the abbess' chamber, Averilla brushed the memory aside. She dried her hands, pulled her scapular straight, and ducked her head into her wimple.

Abbess Emma stood before the fireplace. It was another of Abbess Cecily's extravagances. Of a new design, it was built into the side of the building and had a chimney to take away the smoke. The abbess turned slowly, her eyes steely and withdrawn.

"A convent, my child," she said as she walked to her table and slowly lowered herself into the chair, "is like a hive of bees. Each one works for the good of the others. Each must give herself to the good of the whole. If one ails, so do all the rest. When there is a flutter on one side, those on the other side feel it." She said no more. The implication was obvious. Averilla took the chair the abbess indicated, wincing as muscles she had never known she had groaned in her back and knees.

"You seem to have …" the abbess paused, choosing her words, "uncanny abilities. Gifts, if you will. I little understand them. I am afraid of them. When first I noticed them, they grated on the skin of my flesh like a fingernail on a slate. With reflection, I see that, as St. Paul says, we each have our own particular gifts. Though I understand them not, I will accept that you have them. I will not try to root them out. But only," her eyes rested on Averilla's with steely determination, "insofar as they do not disturb the tranquility of the community."

"I realize that much that you have done has been in response to the need of our community. You were able to help women who were in distress, nay, in grave danger of body and soul. Your dogged concern therewith was very right and seemly. However, as your Mother in God, I needs must caution you. I see in you a lack of control over these gifts. For the good of the community and the good of your soul, they must be harnessed and firmly placed in the service of God." She smiled ruefully and searched Averilla's face.

"I cannot tell you how such is to be accomplished, for I have not been granted such 'gifts.' It is incumbent on you, in prayerful contemplation, to find that means. Uncontrolled, undirected, your gifts will cause you to veer from your path to peace. If you roll free, like a cart's wheel wobbling off the cart, the community will flounder. Everyone around you will then need to alter course to avoid the reckless loose wheel. Most important, the cart itself will falter. It is one of my least happy obligations to point out such things to my sisters. Misunderstand my words not. You have an engaging and yet solemn way about you. Your virtue is without question. Your will is to serve God. I know these things, as do all your sisters in Christ. But you have allowed one of your gifts to flourish untended by your mind, like a blackberry bush gone wild, unpruned by God."

The abbess stopped as if to think, to corner her thoughts and martial them toward her aim. Averilla was sad. What the abbess said not only made sense but also she felt the rightness of it. The wings of her heart beat against the reason of her mind. Who am I to God without these gifts? Aren't these the sum of my value to God?

"I think that, without your knowing it, your hub has subtly shifted. It is important that you search yourself to retake your purpose. Your center must be God. He must be the interest, the only interest, the controlling interest of your life. Your fascination with your 'powers' lies in the way of your peace. To put Him on, you must give yourself up. The aim of your life, and mine, must be to know, please, and honor God, and to walk in the ways of His purpose. These other gifts He has given you must be sublimated to that aim. To those who have much, much will be given, and it follows, as the summer does the spring, that their temptation and their peril will be all the greater."

"The good in the power to heal, the good in comforting the sick and the dying, is helping the sick person to know and to feel the closeness of God. We *all* ache. We *all* die. It is the way God created the world. Everyone Christ healed died. You must not deny God's purposes. Do not weary your fiber in a fight with death. Death is. It is part of God's plan. We do not serve if, in our attempt to succor, we forget to help the person to know of God's love."

The abbess paused, and then, reaching out a hand to the miserable woman before her, said, "I must, therefore, with the coming New Year, replace you in the infirmary. You shall become our sacrist. There you will be closer to God, where you can more easily concentrate on Him."

The abbess looked at the horror in Averilla's eyes with compassion. Averilla, feeling her own plummeting distress, knew that the abbess was right. She grasped blindly at the hand outstretched to her as a tear rolled down her cheek.

"You will have some months to accustom your will to the needs of your soul." Then, more gently, the abbess continued. "While you are sacrist, you will need to teach others what you know of healing. Sister Helewise will be professed by then, and she has expressed a willingness to work in the infirmary. Sister Cadilla has gifts that have too long been sublimated to those of others. She can teach Helewise's immaturity. It will be a good and useful combination. However, when a life in their care sickens beyond their abilities, and such shall happen, then we shall make use of the divine gifts that reside in your hands. But so that this gift does not destroy you, we shall only call upon you in instances of extreme need. As sacrist, your ability to know the thoughts of the members of our community may be of help to them and to you. Dame Edith will, I believe, be happy as an illuminator in the scriptorium. I have been impressed with her talent. We have too few who can so depict God's creation."

Averilla could tell that the interview was at an end, for the abbess rose, rose and came to Averilla. "The lesser matter of your disobedience will be attended to by the obedientaries. In time."

CHAPTER TWENTY-TWO

I.

In the infirmary, Agnes had watched the shadows tick across the ceiling for five days now, had watched the light flicker in and out among them. Time meant nothing. All was light and dark. Sometimes she slept. Then the light would flush the shadows away in a flash of early glory and ease the dark into pure nothingness. The shadows would eventually return, slowly at first, creeping wisps of darkness that gorged on the light, twisted and writhed and bulked into snakes and snarling, thorn-encrusted beasts of frost and winter, naked and gory.

With ultimate regularity and order, though, the light re-emerged. Again and again. And with it, thought. Brief thoughts at first, that struggled through strange, fiery images of a thundered savage rhythm. Bonfires soared dark and melancholy and strangely victorious against the yellow-red glow of the night sky.

Galiena.

The image of the woman glittered menacingly at the edge of her consciousness.

Ease. Promised ease.

Satiated hunger.

So desperately alone.

And unknown. No mark on the wings of eternity.

A puffed, even breathing from the next pallet punctured her engulfing bubble of terror. Dame Maud, barely rumpling the coverlet that pinned her frail body to earth, lay within an arm's breadth. The rhythmic breathing comforted Agnes' restlessness somehow, and once more she slept.

On the sixth day Agnes fully wakened. She was lying on her side, hands clasped under her cheek in an attitude of prayer. Consciousness circled the heavy tails of sleep that nestled in the crevices of her bones. She felt strangely at peace.

Two bird-like eyes, dim with long seeing, fastened on her in interest. Agnes allowed a luxurious stretch to stiffen and tingle her cramped muscles, and yawned hugely, clasping her hands together behind her head and pulling against them. "I have slept," she whispered across the small space that lay between the two beds.

The old dame smiled, her face childish in its joy. "I know. I prayed for you."

"Oh." Agnes opened her eyes wide. Had there been a reason to pray? A coldness gnawed delicately at her heart.

"And so you slept." The squirrel eyes were calm in their certainty.

"I have been...ill?" Agnes faltered, struggling with the memory.

"Sometimes," Dame Maud said, "I don't seem to be here." The words were uttered with a matter-of-fact acceptance. "It happens so when one starts to relinquish the days; a kind of suspense, a sort of endless falling away from life. But you are not there yet, I think."

Dame Maud waited as if the words were a statement, not a question.

"I have been watching the sunbeams during the day, and the moonbeams at night, as they slat through the closed shutters."

"Soon they will allow you into the abbey for the office," Dame Maud's non sequitur was wistful.

Agnes shriveled like a year-old nutmeat. Her lower lip trembled into a rictus of grief. Could she ever again bear the closeness of the choir? Could she ever again stand so open to God? Where He could rest His eyes on her; on one who had allowed a mere feeling to come before Him? She felt tears well and overspill her eyes.

The silence stretched between the two women as Agnes shrugged her mind through the myriad passages she had forbidden herself these long days.

"No," she said after much too long. "No, Dame Averilla would have me rest here. I can see the infirmary chapel from here. Can you not?"

The old woman nodded in resignation. "Yes. I can just see the chapel, but" she plucked fretfully with gnarled twig-fingers, "I miss the choir." Then, "Prayers of a community...when I am with them ... their minds touch mine ... somehow. Bring me to God when I am too frail. Surely you, too, have felt it thus?" Dame Maud's eyes searched the far distance of her memory for the right words. "The — the poignancy, like a wave of golden light. I ache for that blessed companionship... of being more; of not being just one." She paused for a moment.

Agnes tried to still the dead emptiness in her; willed just the tiniest stilted desire for vulnerability to — and need of — God to surface. "Yes," Agnes said. "I remember." Another tear trickled down her face. She could feel the wetness wick onto the linen beneath her head.

"Have you asked?"

"For what?"

"To need God again. Admit that you alone are not enough. Open yourself. Then that other hunger will go."

Agnes watched as a spider knitted its legs together around strands of being, creating, recreating. "Remind me, dame," Agnes said after a long moment, her eyes still glued to the spider, "for I have been far away. How do I begin?"

Dame Maud's eyelids drooped closed. "You start," Maud said, "by shutting your eyes. The eyes have a way of being busy, of taking away the mind and the heart."

"But the paintings on the walls, the carvings on the rood screen, the cross?" Memories flickered dimly.

"They are a start — a prick to the mind. Choose an image. Think about it. Put yourself in the scene."

Maud settled back against her pillow. Her tiny head with its vulnerable scalp was pink against the coarse linen. They were quiet for a moment. "Remember when our Lord was by the seashore and the crowd pressed in on Him?"

Agnes saw it.

She stood on the sand and saw a spider building a web between the gunwales of the roughhewn boat. It was a corner web, one line stretching all the way across.

"You can see the crowd of people, feel them press against you."

Agnes felt the soft swell of a belly pressed against her arm, smelt the onions the man had eaten, and the stench of his sweat.

"You can hear the waves…"

The day was calm, with just a tiny breeze lifting the waves as they sloshed toward her and brushed between her toes. She was barefoot and wiggled her toes into the grit of the sand.

She heard a voice then, over the waves, deep and kind

and full, and she slowly, reluctantly tore her eyes from the web, and the pitch that caulked the bowed boards, scared to look too deeply, afraid of what the eyes, when she found them, would reveal.

2.

SOME TWO WEEKS LATER THE ABBESS summoned Averilla, Agnes and Father Merowald to her rooms. Averilla hadn't questioned the presence of the old man. He had been part of this story from the beginning. "It would be tedious to have to explain this to one of the nuns' priests." Averilla had understood the underlying message. "This is something far beyond their sheltered minds." Even with the bulwark of Father Merowald, Averilla hadn't wanted to be there; didn't want to hear the confession of a sister, of one older in religion than she. Such was for the ears of the abbess and the confessor. The abbess had insisted that Averilla come. "You have dealt with what you thought a malady, so it is necessary for you to know what transpired with her."

Sitting in a brazen patch of sunlight, Agnes was thin and pale. Even so, Averilla felt herself exult. Oh, thank you for giving her back to us. When a sense of accomplishment niggled at the back of her mind, she tried to erase it. Again, thank you, God.

Agnes ran her tongue over still dry lips. No one said anything. The fire murmured to itself. She opened her mouth and shut it again. Then, eyes on the floor, with no word of encouragement she whispered, "It started with a pain. Down my arm and across my shoulders. You," here she looked at Averilla, "thought it might be the dropsy and gave me lily of the valley." Averilla nodded at the memory.

235

"Dame?" Dame Agnes had had an almost furtive look.

Averilla had been rubbing an ointment of monkshood and lamb grease into the shoulders of wizened, toothless old Dame Athelia. There was nothing like it in the cold, damp days of autumn to lessen the rheumatic pain that gripped the old woman like a vise. At the troubled voice, Averilla had carefully put down the pottery jar and turned.

She had seen the look before, on the faces of some of the lay servants of the abbey. More oft than not it would be a fifteen-year-old, unwed and with child. There had even been that strange case earlier in the year. The young girl had been given castor seeds to prevent conception. The infection had been horrible, the poison so potent that Averilla had been unable to save her. But, Averilla had then wondered, where had the girl found those seeds, and why did she even think of using them in that way?

Averilla had taken Dame Agnes by the arm and led her to the officina where there would be some privacy. Agnes had stood, listless, in the center of the room.

"Dame? How may I be of help?" Averilla had asked.

"I-I have a shortness of breath. When I climb the stairs. And I get so tired..." she didn't even seem to have the energy to finish the sentence.

Averilla had furrowed her brow and reached down a beaker in which gold flakes winked and shifted like sand in the clear depths of the tide. "I think...lily of the valley...and gold. I can give you more of this. Perhaps you should rest in the infirmary?" Averilla had poured a thin stream into a horn cup and proffered it to older woman.

"No, no, thank you, dame." Agnes had wiped her lips

delicately. "My duties require me to sit." With a bow she had departed.

As Dame Agnes hastened through the hedges and pleached trees, toward the inner court, Dame Averilla had watched her with some concern. There seemed to be something more, something troubling Agnes over and above the pain, something Agnes was not yet willing to disclose. As she always did when presented with such a conundrum, Averilla had sifted through other possible solutions: hart's tongue in saffron and sugar boiled with white wine? Some used that. Others swore by borage steeped in oil of sweet almonds, wrung out and applied to the heart.

AGNES' VOICE PULLED AVERILLA BACK into the present. "You said that though lily of the valley was not as strong as dead man's bells, it was more certain. You feared to use the stronger potion; feared the dose might kill me. I pleaded. Do you remember? I told you that my father had had the same malady, and that the Jewish medicus he saw had given him dead man's bells. He had called them witches' bells, but you said they were the same."

"As I had feared, the lily of the valley made few inroads on the malady. I was so tired. And frightened. Mayhap it made it worse. The fear. I hungered to do a good job as cellarer. I knew that I was peculiarly suited to the job. The cellarium was disorganized — more than that — it was chaos. It had been way beyond Dame Isobel's capabilities for many years. Abbess Cecily should have given her a rest." Agnes lowered her eyes to her hands. "We must not be asked to accomplish more than we are able." When she raised her eyes, pain clouded them. "At any rate, as I read the account rolls," she continued, measuring her words, "I became more and more concerned. There were errors — inaccuracies — accounts that didn't add up. And there seemed to be huge debts. Debts, if I was reading aright, about which the chapter did not know. Had not acquiesced to. What I suspected, what I feared frightened me so. I feared that to pay for the rebuilding of the abbey, Abbess Cecily had borrowed huge sums. I knew not how we were to repay them. I foresaw the death of the abbey. I should have prayed about it. I should have put my faith in God. At the very least I should have brought my fears to the chapter. But I wanted to do it myself. I thought I could solve it and save everyone else worry and save Cecily's memory. I was just starting to untangle all the conflicting entries when, in the inner court one day, I was caught by a pain. My jaw ached and there was pain in my arm. My heart was beating like a caged bird against the insides of my ribs. A strange breathlessness crushed the center of my chest. There is a bench outside the Brode Hall. I reached it and sat down, gasping for breath. Someone had seen my distress and came to help. It was Dame Joan."

Agnes took a deep breath. "Dame Joan and I have never been ... close. The whole convent knows of our antipathy. Like oil and water, we are. Both of us have tried, since our days in the novitiate, to avoid one another as best we might. But since I had been given the job of cellarer and because she was assistant to the prioress, we had been increasingly forced to work with one another. To her alone I had confided the problem of the debts. At the time she looked momentarily alarmed, and then she dismissed it. Joan thought Isobel must have made a wrong addition somewhere. She encouraged me to try to work it out myself. That day, the day of the pain, she showed much solicitude. Real concern, I thought. In my gratitude I wondered if perhaps all had changed. Perhaps now that we were older we could better understand one another. So I explained to her my fears for my health and explained that Dame Averilla could not, in good conscience, give to me what I needed."

"She told me of Galiena. Said it was the same Galiena who had been with us in the convent school, the daughter of Thomas the wool merchant. Galiena had been recently widowed, and was sent back to her father's house, it was rumored, by an ungrateful stepson. According to Joan, Galiena was a wise woman, versed in the herbal arts. Galiena would give me things that Dame Averilla would not. Galiena would give me the witches' bells."

"So you went to her?" The abbess' voice was sad.

"It was easy for me to slip away. I was in the market every week, you see."

"And the pain went away?" Averilla's voice broke into the tired monologue with the misplaced eagerness of the scientist.

"Yes. For a while. She gave me an infusion to take with me and to drink when the pain came on. And it seemed to work. When the vial was empty, of course, I returned to her house for more. But- but in returning to her, my problem became something else entirely."

The abbess had been looking at Agnes as she talked. At these last words, the abbess felt the tiny hairs on her arms rise.

Agnes sighed as if there was a weight on her soul. "When next I needed the mixture — even I realized that the time span was shorter — she asked me in and had me sit in a chair. Not in the hall, but in an inner room, behind an arras. She gave me the liquid in a cup. To drink there. With her. I questioned it." 'You want to be rid of the fatigue and of the pain?' She sounded exasperated. She seemed hurt, offended. I didn't want to irritate her. I didn't recognize the thought to myself,

239

but I was frightened of her. She handed me the liquid. It seemed somewhat darker in color; brownish, as if mud had been added to water and was held suspended, but I assumed that it was picking up the color of the wooden cup. As I sipped the draught, Galiena placed objects on the floor, things common enough, such as salt and water and an oak twig. I knew it was strange that she should do such a thing, but I was muddled by then. I remember asking her about it. She muttered something about wortcunnings, that certain herbs required actions to be fulfilled. That Averilla had shown her Alfred's *Laece Book*, and that it was filled with such prescriptions as 'take under the light of the moon; turn around when the sun is in the west.' Surely, she insisted, I knew of such things. I should have wondered that she knew of the *Laece Book*. I should have been alerted by the absurdity of Averilla showing it to her. But I was not. Instead, what she was doing seemed weirdly fitting. She dipped the oak branch in something, I remember. It looked like water. Then she circled my chair, drawing designs on the floor and in the air with the branch; holding it like a quill. In my mind I see the branch trailing a greenish glow through the air, as does a lighted brand when you swirl it aloft. But that must have been my muzziness. She told me to finish the draught. It was bitter. Didn't taste as it usually did. She said I would now finally be at ease. By then I couldn't remember what she was talking about. I think I knew I shouldn't drink it. From the sensation I had. Part of me wanted to run away from her. I held my spiritual breath and drank.

"After that, I am unclear. The hall left my sight. I felt as I had at thirteen, restless and fiery with longing. My vision was blurred. It was like butterflies in the trees. I saw a swirling nimbus, like a rainbow. I heard a voice. There was mist in the way, like fine cloth from Gaza. A foggy distance. And then I - I don't remember. I awoke from this sleep of strange dreams in the infirmary."

Averilla pressed her back against the cold stone of the wall and sank into her habit. She should have seen it. Her fault. She thought back, remembering the abrupt change that had come over Dame Agnes. That day, when Agnes had come up from the market, she had wobbled along the Bimport, eyes unfocused, habit in disarray. Those at the gate had brought her to Averilla. It was then that the raving had started. Agnes had tossed and turned, screamed and babbled for two days or more. Then she had gotten better. They hadn't understood. Dame Edith was certain Agnes was mad. Averilla was inclined to agree, although something, even then, had nagged at the back of her mind. The abbess had not removed Agnes from the position of cellarer at first, hoping the madness would pass.

"I visited Galiena as often as I could, yearning for more of the draught." Agnes stared into the fire before continuing. "Soon," she added, "I began to like the feeling of the draught. I knew I shouldn't, but that didn't seem to matter anymore. The elixir released me. It had become enough for me to dissolve my pain and fears for the abbey in the sweeping mists of oblivion. You," she turned her eyes and fastened them on Averilla, "you thought I was mad, didn't you? It began to amuse me. To stay in the infirmary as the uproar gripped me, and then to be myself for days or weeks before I chose to go again to Galiena. I even asked you to protect me from the voices. I thought I was in control. But I wasn't. I did not know of the days of raving. I refused to know them. I thought only of the sweet dreaminess. I was going more often. She was mixing the infusions so that I could relieve the ache any time I so desired. The cellarium saw me no more. I didn't even think of it.

"After that I remember only images, prisms of color like the colors in a raindrop and blurry mists, like the nimbus around

241

the moon after a rainstorm. But- but then something changed. I know not what. When I awoke I was in a strange place. A place I had never seen. That scared me. Somewhere I was, but I knew not where. It was a shelter, like a stone shed, but small. I had come in out of the rain, I thought, for there were drops on the cobwebs. I was in the forest, I think, a hut, mayhap. They — they… someone found me … I — I don't know," her voice cracked, "I remember. I…remember…I think I had no clothes on, for I was cold, and, and, oh, my God. They came at me. Threw me against the wall. Hissed at me and pulled my shift up on my nakedness. One kissed my face greedily with biting harshness…No. No." Agnes' breath came in tattered sobs. "No, nooooo." She shook her head and shrank into herself, her eyes wide with terror.

The abbess went to Agnes, cradled her head, and crooned to her as if to a baby. After awhile, the horror went from Agnes' eyes and she continued, her words punctuated by gulps. "Next I remember being somewhere else. A fire was there. No. More than one fire. More than one place? Real, though. Both of them real? Just one? I don't know. After more time, I know not how long, there was a pounding rhythm. Galiena gave me a huge beaker of the draught. I knew nothing else. Cared for nothing else. Had forgotten God. I must have raved."

The abbess got up and walked over to the fire, trying to hide from Agnes the anger in her eyes.

"I know I sinned. I confess it." Agnes looked wildly from the abbess to Father Merowald. "My soul. Oh, my poor, poor soul. In the place God should be I put something else. God forgive me." Tears trickled down her pale face. "I lusted after a feeling, an animal sensation — real lust. Pity me, Father, I have sinned." Father Merowald got up and put a hand on her head and, bending back his thumb, gently made the sign of the cross on her forehead. "You have seen to the depth of your sin and you have repented. Rise now, for your sins have been forgiven."

She struggled to her knees and sought the abbess with her still-streaming eyes. "Mother, may I try again? Will you have me?"

The abbess stretched out a hand to Agnes, helped her to her feet, and then kissed her on both cheeks. She said not a word, and would have dismissed Agnes had not Averilla's curiosity gotten the better of her.

"Mother, please, may I be permitted to ask of Dame Agnes one more thing?" They all turned, startled by Averilla's voice, shocked at her terrier persistence.

Dame?" the abbess pressed her lips together.

"Could you tell me, Dame, for I need to ..." Averilla, heedless, persisted, "I, we need to know. Had Sister Julianna any part of this?"

"Sister Julianna?"

"She has been going to Galiena's house. Secretly. Since she has been accompanying Dame Edria. I wondered if this were somehow connected. Galiena said Julianna only wanted her fortune told, but somehow I think there may be more."

Agnes shook her head in bewilderment. "No. I never spoke to her of it. I am unaware of any connection. But then, I have not been always aware."

"Did you steal the *Laece Book* from the officina?"

The horror in Agnes' eyes was answer enough. With a furrow in her brow she replied. "As I said earlier, I should have known something when Galiena spoke of it, but no, I did not take it."

It affrights me, the abbess thought, when the others had bowed and left, that so much goes on in this abbey without my knowledge.

A few minutes later there was a knock at the abbatial door.

At her 'Deo Gratis,' Sister Clayetta poked her head around the door. "You called?"

"No, sister. I did not."

"I thought I heard you."

"Well, if I did not summon you, I should have." The abbess sighed. "Dame Averilla is right. There is definitely more to this whole matter."

"I beg your pardon."

"Nothing, sister, I but speak aloud my thoughts. Please have Sister Julianna attend me here."

"Sister Julianna?"

"Sister Julianna."

While she waited, the abbess traversed the width of the room, and, as if ticking off her beads, recited the names aloud. "Agnes, Julianna, Joan. And then Averilla. One right after the other." Her thoughts stumbled around in her mind as she stood watching the doves trying to catch the dreary wisps of sun on the dove house roof. Connected? she wondered. By Galiena, certainly. Like a web. But none of them with malice. Except perhaps Joan. Mailice. Intent to harm. Mayhap. But not Julianna. Surely. The child is undoubtedly lacking in vocation. When was it that I heard her, as I passed, lamenting the absence of baths? It must have been January last. 'Oh, the warmth,' she said. I remember it, for she gave me that impish smile, knowing I had heard, and then continued, rather boldly, daring me to chastise her, 'Surely, lady, you remember. And the fur.' And I said nothing by way of reprimand. Why was I so tongue-tied? Because I didn't see what harm the remark was, probably. That was what I told myself. Father Merowald would have none of it. 'Harm?' he had croaked. His brows had touched each other in his agitation. 'No, lady. No harm to her, probably. But insomuch as she might scar the vocation of another, might lead that other to focus on the loss of luxury, then... 'The least of these my little ones ... No, not lack of insight, lady,' he had continued, 'lack of courage.' She, the abbess of Shaftesbury, had been afraid of being laughed at. And it wasn't just that one time. She remembered a time when the novices were recessing from chapter and Julianna had hissed, for all the chapter to hear, as wind swirled around the cloister and lifted the scanty novice veils. 'Impossible to live here. This miserable wind. If God really cared about us...' But the porter had closed the door and the chapter had heard no more. And Julianna had been reproved, Lord. And again after that. More times than can be counted. And that is the problem.

When Julianna entered, the abbess allowed a silence to permeate the room. Finally she spoke. Julianna raised an eyebrow at the firmness in the abbess' voice.

"You don't wish to be here, do you?"

Refusing to be cowed, something glinting behind her eyes — was it fear — Julianna answered. "That is not so, my lady. Or not entirely. I did want to enter, I— "

"— have no more vocation than a sow in the ewery." The abbess' voice cut surprisingly harsh across the girl's blatted excuses. "So my question is: Why are you here?"

Julianna shut her mouth.

"Speak when you are spoken to."

"You didn't want to hear what I first had to say, so why should I answer anything?" The girl's eyes flashed with imperiousness.

Emma gave no ground. "Nevertheless, no one with a vocation would speak to me as you have just done. There is a reverence, not for me, but for my position. You seem to feel nothing of that kind of awe. I would guess that you are at Shaftesbury Abbey because the alternative, whatever it was, is...unacceptable to you."

Before Julianna could shield her eyes, the abbess saw the fear in them. She continued, "I would hazard that King Stephen offered you a choice. An old man, perhaps? Perhaps he was brutal? And then you were told that if you wanted not this man, you could become a nun. I warrant that the life here seemed to you somewhat more palatable."

Julianna looked surprised. "Aye. How knowest thou of that?"

"Your dowry to us was generous. Probably but a fragment of the worth of your lands. When you chose to come to us, the balance stayed with the king. The king is waging a war."

"Can it be so? Can King Stephen…"

"Oh, aye. A ward can be a very profitable possession for a king. But for you, given the choice, convent or life with a brute, the monastery seemed the better choice?"

"Much better. I had feared. I know what you must think of me, lady, to use God so, but I knew not what else to do. Then, when the fear had worn off I was honest with you in my feelings."

"Indeed." The abbess arched an eyebrow.

"Remember you? We talked about it. About the restlessness. I thought then, really expected, that going to the markets with Edria would ease this feeling of enclosure, of imprisonment. I love God. I do. But I don't seem to want to spend so much time with Him. The obedientaries and those who have taken their final vows seem to find their joy in God. But I, I find joy in the eyes of a knight, in a fast canter in the spring, in secrets and confidences, in a rose left on my cushion with a note. I am still a maid."

"So it was torture to me to go to the market and see that which I could no longer have. I reached out to touch silks and knew I could never more feel the ease of them against my skin. The ribbons dangled in the wind, but for hair that I no longer had. The pots of cosmetics that I could no longer use. I found myself standing, staring openmouthed at a babe nuzzling its mother's breast, looking for the nipple, and felt a very real pain start. Oh, Dame Edria was kind. She took my arm and tried to distract me. It was no good. And each week it became worse. The novices knew, of course. They found it exciting. They listened to me because I said and did that which they could not, would not."

"We noticed."

A rush of color flooded Julianna's face. "They wanted to know all about it," Julianna replied stubbornly. "It was so unfair, you see. We spoke of it as we helped with the threshing and winnowing during the winter last. Do you remember? We were restless, like kittens long penned by the interminable stretches of rain and snow. You sent us, the novices, to help the folk thresh in the tithe barns. None of the professed was there to hear us. Nor could they have above the swish of the flails as we beat the grain. I remember we jousted at first with the flail-poles and then chased one another about, whipping at skirts and legs with the dangling ox-hide straps, and waving the willow swingles about like marsh weeds in a firm current."

"It was during the winnowing, as we scooped the grain up in the large shallow baskets and tossed it into the air that I told them. It was a dare to start. Given laughingly. 'If God won't help you,' one of them said, the chaff floating around her head, 'seek counsel of the witch.' That's what she said. At that they all stopped, of course. Witch? What witch? We clustered around. 'It is said that she can make things happen. The man who offered for you is old. He could die. And then you could choose someone new, someone younger.'"

"And so you chose to take matters into your own hands? You wanted Galiena to set a spell on him that would cause him to die?"

247

"Not die, not at first. Galiena gave me choices. At first we tried easy remedies. We thought to have him lose his memory by placing pins in the head and feet of his image. She had me hide the image in a secret place in a time when thunder was in the air. I was so excited. I wrote to my sister, but she knew naught of his loss of memory. Said he still licked his lips when he spoke of me, as if I was but some tasty morsel for his delight."

"So then Galiena tried a spell for making a coolness come between a man and woman. I had to find seven snail shells. I brought them and she crushed them in a mortar with seven foxglove bells, the feathers of a cock and the blood of the same."

"Blood of a cock?" Emma's face scrunched in disgust.

"Aye. 'Twas naught, coming from the market. Easy enough to buy a dead rooster."

"So you chose to bind him with a spell that would kill him?"

"Yes. Yes, but she would not let me watch that one. Made me pay in gold."

"Gold? You had gold about you?"

"I had brought some with me. But, but it was not enough." The words tumbled forth in a rush as Julianna hurried to make the confession complete. "She wanted the *Laece Book* as well. I—I stole it."

"And we found you that night by the nave altar."

A moment of silence passed as the abbess absorbed the enormity of it all. Finally she said, "And she performed that... that spell to cause his death."

"Aye. Or so she told me...but what matters it?"

"What matters it? To will someone's death?"

"Not I. The witch."

Emma was appalled. "But this was a man's life."

248

"He had no right to live. He was brutal. And he kept me here. And I couldn't stand it anymore."

"Indeed. But that is why there is an abbess here, someone in whom you can confide. If you had come to me..."

"But I had."

"Yes. Well, the milk has already been spilled. Actually you managed to overturn the whole pail." The abbess steepled her fingers. "I think we both agree that Shaftesbury does not entirely suit you."

"Perhaps—" Emma paused and tapped her mouth with her index finger as a thought struck her. Then her eyes lighted as if with a joke, and she smiled 'rather wickedly for an abbess,' Julianna would tell the novices, "— there is an another resolution. Did you know that our former abbess, Cecily FitzHamon, was sister to the wife of the Earl of Gloucester?"

Julianna looked at the abbess warily, unable to follow the train of thought. "No."

"I believe that Amabel can be persuaded to take you on as one of her ladies. That would take your lands and the power over you out of the hands of Stephen. Since the crown is in contention, the empress has as much right to be your guardian as Stephen does. More, perhaps. You would be quite safe in the train of the empress' brother. And I am quite certain that Amabel would listen to your request as to the choice of husband."

"Oh, my lady. Can it be? You would do this for me?"

Julianna's face was transformed, her obeisance low, the kiss to the abbatial ring fervent. But behind the genuine gratitude, the abbess thought she saw a small smile of satisfaction and success flicker briefly as Julianna turned to go. When her hand was on the latch, the abbess added, low, almost a growl in pitch. "Do not, however, presume that the spells Galiena laid to assure this outcome have had the desired effect. It was your own actions that precipitated and my good will that have accomplished this release. Be not deceived. We no more want a recalcitrant member of the community than you want to be here."

Julianna shut the door behind her and then opened it slowly again. The abbess looked up. "Yes."

"I gave one of Saint Edward's bones to Galiena."

"Well," Father Merowald said later, a twinkle in his eye, "if the Lord Almighty can raise bones, I am sure he can figure out how to put them back together properly."

"But if the bones work miracles here ..." The abbess' face was white.

"My lady, it is a mystery. But I am confident that God has it well in hand. Trust Him."

CHAPTER TWENTY-THREE

I.

T he winter winds had started in earnest, striding to the top of the mound and lashing at the sides of the church. It was as if God were sending out a warning, late but needed, to his people for their laxness. The numbers that knocked on the door of the almonry grew larger; their running sores were more plentiful; the glazed look in their eyes was duller; and the number of bones to be counted as they reached out to snatch away the proffered bread more visible.

With the wind pushing back at her like a giant hand, Abbess Emma took herself down the steep path of the park to Abbess Cecily's garden. The garden was sheltered, and there she would be undisturbed as she tried to pace out the weary dismay that had been tormenting her.

She had watched Dame Joan carefully for the last weeks. Though there had been an unusual numbness about the Sub-prioress, a kind of watchful waiting, nothing had been said about her part in what had happened to Agnes. Why had she deliberately sent Agnes to Galiena?

"I can't be sure," Emma had mused to the old prioress in the same way she meditated now with God. "How can I

251

know? I cannot accuse an innocent woman. Could it have been an simple mistake?"

Finally, Emma decided to prod Agnes on the subject. They were in the oratory. A ray of sunlight, a small sliver of watery early-December light, peeped through one of the high windows of the retrochoir as they talked.

"Do you think that the animosity or competition between you and Joan was why she first sent you to Galiena?"

The question startled Agnes.

Before she could respond, the abbess continued, "Think you Joan feared you so much that she intended Galiena to make you insensible?"

Agnes frowned. "Feared me or feared what I might discover."

The abbess went on without listening to the answer. "And then did she really mean to push you off to the punishment cell or send you away?"

"Lady, truly I know not. But I do remember something that at the time made me wonder. It had to do with Master Chapman. One of the tenants, Peter the metalworker it was, happened to meet me in the market of a Monday. I remember asking about his rent, for according to the account rolls it had not been paid, and his shop is on abbey land. He spoke forthrightly, as is the way of those who know the value of what they create. He stood, legs spread apart under his leather apron, his hammer at his hip. 'Never. Never,' he said, 'would I be late. I pay on time as did my father afore me. After all these years shall I be so accused?' He paused then for a moment and a dawning came over him. 'Ah, but,' he said. ''twas midsummer when I gave the rent to Master Chapman. And not in the gatehouse. 'Twas during the market after I had sold some'ut to my lord of Gloucester's man. Master Chapman asked for it right then, as he knew I had the money by. I gave it to him, then, as he bid me. It seemed a thing of moment. We were not alone, though. John the mason stood by. You can ask him.'"

The abbess was bewildered. "Dame, what has Dame Joan to do with Master Chapman? Truly think thee that Master Chapman has been defrauding us?"

"I do. I think he had been defrauding us for many a year. At the time I was too preoccupied to believe it. But I did ask John the mason and he confirmed all Peter told. E'en so, I was unsure. I told no one. In my heart, I thought some mistake had been made; something soon rectified. I did approach Master Chapman as he strode across the forecourt, busy in his ways. Just to say I had looked into it. He denied that Peter had paid him at all. Said that the accounts could prove it. That Peter had not come at harvest, when the rents were due to be paid. He- he said that I was overwrought. That I needed rest."

"And you believed him?"

"I didn't care. But now that I think on it, Dame Joan must have known what Master Chapman was doing. At least suspected. The rents, these and others, must have been dropping off. She could not have failed to see that. But why told she not the chapter? Why hide it for him? As for Galiena," Agnes continued, "Joan had known Galiena when we were young. We all had, though until Galiena returned to Shaftesbury it was of no consequence. If Joan thirsts to be the next prioress, perhaps she did see me as a rival. Did not want me able."

After Agnes left her, the abbess crunched along on the smooth gravel paths, her head bowed, her hands nested in her sleeves. It had been a mistake to allow Dame Joan to act as bursar. Emma could see that now. This whole tangled mess, Agnes, Joan, Julianna, all stemmed somehow from the accounts. But how? And why?

Certainly, when Agnes was not herself, there had been no one to keep track of what was going on. But Joan shouldn't have needed someone to keep an eye on her. The first question was, obviously, did Joan know? Could she have told from the accounts that Master Chapman was defrauding them? She, Emma, was going to have to stop procrastinating about the accounts. No more pushing around of tally sticks. She, the abbess, needed to understand. Was there someone who could help her with that much? Emma tapped her hand on her mouth, thinking. Yes. Yes, there was. Dame Athelia, the old sub-prioress. Though she was in the infirmary, her mind was still sound. Enough, certainly, to explain the accounts.

Athelia was, as always, glad to see her abbess and honored by the attention. When Emma explained her confusion, the old lady was eager to help. "'Tis not so hard," Athelia said. "The rolls are a kind of notation. Though I always thought Petronella's explaination to the novices rather convoluted." The old lady cocked her head and asked, "Was that your last experience of them? As a novice?"

Emma shrugged and made a small moue of self-abnegation. "They should have asked me if I knew anything about accounts before they appointed me abbess. But they didn't."

Her eyes bright with unasked questions, Athelia explained to her superior simply and with exactness how the account rolls were written.

When Emma returned to her lodgings she immediately asked Wat to bring the account rolls from Dame Joan's office. "Ask Dame Anne to give you those for the past three years." Then she mused over them, bathing her mind in their symmetry in order to spot any aberration. "Curious," she told Dame Athelia later that afternoon, "how dim I was about them before, pushing the tally sticks one way and another, trying to understand."

"Perhaps Joan never meant you to understand," said Dame Averilla in passing, still simmering with anger.

"Anger. Righteous enough after Joan's treatment of Agnes. But she wallows in it." The rest of the nuns were watching Averilla with more than a little apprehension.

2.

DURING ALL THIS TIME, THE INFIRMARY of the Abbey of the Virgin Mary and St. Edward, King and Martyr, at Shaftesbury was overwhelmed by a constant stream of wounded. "They don't just come in once," Edith wailed, "but needs be dressed again and again." During those hectic weeks Averilla had little time to spare for the usual officina tasks. As she dashed in and out for this remedy or that, she was able to keep an eye on the fire so the herbs did not mold or take the damp. She kept the shutters and the door firmly latched so that the chill fogs that obscured all but the closest trees of the orchard were not able to creep under the door.

When the snake of wounded and bruised had somewhat abated, Averilla asked to be excused from Vespers to try to restore a semblance of order to the depleted workroom shelves. As she made her way across the inner court, the newly risen moon glittered a cold blue light on the already frosty earth. A brisk wind harried tatters of clouds across its face. It would be clear tomorrow but probably even colder. Not an easy winter for those who hung about the almonry. She would need to see about storing more wood for the fire. Preoccupied with the cold and the multitude of tasks awaiting her, and mentally assigning the order in which they needed to be done, she pushed on the door to the workroom with some force, and then stopped in confusion.

Dame Joan was standing on the officina stool, searching on the high shelf where the books and poisons were stored. At the sound of the scraping door and the rush of cold, damp air, Joan spun around, a small flask still in one hand. With the other, she grappled at the high shelf to stabilize herself. The shelf, balanced only on a crossbeam, shuddered with her weight and overbalanced. She started to fall. The shelf tipped and, inexorably, the bottles and flasks slid down its length, gaining momentum until they fell, flying in all directions, crashing and spattering potions and draughts all over the room. The fire flared as tinctures containing spirits spattered into it; pottery thudded in pieces onto the floor. Some of the jars, luckily, bounced in the cushioned floor rushes and remained whole. Averilla slammed her body toward the other woman, grabbing her legs beneath the heavy folds of wool. Joan's feet slipped off the stool. As she hit the floor on her right foot, there was a sickening snap, like a pea pod bursting, and she screamed, high and piercing, like a fox caught in a trap. The force of the fall ground her face onto the flags and for some moments she lay still.

Finally, Averilla, caught beneath her, moved an arm.

Joan screeched, "My — my foot," and fainted. Averilla pushed herself out from under the unconscious woman. Her slight movement had pushed the jagged splinter of naked, white bone into the fire. Barehanded, Averilla swept the coal back onto the hearth. Cadilla would examine Averilla's hand later, amazed to find no sign of burning. "I did it so quickly," Averilla would say by way of excuse.

At the time, Averilla pulled a straight branch from the woodpile, wrapped it in a linen cloth and laid it near the sprawled woman. Slowly, glad that Joan was unconscious, Averilla lifted Joan's knee, supporting the dangling foot with her other hand, and guided the broken portion onto the

256

branch. Later she would get a plank. She pulled another strip of clean linen from the bundle luckily kept on a low shelf, and wound it tightly around the break to stanch the bleeding and support the bones.

As she worked, absently mouthing prayers for Joan's health, Averilla's mind was recoiling in disgust. *She will be with me. In the infirmary. For days. Weeks. I shall have to care for her. With my own hands. I cannot. I will not.* She had no pity on Agnes. *She doesn't deserve to be taken care of.*

"I need to fetch Wat," Averilla mumbled to the unconscious woman, an ache of loss for Will crashing through her. She laid a scratchy coverlet over Joan, hitched up her skirts, and ran through the gardens to the stables in search of Wat.

When she returned, Joan was so still that Averilla wondered if her patient had somehow managed to drink from the flask she had been holding. Averilla's eyes sought around the room for the flask and located it finally under the table. Peach pits, dissolved in wine. Empty. *Could she have drunk it before she fell?*

With amazing strength for his age, Wat lifted Joan and carried her through the hedges to the infirmary. He laid her on one of the beds in the aisle closest to the orchard wall. To Averilla's mingled relief and despair, Joan had regained consciousness. As Wat and Cadilla started to pull the bones back into place, Joan howled and again retreated into senselessness. She remained that way as the open wound was treated with burdock and honey to prevent infection.

For several days Joan "just lay there," face to the wall, eyes unseeing, refusing all food and most water. She ignored the gentle efforts Cadilla made to minister to her, allowing her bandages to be changed "as if it was happening to someone else and had nothing to do with her." For her part, Averilla did as little as was consistent with her office. "I honestly tried to leave her to kinder hands," she grumbled to the abbess.

During all that time, the abbess was still struggling with the accounts. Her lack of progress so frustrated her that she ordered Sister Clayetta to refuse most visitors. However, later in the week, Clayetta barely had time to knock before an unannounced visitor brushed past her with the emotional force of a strong man; a force all the more arresting as the visitor was the tiny, rheumatic widow of Thurstan de Huseldure. Her stick thumped as she crabbed her way across the floor toward the startled abbess.

The abbess rose. "Milady. To what do I owe this honor?"

Margaret de Huseldure looked around her for a chair. Spotting the only other available seat, she proceeded to arrange herself on it, perching on the edge like a child with too-short legs. She fixed Emma with her bird-like gaze and said, "I will come straight to the point, my dear." Under a widow's coif, lines of pain scarred the old face, but the eyes were clear and determined. "While my son is in the Holy Land, I have been managing," she waved a crippled hand vaguely, "everything. He should have married, of course, but as he has not, it is left to me to organize matters. Money is scarce. For everyone. But it has come to my attention that recently there have been some irregularities about the abbey accounts." She paused.

How does *she* know, Emma thought, when I myself am just starting to sort it all out?

"And so," Margaret continued, "I thought I should come to find out whether the monies I gave were spent as I had intended."

Emma had no idea what Margaret was talking about. "The sub-prioress, Dame Joan, who usually handles these matters, has had an accident and is very ill. I am afraid you will have to try to explain to me what you are talking about."

"Surely it is simple enough. Has my money been spent as

258

I intended or no?" At Emma's blank look, Margaret began again. "You see, I don't easily give, to the poor or to the church. I believe that charity begins at home. However, Dame Joan reached me when I was at a low point; de Huseldure had just died. I wanted something to memorialize him."

"Which was?"

"You don't know?"

"I am afraid I do not." Emma tried to keep an appeasing note in her voice. "You must understand that the abbess can not possibly be aware of everything that goes on in an abbey of this size."

"I gave one hundred twenty-five pounds for the creation of a reredos. Surely that is a sum that would be noticed." Margaret lowered her chin. "Even in an abbey of this size."

Emma gulped. "Surely— "

Margaret decided to rescue her. "I chose that amount deliberately. It is the exact sum that would be paid in wergild for the life of a man. Since my husband had died, it seemed fitting, in an illogical sort of way, to so memorialize with just that sum. Particularly since he had always wanted to go into the church."

Emma didn't know whether to laugh or cry. Was it very dry humor or was the woman completely mad?

"Anyway, the piece was to be cast in silver."

At this Emma's brow creased into a frown.

Margaret continued. "A sizable sum, of course, one hundred twenty-five pounds. If the reredos is not yet in place, I would like at least to see what has so far been accomplished. Perhaps speak with Master Hugo."

Seeing the look of incomprehension in Emma's face, she asked, "Is Master Hugo yet here? From St. Edmunds? Come my dear, surely this much is known to you? The carver who cast the famous bronze doors?"

Emma did know of Master Hugo, of course. Had heard of the doors. But what he had to do with Shaftesbury was beyond her. Her dismay was becoming deeper and deeper until finally, as Margaret lapsed into silence, the silence itself lay between them unmarred.

Finally she asked, "The money? You gave it to Joan?"

Margaret breathed a deep sigh, "I did know that it was to be a secret. In strictest confidence. That I was to say nothing to anyone about it. But surely you, the abbess, knew? I did not spend my childhood with the nuns at Romsey without learning that no one in a convent does anything without the specific consent of the abbess."

Emma accompanied Margaret out to the main gate with as much grace as she could muster, assuring the latter of a prompt accounting as soon as she, Emma, could ascertain what was being done about the commission. "Dame Agnes, our cellarer, has also been quite ill. And now Dame Joan. I am sure that had we not been so distraught, more could have been accomplished towards the completion of the reredos. And Master Hugo has perhaps duties that cause him to remain overlong at Bury. The abbot ..."

I do believe, Emma thought as she crossed the inner court to the infirmary, that Margaret's sole purpose was to warn me; she gave me the necessary piece of information with which to confront Joan. Dear, meddling, little old lady.

Hearing the quiet footfall of the abbess, Joan turned her face toward her superior with resignation.

When Cadilla had placed a stool for Emma and retreated out of earshot, Joan said, "It was the abbess."

Emma was momentarily confused, and then an inkling of comprehension caught at the back of her mind, "Cecily?"

"Aye. She spent and spent and spent. The abbey. She wanted a monument."

260

"But I thought — "

"That the money came from her family? We all did. Were led to believe so. That was why Dame Athelia was sent to the infirmary. Why I was put in her place, knowing nothing about the accounts. But I loved Abbess Cecily."

"We all did."

"So, when she told me there would be no further monies coming, that her sister had needs elsewhere, that she was convinced that our tithes and rents should be sufficient for our program of rebuilding, I determined to do anything, everything, in my power to find the funds she needed. And it was true our rents should have been enough. In addition to the monies we receive from the crown. Somehow, in my blunderings, I had discovered that it was possible that Master Chapman was not giving us our due."

"So Agnes supposed. But what has that to do with you?"

"By that time I had been taking all the income, every penny that came in from whatever source, to pay for the rebuilding."

"Including that given by Margaret de Huseldure in memory of her husband."

"Including that. Did you never wonder why the construction went on all day long? Was not halted for the Divine Office as it is now? It was to save money. If I never hear another mason's hammer it will be too soon. With every blow hit during the Divine Office, I felt a nail go into the cross. We were giving up Christ for the abbey."

"And Margaret de Huseldure was not the only one who gave gifts that went into the masonry? And Master Chapman knew it?"

"Aye."

"So you couldn't prosecute him without revealing what you yourself had done?"

261

"No." Joan heaved a deep sigh. "And then Agnes was appointed cellarer. I made as much of a mess of the cellarer's accounts as I could, but I knew I couldn't outwit her. I never had been able to. I was so afraid."

"Afraid of what?"

"Everything. That my deception would be found out before the monies could be replaced. That the abbey wouldn't be finished. That it would be found out that I had borrowed."

"Borrowed? You mean, took gifts and used them for other than what they were intended?"

"No. Borrowed. From Master Levitas. As collateral I offered the abbey silver. He said he didn't need it moved from the treasury. He trusted us." Joan turned her head away from the horrified face of the abbess.

"Joan."

"I couldn't bear to have people speak ill of Cecily." A great tear rolled down Joan's cheek.

"Worse and worse."

"Aye, lady."

"So you consigned Agnes to Galiena? And then tried to send her away?"

Joan's face was bleak. Finally she spoke. "Apparently I was content to consign a sister to … a life of unspeakable misery. A misery I had arranged."

"So you were trying to kill yourself?"

"I should be dead."

"No."

"And in hell."

There was a silence between them. The abbess struggled to contain her anger; tried to think of things she herself had done, evils she had committed. With deliberation she finally spoke. "What you did was indeed wrong. That is obvious. But you have repented. Do not wallow in your own sinfulness. Christ remitted your sins, once and for all. A long excommunication will be necessary. Father Benedict is very clear about that. You will eat alone. You will be forbidden the oratory until such time as you will be required to lie spread-eagled before the altar. Remember as you go about this penance, it is not for the community that you submit, but for yourself. You understand that? For your own good. To make you right with God. But do remember, our Lord remitted our sins. All of them. Since you have repented, you will find it easier to forgive yourself."

3.

FOUR DAYS PASSED AFTER JOAN'S CONFESSION to the abbess, and despite the honey and the cleansing of the herbarium fire, her wound started to ooze and fester, swelling into a putrid mass. In desperation, Cadilla cleansed it again and heaped cobwebs onto the yellowing ooze before slathering it with honey. It was then that a fever blossomed. Edith had maintained a distant objectivity through the days of nursing, but with the heightened fever she stepped in and took control from the exhausted Cadilla.

Edith sat with Joan almost constantly, mopping her brow of the fetid sweat and laying wet cloths on the overheated body. Tirelessly, she dripped a mixture of hyssop between parched and cracked lips, trying to bring the fever down.

Deep into the depth of the fourth night, right after Lauds, when Averilla returned to the infirmary, Edith hurried over to her. She plucked at Averilla's sleeve to draw her back outside so that they might speak.

Holding both hands to her wimple to keep the wind from tearing it off, Edith said, "She tosses and turns, dame, with fever, and I fear for her life. She babbles. Father Merowald must be summoned."

"What does she say?"

Dame Edith looked troubled. "I know not, dame. It matters not, does it? She babbles in sickness," Edith gave Averilla a frustrated look, "and needs Father Merowald's hand."

Waiting for Father Merowald to be fetched, Averilla noted that Joan's formerly bulky form had dwindled to the point of emaciation, and one hand continually plucked at the coverlet.

As he shuffled down the steps into the infirmary, Father Merowald looked like nothing so much as a sleepy child awakened. Averilla rose and went to him and took him to Joan. Then she left him and hurried off to other tasks, any other tasks.

After more than an hour, sometime before Prime, he slowly rose and tottered back to Averilla. "I can do nothing for her," he said, "without your help."

Averilla turned to him. "My help?"

Without speaking, he limped the two steps to the door, pulled his mantle from the peg and stepped outside. Averilla made a sign to Edith, grabbed her own cloak and followed him, pulling the door to against the wind. They walked toward the pigeon house.

"She needs your help, Dame Averilla. There is much anger and … perhaps … hate against the woman in your heart. I can feel it … here." He gestured vaguely to encompass the entire building. "You have a grievance against this, the sub-prioress?" he asked.

"I? No, sir, no grievance."

"Dame!" The single word was a reprimand. Averilla turned to face the old man. She looked into his eyes and then dropped her own to the partially iced clods, broken beneath her boot. Then she said, the bitterness edging her words, "No. 'Tis not my anger, but God's."

"Dame!" The strength of the rebuke lashed against her.

Averilla put her hands to her face and rubbed at her wimple as if to run her fingers through her hair. She raised her eyes to him, a jagged flash of anger leaping behind her gaze. "She helped that woman. She aided the witch. She ... one of Dame Agnes' sisters? Consigned Dame Agnes to that torment? And you would have me minister to her? She, whose pride of place ... I cannot." Averilla looked into the murky distance, seeing nothing.

"She needs absolution. Not only from God — even she knows that she can rely on that — but from the community. And from you." Father Merowald paused and gazed at his gnarled hands for a moment. "You do not help her with your anger and hate." He paused again. "It is a wall that you are building around her which forbids healing and restitution. She has confessed. To the abbess. To me. She needs to lay herself before the altar, as is your custom. She needs whatever other penance the abbess dictates. But you, all of you, must forgive her. It is the only path to healing. And you, Dame Averilla, must be the first to forgive. From deep in your own heart."

"I cannot. I have tried."

"You can. *If* you will." A pause. They stood there on the edge of the cliff; the rolling downs to the southeast only a teal-gray blur in the murky light. He sighed, tired beyond his frail strength. He must continue to try to make her see. He didn't have the energy. But he had to try.

"Dame," he said after a moment, letting the words come. In the end it was Averilla's choice to listen. "She *has* repented. Think on her. Put yourself into her skin. Then pray for her. As she would pray for herself. Feel her hurts and her wants as if they were your own. Our Lord requires nothing less. You would forgive yourself this trespass had you done it. So you must forgive her. You would give yourself another chance.

Do the same for her."

Then, as she remained still, gazing out over the vale, not looking at him, with no indication that she had heard, a flicker of anger flashed into his eyes, and his voice gained a sternness she had never heard. "Your penance for this deliberate and chosen abrogation of your responsibility, this willful disobedience, is to lay yourself down, spread-eagled, before the altar until you become Joan. Until you can feel her inner pain in your heart. Then you must minister to her until she is well enough to abase herself." With a slight bow to her still-immobile back he turned and left her there alone in the drawing December night.

Chapter Twenty-Four

aliena had not, at least during the day, returned to her house to retrieve the herbs and medicines she had left. There were stories, told mostly by the older children to scare their younger siblings, about a cold black shape that could be seen flitting from shadow to shadow on dark nights when the clouds scudded across the sky like winged dragons.

Late in Advent, when the mists and storms of December had truly fastened themselves on the bare twigs, when only a withered leaf here and there swirled in frenzied leave-taking, it was then that some of the children noticed Father Merowald heading toward the woods, a heavily laden basket on his arm.

The Widow Otta had fed him well the night before, packing up succulent pasties, floured wheaten bread, two eggs from her barrel carefully preserved, and even some pork to keep him through the following days. The unexpected and extravagant bounty had sparked his resolve. He had procrastinated for weeks. His well-trodden sense of uselessness had assailed and defeated his intention, and he had not done what he ought to have done. The embarrassment of the luxurious basket of food had finally prodded him into action.

"Years too late," he mumbled to himself. "So ashamed."

He thought of her as a lost soul, a soul that had been lost

because he had not given it succor when it so desperately needed it. When Galiena had come back to her father's house, widowed and broken in spirit, he had not offered her his meager assistance; had not seen to her wants. "Our Lord demands few things of us, his lost sheep," he had muttered to himself over the weeks, "but visiting widows and orphans in their distress is one of them. Little enough to do." But he had not done it. Even when he had seen her grow thinner and thinner and had known that she was selling her meager inheritance in order to live, he had done nothing. When the whispers started, he had heard them, and pretended to himself that he had not. He had known that some of his flock visited her. He suspected why it was that they crept to her house under the shroud of darkness; he had let it lie, rationalizing to himself that she needed to make a living. But he knew, as well he should, what the sourness of despair and the loneliness of bare walls can lead one into.

His resolve this day had remained firm, but his body was, as he dragged it through the forest, very weary. The wound he had received at the barrow had never healed, but continued to ooze, sapping his strength. "I have trudged through these woods too often of late," he murmured, glancing without appreciation at the iron-black trees etched against the leaden winter sky. He foundered along now, slipping on patches of unthawed ice hidden under the mounds of mushy fallen leaves. The briars, unsheathed of their coverings, like the claws of the cat, tore at his cassock and entangled him so that he stumbled. "It's because I don't want to go," he grumbled half-aloud as he plowed past the oak, his feet slowing to give it the honor due its grandeur as one of God's creations. He caught himself before he genuflected, but he had started. "Lord help me if I don't half believe in the spirits myself. I need to look to that. Dear Lord," he prayed to the Almighty with the same frankness with which he talked to himself, "here I am trying to resolve one misdeed, and another worms up that I hadn't even been aware of. Forgive me, Lord, and take from me that misbelief."

He had no idea how to knock or announce his presence when he got to the mound. He stood looking at it thoughtfully for a moment, put his heavy basket down upon it and then, gratefully, sat. He didn't hear her come up behind him. Instead he felt her; felt the coldness of complete despair, felt the nothingness and heartlessness of a being foregone. It sapped him; leeched out of him any remaining vigor in a way he had never imagined was possible. Involuntarily, he shuddered.

"What do you want of me, old man? Thanks? Thanks I give to you for my life." Her laugh was sour and mirthless and dissolved into a sodden cough.

He remembered that the widow Otta had packed him some simples. Probably Galiena had some from her plot, but he didn't know. She had been thrown out at the coming of winter with no chance to store up provisions. Without answering her, while he tried to gain strength against her yawning dearth, he pawed through the goods bulging from the basket. When he looked up again, the hunger in her eyes surprised and frightened him. Momentarily he feared the hunger, suspected that she hungered for him, for his soul. He didn't think he had the strength, now, to fight that hunger. The battle in the forest had so taxed his reserves that all he had the strength for now was to endure. He looked again. The black thing that hid behind her eyes was momentarily caged. What peered out at him was naked physical hunger. The bones in her elbows and chin protruded. Age-spotted skin stretched over sinew and bone, like the hock of a deer. Her eyes bulged hugely from drooping circles, and her belly was distended from starvation.

"It's cold. Will you ask me in? I have brought you some food."

"Me? You have brought me food?" The hunger mastered

269

her; overpowered her will. With no further words, she turned and scrambled across the top of the barrow on hands and knees and descended down the half-hidden staircase. The barrow smelled of mold and mouse and despair and felt dank inside, like a crypt. The paved stones were slimy, and drips piddled down from the ceiling. He brushed at one that seeped down his neck, and peered into the murk. He wondered how she could live there, and shuddered because he knew that he would need to do something about it, and was beginning to know what that something was. He settled the basket on the floor. There was a stump beside him, and he gratefully crumpled onto it. She lighted a rush light from a sullen ember on the floor, and it gleamed dispiritedly from a hole where a rock had fallen. Stringy herbs dangled from the ceiling. Runes were scrawled in brown paint on the walls. The remains of a badger's pelt were crumpled near the fire. A whorl of drugged flies circled dispiritedly above the heat. Flies? He wondered. How could there be flies at this time of year? He felt his eyes begin to water with fear. Beelzebub. Living off the death and substance of others. Lord of the flies.

She tore into the basket, holding the wheaten loaf in both hands, cramming it into her mouth, biting hunks out of it and swallowing without chewing, like a dog.

When she finished the bread, she grabbed the pasties, one in each hand. She looked up at him then, quizzically. "I won't kiss the cross. Nor ask for forgiveness, if that's what you are bent upon. If you need another soul to notch your cross with, you'll go away without."

He shook his head. "No, no. That's not why I came," or not all of it, he added, mentally, to himself. "You might want to eat more slowly, though ... "

She chewed reflectively for a moment, trying to figure him out. "Then why?"

270

He gnawed at the side of his cheek and then sighed. "We, uh, took away your means of livelihood, I suspect." He looked toward the back wall. He was uncomfortably aware of the pile of figures beside him, human bones and twig figures stacked grotesquely like kindling against the carved barrenness of the cave. The candle-wax odor of the bones, the smell of fat and marrow, pushed a rush of bile into his throat. He had heard tell of a place deep under Rome where bones were stacked thus, had heard that they were the remains of the early Christians, but those bones had cracked and become coarse with the changes in temperature and the passage of time. He shook his head and tried to ignore them.

"I, uh, I would like to have another chance to, um, be of some help to you." He was having trouble with this. Oh, his precious peace, to give that up. His time with his God. How could it be asked of him? His time of reading. Inexorably, he forced himself to continue, "But, um, if you could find your way to getting rid of those ..." and he motioned vaguely toward the clay and twig figures. "I am much in need of a, of a housekeeper. I would protect you there."

She was gnawing now, on a pork rib, her few remaining teeth on the side of her jaw tearing at a shred of gristle, her eyes crafty, never leaving his face. She stopped. Wiped a dribble of grease from her chin with the back of her wrist. Her eyes slitted, and then a gleam of incredulous triumph flitted across them.

"And live with you? You old fool!"

"I told you the condition."

"Yea, to break the figures. I don't mind that. They were paid for long ago. Any road, they turned on me, those they were made for."

Amazing, he thought, and looked at her in frank wonder. That the physical body could be so used by God, against a

271

spirit that has been lost. Often, too often, he continued to stare at her amazed, a body led a soul into sin. But little did he suspect that the hungers of the body could lead a disinclined spirit to good!

Her voice broke into his thought. "No other condition? What do you get, old man?"

He shook his head and said slowly, "I'm doing it for me. I should have helped you long ago."

The children were the first to see them dragging into the town. The two children, eight and six, were hunting for frogs at the edge of the abbey fishpond. They saw them come, hauling the basket back between them, he hunched with the strain of being near her, she frail but still tall, with something like victory glinting between narrowed lids.

The parson's defiance was monumental, but those who had thought to approach him took one look in his eyes and thought better of it.

As the weeks progressed, the town got used to her. The bailiff and his men left them alone despite the injunction of the steward given at her ordeal. Neither had the steel to take on Father Merowald when he had that look of resolve. In the market, few approached her. Those who did, she rebuffed with a sneer or a battery of curses. The black thing waxed and burned inside her with the sweaty fire of a fever.

Father Merowald made no demands on her other than the light maintenance of his house. The toil of living and battling with the thing inside her took its toll on his frail body.

One week later, just before Christmas, Averilla was awakened from a fitful doze in the infirmary, yanked out of sleep by Galiena, fear and arrogance mingling strangely in her face.

She stood, dripping, on the threshold. "Come quickly. I can do nothing. I think he dies."

Averilla ran behind Galiena through the rain and into the

old town. She could feel the sodden despair Galiena dragged with her, and knew, without asking, what it was that was killing the old man. This ailment was beyond her power to cure. That was what the abbess had said, hadn't she? What the priest now needed was peace in his soul.

They nursed him, the two of them, side by side. Galiena used the herbs Averilla brought, in ways that Averilla herself wondered at. The next night they both stayed and watched, and Galiena fiercely held the old man's body. Averilla couldn't tell whether the fierceness was of love or hate, or both mingled and intertwined, like a canker around the strong muscles of the heart.

"I hoped that love was blooming inside her for him, just a flicker of love for this one human being," Averilla would tell the abbess.

On the third night, Averilla was praying quietly to herself, there beside the pallet, for the soul of the priest. He was going, she suspected, where he had always wanted to go, but she wanted him to get there as easily as possible. Or mayhap he needed more time. She didn't know, but knew she needed to pray. She could feel Galiena's eyes upon her but the other was silent.

Leaving Galiena alone with him, Averilla went to wake the nuns. The whole convent would rouse itself, she knew, even though they had just retired from Compline. With the force of one will, they would pray.

By morning, the fever had broken, and the little man was cool and breathing easily. When he opened his eyes to the dreary December light and blearily searched the room, Galiena was away on some errand. Averilla was alone with him. He tried to speak, but the sound gurgled against his throat. He paused. She saw his Adam's apple move as he tried to clear his throat.

273

Like light leaves trembling, his fingers moved against the coarse coverlet. There was something he wanted of her. She put a hand over his, feeling the bones, the swollen joints and the veins straining up through the parchment-like flesh.

"Not ... much longer." He paused and again struggled with the phlegm blocking his air passages. "Take this," and he patted at his chest. Averilla thought that he was patting at his body. Take his body? It made no sense. In frustration, his fingers scrabbled and plucked at something under his tunic. The cross, the heavy silver cross. She remembered it now. She reached over and gently drew it out, barely warm from the wreck of his body.

"Take it ... to Master Levitas. Have," he coughed and lay panting for a moment, sweat beading his forehead, his face gray, "minted ... into coins. Give ... to her. To go away." He stopped and shut his eyes, and Averilla reached over and undid the heavy clasp. As she drew the links from the scrawny folds of his neck, he wheezed. "Mayhap ... that ... mayhap that ... save her."

It was a Celtic cross. Yet not entirely. The figure of the Man was superimposed upon its surface — a bas-relief imposed and yet integrated onto the flat surface so that the rounded lines of the figure melted and flowed from and into the vines and leaves traced on its surface. The figure gleamed, polished by the old man's skin oil and buffed by the hair shirt he always wore. Averilla had never seen its like. Celtic crosses she well knew. Her old priest had explained their significance to her as a small child. "The circle," he had said, "represents the cycles of creation and nature. The cross of our Lord is the bridge between heaven and earth." It was beautiful. She hesitated.

"Go" he whispered, "I ... not long. Not sold. Melted."

Averilla drew the bolt. The door opened, pushed from

the other side. Galiena shoved past her. The smell of wet wool clung to her threadbare cloak. Rain spattered the hard-packed dirt of the floor. The two women had kept apart as they nursed, like two cats sharing the same hearth. It was all Averilla could do to stay in the same room with her. As she had done to Father Merowald, Galiena battered at Averilla's soul with the clinging force of nothingness and rage. If a sliver of love had pierced her heart, it had not vanquished the blackness. The woman still had no peace.

She gave Galiena a hasty nod, then hurried along the Bimport to Gold Hill and descended to the goldsmith's. Rain had lashed the town in sheets since the first of December, and the streets squelched and ran like so much gritty porridge. Beside the abbey wall that bordered Gold Hill on one side, torrents of water cascaded down from the park. Averilla had clogs, but even they sank deep into the mire.

She threw back her hood as she entered the shop. The shop was small but very tidy, everything arranged with an orderly precision. In the center of the floor, upon a hearth of vertical tiles, was the white-hot fire. Holding a bent hammer, Master Levitas sat astride a bench before an anvil. He was a dark man with a heavily lined face, a black beard, and the black, compassionate eyes of one who has seen much of life. He looked at her blankly for a moment and then, recognizing her, a seemingly unaccustomed smile cracked the caverns of his face. Because of the freezing rain, Master Levitas worked cloaked and with half-mittens on his hands for warmth.

"I would have you melt this down and mint it for me. Can you do it? Quickly?"

With a quizzical glance, he took the silver cross from her and turned toward the candle next to which he had been working. His table held several rush lights and the candle to help him see within the trembling dark of the short winter's day. The fire glinted and danced on the pieces of silver on which he labored, giving the room a depth and breadth it did not have.

He raised his eyes from the silver with a frown of concern and a look of dismay. "This is a beautiful thing," he said. "The workmanship. A very great master." There was a question in his eyes that he was too polite to voice.

She could well imagine what he was thinking. A nun. In the wet. Having a cross melted. "It is not mine. It belongs to Father Merowald. He would have it melted and minted. Into coin," she finished unnecessarily.

"I would buy it from you," he responded, "I would give you more than the worth of the silver. For the beauty of it. It would be a desecration to destroy it."

Father Merowald had said melted, but Master Levitas was right. It was a sacrilege to destroy something of such beauty; something created from the mind and fingers of genius.

"Besides, the dies have already been safely stored in the strongbox in the church."

She looked at him blankly, not comprehending.

He saw it. "By order of the king. The dies, stamps with which I make the coins, must be put away each night. In the church."

"Oh," she said, finally comprehending. "Yes. Then there is no choice." He counted out some silver pennies and farthings for her, and she put them in her purse and ducked back out into the rain. Going up the hill was even harder, for she slipped in the mud and slid, finding it almost impossible to remain upright. She thrust open the door of the hut. The rain lashed across the room and blew against the meager fire, drinking in its warmth. Galiena whirled around in irritation at the draft of icy air, saw Averilla and, without a word of greeting, turned back to the pallet.

Taking the coins out of her purse, Averilla knelt down next

276

to the bed and jangled the coins down onto the frail form. "I have the coins," she whispered, afraid that he was asleep, trying not to wake him.

"You ... were ... not ... so ... long."

"It is true. I hurried."

"The same silver? Minted?"

"No. No, Father. I, I let Master Levitas buy them from me. I thought that it was so — "

His voice interrupted her, the voice of a very old man petulant and querulous with the last pinch of strength. "Minted. Same silver. Go. Not ... time."

Bewildered, Averilla trudged back out into the muck. Her cloak was too wet to be of any use to her, and the mud was a heavy liquid clay with the constant rain. It eddied around her feet like a river, oozing over and around her clogs. She waded through it, more slowly this time, exhausted by the forces against her.

Master Levitas had bolted the door after she left, so she knocked and then stood, wondering if he had heard her, while a stream of water dripped from the thatch to trickle down her back and wet her habit.

She heard the scuffling of his felt slippers through the rushes, and finally the cautious clearing of his throat before he asked, somewhat pettishly, "Who is it?"

At her answer, the bar of the door grated against its iron casings, and he pulled it open by a ring attached to the solid wood.

"He wanted it minted," she said. "The same silver."

He scowled at her. "A shame. To waste such beauty. An expense of love." He shook his head, disgusted. "You must get the dies, then."

She struggled back up the last bit, the steepest part of Gold Hill. The gatekeeper at the east gate had nodded off and took some time opening the gate. The nuns were still at Matins. Midnight. Thank God, she thought. I won't have to try to find someone with a key. The antiphon stopped and the voices trailed off one by one as the nuns saw her. It was the abbess herself who went to the north aisle, where the stairs led to the crypt and the nun's strongbox. All Averilla had had to say was that she needed the dies. The abbess had given her one piercing look and had hurried to get them.

Averilla didn't bother to knock, just pushed the door open when she again arrived at Master Levitas'. She followed him across to his table and stood, dripping, as he started to work. She waited silently as he added more charcoal to the fire and brought life to it with his bellows. He had put his things away for the night, but while she was gone he had replaced them again on the table. He beckoned her over and she took the bellows from him to increase the heat. The fire was intense. He had already placed the cross in a iron pot over the fire. The figure of the man on the cross writhed and thrashed as if in torment, and finally swirled into the molten mass to become one with it. Master Levitas poured the silver into the circular molds. It took no more than a moment for them to cool. The lower die, or pile, made of iron, was fixed in a block of metal directly to the table to keep it stable. The upper die, or trussel, which Averilla had been sent to retrieve, was held in the hand. With a movement both swift and sure, Master Levitas hit the trussel with his hammer, imprinting the coin with the most current image, that of King Stephen.

When Averilla returned to Father Merowald's, she dropped her sodden cloak on the floor at the door and crossed to the bed. For a moment she thought he had already died, so still was he. She dropped the coins onto the blanket so that he could feel the clinking weight of them. He had wanted them before he died. He needed to know that they were there. At least at some level of consciousness. There were only three of them, not thirty; three small pieces of silver glinting in the sallow light of the hissing fire.

As if coming from a long way off, he opened his eyes, blinking to remove the gunk that had started to gather at their edges. He fixed his eyes on Galiena — crouched on the other side of the thin pallet — and held her gaze. He lifted his hand just a bit off the coverlet, and swirled it vaguely above the fall of silver. "Take these," he croaked. "Take these. Flee. Not ... safe. Not allow you ... " He stopped, and there was only the spitting of the sorry fire to be heard over his labored breathing. His hand fell limp onto the coverlet and he gave a gasp and was no more.

Galiena looked at him for a moment, her face expressionless. She bent and swept the coins from the limp body into her purse, and placed it carefully in the bundle of necessities she had gathered. "I won't help you lay him out." She turned, and the thing behind her eyes burned so fiercely that Averilla feared it and its strength.

Galiena tore the old cloak of the parson's from the peg on which it hung. It was green with age, but it was better than her own rags.

IN THE NEXT YEARS, THERE WERE MANY STORIES from Gloucester of evil and hate and death. As the coils of war tightened around the country, these stories were a mere ripple upon the universal pall of misery. Averilla prayed for Galiena daily. At Matins, in the deepest part of the night, when her arm hurt the most, she continued to fix her prayer on the tormented woman. She prayed that the love that had flickered so briefly for Father Merowald might have grown into something stronger, mayhap strong enough. He had done, finally, all the hand of man could. The rest was up to God.

I choose
The selflessness.
The pain of feeling.
Sadness.
Prisms of color.
Come - Oh! His voice.
Here. Here He is.
Misty veils, webbed.
Foggy distance.
Where?
Here.
New vision
In the rainbow.
See Him.
One.
Chrysalis to butterfly.
Swirling nimbus.
I am following.
Wait for me.

THE END

I am the Lord.
That is my name.
My glory I give to no other.
Isaiah 42:7–9

ACKNOWLEDGEMENTS

I would like to express my heartfelt thanks and gratitude to the following, who kindly read and interpreted the various incarnations of this novel:

Julie Duff, Mary Ann Shaffer, Bobbie Maschal, France Bark, Carolyn Cavalier, Jean Cacace, Dorothy Slaton, Jack Schanhaar, Kathy Isaacson, Kathy Dublin, Kathy Lewis, Jane Houton, Mary Piper, Julia Skinner, and Rita Ching.

NOTES

THE ABBEY

SHAFTESBURY ABBEY WAS INDEED BUILT by Alfred the Great after the Battle of Eddington, around 888. The abbey was later rebuilt. I postulate that it was rebuilt under Cecily FitzHamon because of her father's support of the church, particularly at Tewkesbury. Though this is speculation, there is physical evidence to bolster the supposition of the existence of an abbey of that size at the time. Many buildings were commissioned by ecclesiastics such as Henry of Winchester, thus it is not unlikely that Cecily would have undertaken such a project. These buildings were built surprisingly swiftly; Winchester was completed in only thirty years.

Shaftesbury Abbey is now a ruin. It is significant that when the great monasteries are currently spoken or written of, Shaftesbury is rarely mentioned. Yet it was one of the biggest and richest in the country, with a nave rivaling that of Winchester and a size near to that of Glastonbury. Is this silence due to the destruction accomplished under Henry the Eighth, or is it perchance because Shaftesbury was a convent for women?

The Characters

WHILE MOST OF THE CHARACTERS in this book are fictitious, some are real, especially those not related directly to Shaftesbury Abbey. From the abbey, the only names we actually know are those of the two abbesses, Cecily (a.k.a. Cecilia) FitzHamon and Emma. Although we know their names, we do not have the exact dates of their tenures. Cecily FitzHamon was of a well-connected family in the Norman hierarchy. Her father, Robert Fitzhamon, had been a friend of King William I and of William II, known as William Rufus. He is said to have moved a house of monks from the Blackmore Vale and built a new house for them at Tewkesbury. Cecily's sister Mabel, or Amabel FitzHamon, was the wife of Robert of Gloucester, the bastard son of Henry I and therefore half-brother to the empress Matilda, whose armies he commanded during the civil war.

Under English law, women enjoyed a near equality with men. Women held office, owned property, commanded armies and even ruled. With the advent of the Normans, however, the civil liberties granted women were abruptly curtailed. Matilda would be the last woman to rule in her own name for four hundred years. English spoken at the time reflected this lack of emphasis on gender and is in stark contrast to Norman French where words were designated to be male, female or neuter.

WITCHES

DORSET, ESPECIALLY THE CRANBORNE CHASE, has a long history of eerie and supernatural occurrences. People clung to pagan superstitions and worship, strange rites and initiations in underground caves long after such had been discarded elsewhere.

The twelfth and thirteenth centuries, however, saw very little of the persecution of witches that occurred during the seventeenth century. There were "wise women" and some "anchorites" who were versed in the healing arts; some of them undoubtedly solved problems with little regard for moral niceties. As always, it is not the tool, in this case mushrooms and frogs, but how it is used. The choice is always: to do or not do harm.

TOADSTOOLS AND TOADS AND OTHER TOOLS OF MAGIC

AS SHAKESPEARE NOTED IN *Macbeth,* no self-respecting witch was ever without her toads and toadstools. Continuing research by herpetologists has discovered that many old "superstitions" hold merit. One researcher working at the National Institutes of Health had studied frogs for a number of years when he started to wonder why these small amphibians failed to contract infection when sutured and reintroduced to an environment full of bacteria and feces. He discovered that the skin of frogs and toads is well protected by antibiotics and fungicides. There are, indeed, actual migrations of frogs such as Galiena witnessed, in Gloucester around the vernal equinox. In the twenty-first century, they present a writhing, squirming mass to unwary motorists.

Magic wands are another reality-based element of sorcery. A magic wand was a twig covered in a lichen that phosphoresced at night. Two were of use; *Omphalitis olearius,* which is associated with oak groves and gives off a green light and honey fungus, or touchwood, *Armillaria mellea,* which has black, thread-like, bootlace structures, which reach from the roots of one host tree to infect another. A wood so infected glows phosphorescent.

Fomes fomentarius, or witches' brimstone, was used for a long time for stage lighting. In another lighting device the spores of *Lycopodium* were mixed with the giant puffball, or *Langermania gigantea,* which together ignited with a dramatic flash.

The death cap mushroom, *Amanita phalloides* which Galiena used on her husband, causes death, but only after several days. The first symptoms occur ten to fourteen hours after eating, then subside. After two or three days, splinter-like hemorrhages occur under the skin, followed by convulsions and damage to heart, liver and kidneys. Death is in seven days.

For more information on this fascinating subject, I recommend *Toads and Toadstools,* by Adrian Morgan, (Celestial Arts, 1995.)

LEECH BOOK

KING ALFRED'S LEECH BOOK, or *Laece Book*, does exist and can be found at the British Museum. Known as *Bald's Leechbook,* it was a compendium of medical knowledge sent by the patriarch of Jerusalem to Alfred the Great in the 800s. Whether the abbey at Shaftesbury had a copy is not known. I have assumed that one did reside there because Alfred built Shaftesbury for his daughter, who was the first abbess. Alfred, the only king to be called "The Great," had many ancient texts translated into English. His biographer, Asser, writing some 200 years later, asserts that Alfred himself translated these works from Latin to English. He then had the translations copied in the scriptorium at Winchester and sent all over Wessex to libraries in other abbeys and cathedrals to save them from burning by the marauding Danes.

RELIGION

THE TWELFTH CENTURY WAS A TIME of economic growth and expansion and also a time of incredible religious fervor. It is likely that the nuns at Shaftesbury were indeed the devout ladies here portrayed and not the languid creatures portrayed in stories of convents of the fourteenth and fifteenth centuries. It was a time when the Benedictines themselves tried to strengthen and purify their practices. But, as I have tried to show, Christians, even nuns, are prey to temptation. We are not perfect; just, if we repent, forgiven.

Dean Church wrote: "In an age when there was so much lawlessness and when the idea of self-control was so uncommon in the ordinary life of man, the monasteries were schools of discipline. And there were no others. They upheld and exhibited the great and original idea that men needed to rule and govern themselves and could do it and that no use of life was noble without this ruling."